NDIVISIBLE, VIE

"INDIVISIBLE, an intensely powerful portrayal of the emotional stress of combat and military separation impacting faith and family. It depicts the struggle of a young chaplain and his family as they confront the realities of war with an idealistic perspective of faith. INDIVISIBLE views their journey coping with various losses which challenged the very foundation of their faith. Yet, through a greater spiritual awareness and understanding, provided by seasoned chaplains and mentors, they were able to overcome these challenges of faith and continue their ministry to the military."

—James E. Agnew, Chaplain (Colonel), US Army Retired

"A masterful movie bringing to life God's ability to restore war-damaged marriages and families. A great story of hope and restoration."

—Clair Hoover, National Coalition of Ministries to Men

"Service, mission, sacrifice, brotherhood, loyalty, family, and God all wrestle for a man's top priority in the action-packed movie INDIVISIBLE! Terrific!"

—Brian Doyle, president, Iron Sharpens Iron

"As a retired army chaplain, watching INDIVISIBLE was like experiencing reality for me, because I lived through much of what it portrayed. I cried at numerous points while viewing INDIVISIBLE, because the movie tapped into my emotions, experiences, and the tragedies I have experienced and personally helped many soldiers work through. INDIVISIBLE was indeed true to life, reflecting the experiences of tens of thousands of soldiers. I highly recommend INDIVISIBLE to all military personnel, and to every family, church, synagogue, mosque, or organization—secular or religious."

—Chaplain (MAJ) James F. Linzey, USA (Ret.), founding president, Military Bible Association

"INDIVISIBLE is gripping and poignant in its open portrayal of real-life challenges. Learn how community, asking for and accepting help from others, and the gift of faith can help you face your own trials with courage. A brilliant reminder that we are never alone."

—Lisa M. Hendey, founder of CatholicMom.com and author of *The Grace of Yes*

"As America's longest war carries on and couples face struggles in an ever-changing world, this film points to how we can remain Indivisible in our marriages and in our walk with God."

—Justin D. Roberts, director of *No Greater Love*, former army chaplain

"INDIVISIBLE is an authentic story of God's enormous power to heal marriages, elevate faith, and strengthen families. A must-see movie!"

—GJ Reynolds, CEO, Women of Faith

"Military couples have an uphill battle to maintain healthy marriages, whether in deployment or stateside. INDIVISIBLE is one of the best films on marriage I have ever seen. It is an honest look inside the homes and hearts of our heroes bringing hope and encouragement that they can win the battle!"

—Dr. Gary Rosberg, America's Family Coaches, author of *6 Secrets to a Lasting Love*

INDIVISIBLE

A NOVELIZATION

WRITTEN BY TRAVIS THRASHER

FOREWORD WRITTEN BY DARREN
TURNER AND HEATHER TURNER

THOMAS NELSON
Since 1798

Indivisible

Published in Nashville, Tennessee, by Thomas Nelson. Thomas Nelson is a registered trademark of HarperCollins Christian Publishing, Inc.

Published in association with the literary agency of WTA Services, LLC, Franklin, Tennessee.

Images in photo section are courtesy of © 2018 Provident Films LLC and The WTA Group, LLC. All rights reserved.

Quotes taken from *Wild at Heart* by John Eldredge Copyright © 2001 by John Eldredge. Used by permission of Thomas Nelson. www.thomasnelson.com.

Thomas Nelson titles may be purchased in bulk for educational, business, fund-raising, or sales promotional use. For information, please e-mail SpecialMarkets@ThomasNelson.com.

Unless otherwise indicated, Scripture quotations are taken from the Holy Bible, New International Version®, niv®. Copyright © 1973, 1978, 1984, 2011 by Biblica, Inc.™ Used by permission of Zondervan. All rights reserved worldwide. www.zondervan.com. *The "niv" and "New International Version" are trademarks registered in the United States Patent and Trademark Office by Biblica, Inc.*™

Scripture quotations marked nlt are taken from the Holy Bible, New Living Translation. © 1996, 2004, 2007, 2013, 2015 by Tyndale House Foundation. Used by permission of Tyndale House Publishers, Inc., Carol Stream, Illinois 60188. All rights reserved. Scripture on pages 38–39 is from Psalm 18:2-3 nlt. Scripture on pages 84–86 is from Psalm 55:1-7, 16-17 nlt. Scripture on page 219 is from Psalm 39:7 nlt. Scripture on page 289 is from Psalm 51:10 nlt.

Lewis, C. S. *A Grief Observed*. New York: HarperOne, 2015. First published 1946 by Geoffrey Bles.

Publisher's Note: The novel is a work of fiction. Names, characters, places, and incidents are either products of the author's imagination or used fictitiously. All characters are fictional, and any similarity to people living or dead is purely coincidental.

ISBN: 978-0-7852-2405-1 (trade paper)

Library of Congress Cataloging-in-Publication Data

CIP data is available upon request.

Printed in the United States of America

18 19 20 21 22 LSC 5 4 3 2 1

This book is dedicated to the chaplains of the United States Armed Forces and the soldiers who valiantly serve to protect our freedom.

A wound that goes unacknowledged and unwept is a wound that cannot heal.

—JOHN ELDREDGE, *WILD AT HEART*

Finally, be strong in the Lord and in his mighty power. Put on the full armor of God, so that you can take your stand against the devil's schemes. For our struggle is not against flesh and blood, but against the rulers, against the authorities, against the powers of this dark world and against the spiritual forces of evil in the heavenly realms.

—EPHESIANS 6:10–12

FOREWORD

BY DARREN AND HEATHER TURNER

In January 2008, a reporter from the *Atlanta Journal* shadowed our battalion for a few weeks during my (Darren) deployment. She wanted to focus on the chaplain's role in combat, since there was plenty of war coverage in other articles during that time. She thought it would be unique to see things through a chaplain's angle. So she shadowed me and got an eye full (we had mortars come into our camp often, casualties from missions outside the camp, I traveled a lot to remote locations, I conducted Easter services and baptized guys, etc.). She then returned and published eight different articles in a row that told the story of her trip. When she contacted us a couple of years later and heard about our marriage problems and how we patched things up, she added that last part to what became an e-book called *Chaplain Turner's War*.

In the summer of 2011, filmmaker David Evans contacted us after seeing our story on a news website. His idea of making a movie about our story sounded interesting but unrealistic. We didn't think it would really happen.

After David contacted us, we wanted to meet him and hear his pitch. So he and his wife, Esther, drove to Fort Campbell and we had a long lunch. After that meeting, Heather and I felt very comfortable with David and Esther. They were sincere, cared way more about our story than we did, and had a passion to share this on film. Most importantly, they saw this as a way to glorify the grace of Jesus Christ. After that lunch meeting, we waited a few days before responding. We wanted to pray about it and not make an emotional decision in the moment. I talked with our army folks to get their opinions, and once everything looked right, we said yes to David's offer and also shared our personal journal from the deployment to use for development of the screenplay.

For David and the rest of the filmmakers, their passion and persistence ended up resulting in the film and book for *Indivisible*. We could never have conceived and developed this, especially since we simply don't have the time or space to do something on such a scale like this. We simply agreed for them to use our story and names, and David and his team did all the rest. We have watched everything unfold in amazement, and we are proud of the results.

Having seen the movie, it's still very strange to see and hear our names and watch our lives unfold onscreen. Of course there were artistic licenses taken, but for the most part it's pretty accurate. Some of the scenes brought back a lot of unexpected emotions. We were surprised by that. It was good to recall some things that we needed to remember again, especially God's wonderful gift of redemption.

We have many hopes with *Indivisible*. First, we hope those watching the film and reading this book can be honest with themselves, others, and the Lord. Second, we hope that nonmilitary Americans will understand our vets better and maybe even get involved in their lives.

Ultimately, we pray our story blesses folks and frees people to be real and honest about where they are in life. Our desire is for people to consider *the* solution to our fatal condition of sin and selfishness.

It's the summer of 2018, and we're spending some of our days and evenings relaxing on or near the lake we live by. We're looking forward to a busy fall when the film and book are released. It's going to be a lot of fun to see people's reactions to the incredible film David and his team have made. We remain honored and humbled to be part of this amazing journey.

God still has big plans for our family as He does for you, too. We thank Him for His many blessings, including continuing to help tell His story throughout our lives.

PROLOGUE

She carries the memories and always will. She doesn't need to think long when the chaplain asks her to pick a moment from the past.

So many special times to choose from. I have hundreds of good memories. But we've stopped making new ones.

She glances over at her husband, sitting in a chair only inches away from her, yet miles removed from her life. Heather forces a smile as she turns to the chaplain.

"The day we met," she begins, "I was taking photos on campus when he drove by, looking at me, just as he ran his motorcycle into my shot of the chrysanthemums. And ruining both the photo and the flowers! He just kept going too, and I thought, *Who is this hotshot?* But later that day I saw him again. It turned out he was the guest speaker for Campus Ministries, and as he shared his mission work, I saw a man with a heart for God. *And* he was hot, so—"

"What do you mean, *was* hot?" Darren shoots back, the first sign of any amusement from him during this counseling session.

"Hey, don't push it," she says.

Chaplain Rodgers gives her a steady nod and grin. "Okay, time—Darren? Whaddaya got?"

Her husband's silence feels like nails pounding into her, one second after another. She looks at him, waiting, willing him to say anything, watching him trying to find an answer but unable to say a single, simple thing.

"And this is where we are," she finally says. "Anything that truly matters—he shuts down."

Darren tries. "Memories have just been . . . I mean, every time I try to think back, what I don't want to remember takes over. Like there's a wall in my timeline, or . . ." He doesn't finish.

Heather closes her eyes, swimming in the familiar emotions she wakes up to and falls asleep with. A lonely and drifting sensation, bobbing up and down in the middle of the ocean, with no land in sight and nobody around to hear her cries for help.

"That's very normal, Darren," the chaplain says. "And Heather, post-traumatic stress is a mind inhibitor that requires time and intentional rebuilding of the muscles and tools we use to control our thoughts."

"But I'm pretty much outta time," Darren says.

Heather never could have imagined such words of defeat coming from her husband, much less hearing the tone in his voice. But he's right. They have run out of time.

She hopes—no, she desperately *needs*—the Darren she fell in love with and knew so well to come back home.

PART 1

PREDEPLOYMENT 2007

WINTER AND SPRING 2007

1

Twenty-one days before signing into Fort Stewart, Darren Turner listened to the president addressing the nation on television, not to hear what America was doing abroad, but to learn where he might possibly be headed in a few months.

"Good evening." President George W. Bush spoke from the Oval Office in the White House. "Tonight in Iraq, the armed forces of the United States are engaged in a struggle that will determine the direction of the global war on terror and our safety here at home. The new strategy I outline tonight will change America's course in Iraq and help us succeed in the fight against terror."

The children were asleep, Elie and Sam in their beds, infant Meribeth snug in Heather's arms. Darren turned up the volume and shifted on the couch, his focus solely on the president as he spoke about the historic elections in Iraq two years earlier and the hope that they might bring the people together—resulting in a need for fewer American troops.

"But in 2006, the opposite happened. The violence in Iraq, particularly in Baghdad, overwhelmed the political gains the Iraqis had made. Al-Qaeda terrorists and Sunni insurgents recognized the mortal danger that Iraq's elections posed for their cause. And they responded with outrageous acts of murder aimed at innocent Iraqis."

Darren glanced over at his wife as President Bush continued. He could see the concern in her expression.

"The situation in Iraq is unacceptable to the American people, and it is unacceptable to me. Our troops in Iraq have fought bravely. They have done everything we have asked them to do. Where mistakes have been made, the responsibility rests with me. It is clear that we need to change our strategy in Iraq."

Darren knew there was a big reason for the president to be talking to the American public on this Wednesday night in January. He was leading up to an announcement.

Only a year ago, he and Heather would have been watching like the rest of the country, listening to hear what was happening to other men in foreign countries. Now, however, he watched and waited to hear what might be happening to him.

"Our past efforts to secure Baghdad failed for two principal reasons: there were not enough Iraqi and American troops to secure neighborhoods that had been cleared of terrorists and insurgents, and there were too many restrictions on the troops we did have."

The president spoke about a new plan that could work, how the Iraqi army and national police brigades and local police would be engaged in operating locally to conduct patrols, set up checkpoints, and go door-to-door to gain the trust of Baghdad residents.

"This is a strong commitment," President Bush stated. "But for it to succeed, our commanders say the Iraqis will need our help."

This time Darren didn't look at Heather. He stared at the screen, anticipating what was coming next.

"So America will change our strategy to help the Iraqis carry out their campaign to put down sectarian violence and bring security to the people of Baghdad. This will require increasing American force levels. So I have committed more than twenty thousand additional American troops to Iraq. The vast majority of them—five brigades—will be deployed to Baghdad. These troops will work alongside Iraqi units and be embedded in their formations. Our troops will have a well-defined mission: to help Iraqis clear and secure neighborhoods, to help them protect the local population, and to help ensure that the Iraqi forces left behind are capable of providing the security that Baghdad needs."

Darren moved over and reached for Heather's arm that held the sleeping baby. He smiled, letting her know that things were going to be okay, that God had this taken care of and they shouldn't worry. He knew she was thinking the same thing, yet both of them felt the gravity of this moment sink over them.

Twenty thousand additional troops.

Will I be one of them? Darren wondered. He pictured their children and what it would be like to say goodbye to them.

This is the choice I made. The choice we made.

President Bush was still speaking. "Will America withdraw and yield the future of that country to the extremists, or will we stand with the Iraqis who have made the choice for freedom? Let me be clear: The terrorists and insurgents in Iraq are without conscience, and they will make the year ahead bloody and violent. Even if our new strategy works exactly as planned, deadly acts of violence will continue. And we must expect more Iraqi and American casualties."

This is our new reality. And we've known about it ever since I chose to join the army.

2

What am I here for?

The question whispered deep inside of him once again. It was a question he'd been born with and carried around like a shadow his entire life. During his wild and reckless days in college it grew louder, trying to get his attention, urging him to want more out of his meaningless life. So one spring break, instead of continuing to party with his classmates on a beach in Florida, Darren returned home to Canton, Georgia. He also returned to the pages of the New Testament.

He didn't need to "find himself." Darren needed to find faith in someone else. Realizing it might appear to be foolish and against all that common sense might suggest, he turned his heart over to Jesus Christ, deciding to follow Him. In whatever fashion and form that meant.

What am I destined for? This was the new question that he began to ask.

It remained with him as a student teacher during his senior year at UGA. After graduating in 1997, the question followed him all the way to a teaching position in Mongolia, then back to his alma mater a year later, where he became a part-time campus pastor. After two years, as Darren continued to wonder what God wanted for his life, a door opened for a full-time assistant pastor job at a church in Athens, Georgia.

Deciding to follow Jesus meant saying "Not my will, but Yours be done" . . . and Darren knew it could get messy and uncomfortable sometimes.

After four years of marriage, Darren and Heather began talking about options other than what they were doing in their church ministry. One of Heather's college friends had married an army chaplain, but at the time that hadn't stirred their interest. They wanted to invest their time and family with a group they could live life with.

Yet Darren always continued to ask: *How am I supposed to serve, Lord?*

One morning in early January of 2004, he was reading from Psalm 27 when the verses grabbed him. David wrote that even though an army was camped around him and war rose against him, he would be confident in the Lord and not fear. "One thing I ask from the Lord, / this only do I seek: / that I may dwell in the house of the Lord / all the days of my life, / to gaze on the beauty of the Lord / and to seek him in his temple" (Ps. 27:4).

Darren knew right at that moment that this was what he

wanted to do. He wanted to bring faith and confidence in Christ into a place of war. Not long after that, he and Heather spoke to the chaplain who was married to her friend, and then they called an army recruiter. Everything happened quickly, and by August Darren had resigned from his church position and enrolled in seminary.

Now, as he lay awake thinking of President Bush's words to the American public earlier that night, he asked himself another question.

What am I made of?

Each step on the ladder of his life had led to this place. He believed the president's words when he said, "In these dangerous times, the United States is blessed to have extraordinary and selfless men and women willing to step forward and defend us." Darren knew it was true that they "serve far from their families, who make the quiet sacrifices of lonely holidays and empty chairs at the dinner table. They have watched their comrades give their lives to ensure our liberty."

Darren knew who he was, and that God had shaped him with His hands to bring him to this point in his life. Not only had he been called to serve, but he knew he was called to help soothe the souls savaged by the war.

Would he be headed overseas to serve? If he went to Iraq, what would he find there?

What am I made of? He shifted in the bed.

He looked at his wife, sleeping peacefully beside him, and prayed they would both be steadfast and strong as they faced the future.

3

The noise of the four children playing in the living room gave Heather a feeling she hadn't experienced since moving into their new home: normalcy. For the first time, she felt normal again, even though sheets were still draped over chairs and tables and they were still searching in moving boxes for items like the coffeemaker. The rowdy fun the kids were having with the tent they had set up in the living room and named Fort Bumblefoot was something they would have done back at their old house. It had only been a few days, but slowly and surely, she knew they would grow used to living on the army base.

When they had first pulled up to Fort Stewart, she had read the sign at the front of the base: *Welcome to Fort Stewart, Georgia, an Army Community of Excellence.* Below its logo were the words *The world's best installation to train, deploy, live and raise a family.* The February morning had been like today, a cool forty-five degrees with clear skies that showed off the 280,000 acres about an hour west of Savannah. The base contained everything, from ponds and waterfronts to the Heritage Chapel and medical and training facilities. Their neighborhood consisted of pretty suburban houses with small and well-maintained lawns and lots of young families like theirs.

Normally Heather might have suggested that the children set up their tent somewhere other than the living room, but since everything was still in a bit of disorder, she figured they might as well have some fun. As she peered into the room, looking for her husband, she was greeted by almost-four-year-old Sam's shouts of "Pow pow pow!" He was guarding the entrance to the fort, his Armor of God costume hanging off his shoulders while he swiped the plastic sword in the air and made swishing sounds as he fended off the artillery from the unseen enemy. He waited for his big sister to come around to the front and join him.

"No one gets past Electric Elie!" she shouted as she adjusted the tinfoil wrapped around her forehead and wrists.

"Or Samurai Sam!"

Even though Elie was eight, she wasn't too big to play with her little brother. She spun around and saw six-month-old Meribeth crawling on the carpet toward the tent.

"Oh no!" Elie cried out. "An in-surgeon!"

Sam steadied himself at the base of their fort. "Quick. Secure the gate!"

Heather watched all this with a grin on her face. "Okay, send the commander back to HQ," she told the kids. "He has three more boxes to unpack. And stop calling your sister an insurgent."

"The commander doesn't have time for boxes," Sam called out. "Fort Bumblefoot is taking fire." He tossed a pillow high into the air, shouting, "Incoming!"

Just then her biggest "child" bolted out of the tent, wearing his army combat uniform and commanding, "Pull back! Pull back!" Darren quickly scooped up Sam and then Elie, pulling them into the safety of the tent, while three children giggled and screamed in joy. Then silence covered the room, with a round of shushes coming from the soldiers inside the fort.

Heather shook her head and tiptoed over to the back of the

tent. She burst through the flaps and startled them, howling as she began tickling the kids.

"Sneak attack, sneak attack!" Darren cried. "Evacuate!"

While the kids piled out of the tent to escape, screaming and laughing, Heather called out behind them. "Careful. Don't tear my sheets." Then she leaned over and fell into Darren's lap.

He gave an exaggerated "Oof" and called out, "I'm trapped! Save yourselves. Run!"

The pitter-patter of feet running down the hall followed by echoes of laughter were sounds she would never grow tired of. Meribeth tried her best to keep up, crawling in her own little way to chase Sam and Elie. Capturing her breath and looking up at her husband, Heather once again felt normal, resting there in Darren's strong arms.

"And don't come back for fifteen minutes!" she called, as Darren smiled his approval. He gently kissed her, then studied her for a moment. She felt like she was a kid again too, and was making out with the homecoming king.

"It's good to hear you guys having fun," she said in a soft tone.

"It's good playing with them. Especially Elie."

The move had been toughest on their bright second grader, who had hated saying goodbye to her friends.

"The house feels cozy," Heather said.

"Or maybe it's just me," Darren said as he snuggled closer to her. "I kinda like Fort Bumblefoot. What about you?"

Before she could answer, a high-pitched squeal of tires came from out in their front lawn. They gave each other questioning glances, then she led the way out of the tent to see what was going on. Looking through the front window, they saw a truck in the middle of the lawn at the house directly across the street. A man in uniform was at the door, pounding on it and shouting.

Darren quickly headed to the garage, no doubt wanting to see if there was anything he should do, so Heather followed. They navigated past stacks of moving boxes and other items filling up the garage as they heard the shouting across the street.

"Tonya! If you changed these locks again on my own house—"

The door opened and a woman appeared, staring up at her husband and refusing to budge an inch.

"Really?" she said. "This is what 'I promise to do better' looks like?"

"Just let me in," the man said, trying to shove past her, but the woman stood her ground.

Heather felt like they should go back inside, not watch and listen like nosy strangers.

"You smell like a whiskey plant," the woman said.

"I'll sleep it off, don't worry."

"After a long walk, maybe, because it won't be here."

The woman looked about Heather's age, short with caramel-colored skin and an expression on her face that said she would not suffer fools lightly. Heather doubted this was the first time the couple had argued like this. As the woman started to shut the door in her husband's face, his arm stopped it from closing all the way.

"You know I got your commander on speed dial?" she said. "So help me, Michael, you can quit caring about me, but you better find a way to be the man those little girls in there need you to be. No—*deserve*—for you to be. Or more than the old door locks will disappear."

For a moment the man stood there, then he turned around and strode to his truck, which was still running. As he was climbing in he noticed Heather and Darren watching.

"Hey!" he called out to them. "Mind your own business!"

Heather quickly grabbed a box to at least pretend like she was in the garage for some other reason than to snoop. Darren was still standing there, his gaze unmoving.

"Honey, he's staring right at you. Pick up a box."

Instead Darren waved while the truck accelerated down the street. Heather couldn't believe it, yet she felt a little better seeing the driver's hand giving a subdued wave back. As the sound of the truck faded, the woman on her doorstep was joined by two girls, one at either side.

Darren turned around, his friendly expression not having changed a bit.

"Well," he said to Heather. "Guess we met the neighbors."

4

Darren believed these words from one of his favorite books, *Wild at Heart* by John Eldredge: *Every man is a warrior inside. But the choice to fight is his own.* Yes, the choice to fight was his own, but the choice facing him now was when he would actually decide to go. That decision wasn't his alone to make. Heather needed to weigh in as well.

Two weeks after signing into Fort Stewart, Darren met with the division chaplain to see where they would be putting him. Once President Bush announced the surge, it was a foregone conclusion that he would eventually be heading over to Iraq. The only question was when.

After taking his first couple of weeks to in-process into the army, Darren learned he would be deploying with a unit at a later date. He met with fellow chaplains and his future chaplain's assistant from this brigade. Everything seemed set; he knew the brigade he'd be serving with and started to get to know the men and women in it.

Then suddenly everything changed. He was told they were putting him in an infantry brigade, one that was surging. Both the division chaplain and the brigade chaplain asked him if he was okay with the change, and he said yes—but he wanted to talk with Heather about it first.

As always, his wife's response was levelheaded and thoughtful.

"Do you remember after we first met," she said, "when you were still working in Athens and I was preparing to go back to China to teach English?"

"Yeah," Darren said. "You were going to be gone a few years."

"But after we got engaged, I decided I would only go for a year, then come back and get married."

Darren nodded. They both knew Heather didn't, in fact, return to China. Instead, they proceeded to get married just a few months later.

"I remember talking to Cindy about it one day and crying about that decision. About how long I'd have to be gone. I knew that at the end of our lives, I would look back and say I wished we'd taken every opportunity to spend it together." She took his hand in both of hers. "I think that maybe this is the Lord's way of getting that year back from each of us. He simply had another destination in mind. Not China, but Iraq."

Darren couldn't help but kiss his wife, still feeling like the luckiest guy in the world to have her by his side.

"Maybe you're right," he said.

The next day, he went back to talk to Chaplain Colonel John Rodgers to give him an official answer. He could tell by the colonel's face that this was a monumental decision; the stakes were high.

"The timing is not ideal, son," Chaplain Rodgers said. "I know you just finished basic, and I'd like to see you get more noncombat experience first, but a military-wide shortage on chaplains says otherwise."

"I understand, sir. They're putting me in the infantry battalion. Under Lieutenant Colonel Jacobsen."

Rodgers gave him a somber nod. "Surge unit. Serving folks who spend their days clearing roads laced with IEDs. Means they have confidence in you."

That's where I'm meant to be. Where God wants me to serve.

"I'm ready, sir."

"The 1–30th is going be at the tip of the spear in Iraq," Rodgers said. "There's going be a high risk of casualties."

"I understand that, sir."

"Look, Darren—the death of a soldier is the toughest thing
you'll face as a chaplain. There are other meaningful ways you
can serve the army without heading straight into the thick of it."

"I signed up to be where the need is, sir," Darren said. "And
twelve months'll go by fast."

"Bit faster than fifteen, for sure."

"Fifteen, sir?"

Rodgers gave him a short nod. "Fifteen."

"Yes, sir."

"The infantry unit's already been out in the field training,
but you can join them for their final week. You'll have March
and April to get ready before deploying. You'll be doing lots of
boring stuff like sorting out your medical and legal things. But
the good news is you'll have two weeks of leave for a final vaca-
tion before you go. My suggestion is you enjoy every second of
your time here before May arrives."

5

There was something thrilling about taking a broken and abandoned piece of furniture and restoring it. Heather loved finding
pieces from Goodwill and fixing them up, turning them into
beautiful furnishings for their home. Friends had even asked her
to do this for certain pieces they had found. Today she was finished with her latest big project: restoring a dresser. She couldn't
wait to show it off to Darren when he got home.

The original was a bulky piece with loose drawers and an

ugly faded brown color. After painting the dresser, she put in new metal drawer slides and handles. The white chalk paint allowed the detail and hardware to pop, especially the intricate wood carving along the top edges.

When she heard Darren open the door and greet the kids, Heather walked into the family room to meet him.

"Hey, babe," she said as he leaned down and gave her a kiss. "I want to show you something."

Leading him to their bedroom, she threw out an arm like the hostess on a quiz show to point out the new centerpiece of their room.

"Did you just buy that?" he asked.

"No! It's that dresser I picked up a month ago. The one sitting in the garage taking up space."

Darren walked up to it and felt the edges. "It looks brand-new," he said.

"See? I told you it had potential. All it needed was some TLC. And a little time to make it happen."

"I think you should start doing this for a living," he said with a smile. "Open up a little shop. Sell these for ten times the price you make them for."

"So does that mean you'll stay at home with the kids and homeschool them?"

"Oh, that's right," he joked. "Details. This really is something, though."

"Little by little we're getting there." She was making the new house their own, slowly but surely, in small and significant ways.

6

They may be misplaced, forgotten, or misdirected, but in the heart of every man is a desperate desire for a battle to fight, an adventure to live, and a beauty to rescue.

The writing leapt off the pages and into Darren's heart. He didn't simply feel *inspired* to action; he felt *ignited.*

As Darren scanned through highlighted portions of *Wild at Heart*, he remembered why he had felt so strongly about joining the army and serving with men and women. He knew his calling, and a big part of him was excited to be taking this next step.

So there comes a time in a man's life when he's got to break away from all that and head off into the unknown with God.

It spoke to him as a man, but a man made in God's own image. *Yes, a man is a dangerous thing,* Eldredge wrote, using the scalpel as an example of being able to both wound and save a life.

Chaplain Rodgers had initially thought he would be better suited sitting behind a desk in a safer environment, but Darren knew he was ready. He believed he would be strong and brave. He would provide important emotional and spiritual support for soldiers after their combat missions.

With a stack of books next to him on his desk, Darren knew there would never be enough time for him to spend studying. First and foremost, he spent hours in the Word, knowing how vital it was not only for his position but for his very being. There was a battle going on even greater than the one in Iraq: a spiritual battle raging every day, and the only way to survive and win was spending time with God. Seeking Him required discipline and determination. And now that he would be heading overseas, Darren knew he needed to arm and prepare himself even more.

Eldredge encouraged all men to take journeys like this. Not necessarily physical ones, but spiritual ones: *To recover his heart's desire a man needs to get away from the noise and distraction of his daily life for time with his own soul. He needs to head into the wilderness, to silence and solitude. Alone with himself, he allows whatever is there to come to the surface.*

As he turned off the lights in his office to head to bed, Darren wondered what the wilderness would feel like, and what things were going to come to the surface.

He couldn't wait to discover them.

7

The days are long but the years are short. The longer time went by, the more Heather thought of this quote she had heard from another mother once.

As she looked for candles in the kitchen to put on Sam's birthday cake, she couldn't believe how four years had simply blinked by. One minute she was holding her little baby boy, who wasn't that little at ten pounds. The next minute he was wobbling desperately to walk, then he was running and climbing over everything. Sam was all energy and excitement. He spoke more in his actions than with his tongue, except, of course, when he was giving his older sister a hard time.

The days are long . . .

After looking for the candles for fifteen minutes, she gave up and called for reinforcements.

"Babe, could you do me a big favor?" she asked after reaching Darren on his cell phone.

"Sure."

Today he was meeting with a financial adviser who was helping them get all their accounts and banking issues in order before he left for Iraq.

"I need you to pick up some candles for the birthday cake. I know I had a box of them but I can't find any."

"They must be in that missing box. You know—the one with those picture frames and my Bulldogs socks."

"Yep," she said. "We'll add candles to the list."

There were still quite a few boxes in the garage waiting to be unpacked, but she had already skimmed through them and couldn't find the half dozen framed family photos she had carefully wrapped and boxed herself. For some reason, the one box she had made sure to keep track of herself during the move had vanished.

As for Darren's nasty Georgia Bulldogs socks . . . She might have "accidentally" left them back at their old house. And they might have somehow made their way to one of the garbage bags they filled with stuff to throw away.

She didn't mean to deceive him. Heather planned to go out and buy him some new socks. The old pair had holes in them and seemed to smell even after they were in the wash. Some things did *not* need to come with them with this move.

"Any particular type of candles?" Darren asked.

"I'm sure your choice will be perfect."

When Darren arrived back home an hour later, he showed off the candles he'd bought with a boyish pride. They were green army men candles.

"The set came with five, so we'll have an extra," Darren said. "Look—each guy has a unique pose."

One soldier carried a rifle, while another was talking on the phone.

"Should I be worried there's someone throwing a grenade on our son's birthday cake?" she teased.

"My personal favorite is the guy with the rocket launcher."

It was no surprise that this was Sam's favorite army man candle as well. He seemed almost more excited by the candles than the cake itself.

Darren had picked up not only the candles but also some pizzas from a new favorite joint near their house called Maciano's. Sam loved bacon, so one of the pizzas had bacon, pepperoni, and sausage on it. Before eating, Darren asked God's blessing on their meal.

"Dear heavenly Father, thank You for this day and for this celebration of life. We thank and bless Your holy name for giving us Sam. We praise You as we watch him becoming a young man before our very eyes. Thank You that he replenishes those around him rather than depletes. Please, Lord, help Sam continue to grow up being a person who gives to people. We ask this in Your Son's name. Amen."

"What's *replemish*, Daddy?" Sam asked.

"Well, a lot of people in this world don't give to others;

they only take," Daddy said to him. "They don't think of others. But you do. And we think it's a great thing to see you be kind."

"He's not always kind to me!" Elie chimed in.

"Be nice," Heather said. "It's his birthday."

When they were ready to sing "Happy Birthday" to their little man, Heather found herself getting choked up. She stared at the lit candles and the joy in Sam's face as his big sister proudly looked on and the little sis sat in her high chair, mesmerized by the flames.

It was a simple thing, Darren swinging by a store to get the candles and picking up the pizza. A simple and easy thing to do. But it was help.

How am I going to do all of this on my own?

As they sang to Sam and laughed throughout at Daddy's voice thundering through the kitchen, Heather knew the days were about to get longer. But . . .

I hope the next year is short. The shortest I'll ever have to experience.

8

"I'm going to miss these walks," Darren said as they strolled through Freedom Park on the picturesque afternoon.

"Me too," Heather said. "I can't believe it's only a month away."

"Yeah. I can't believe how busy the battalion has been."

The "surge" announcement really sped up the timeline for getting ready for deployment. He had already been able to do some overnight exercises with the battalion, going for five nights to do training with them. When they weren't in the field, the days were full of packing containers, getting uniforms and equipment ready, and prepping vehicles. There was an element of anticipation in seeing soldiers running around town buying everything in sight.

"It'll be fun going to see your family this weekend," Heather said, thinking about their upcoming trip to Atlanta.

"I can't wait until we have our block leave."

"You just can't wait to go to Disney," Heather joked.

Everyone was encouraged to take personal leave before deploying for Iraq. They planned to visit Disney World for a few days, while the rest of the time would be spent packing his personal things and trying to have quality family time. There were still lots of "honey-do's" that needed finishing around the house.

They walked toward the gazebo and sat down on the steps. It was nice to be together and alone, with the kids at home with a babysitter.

"I'm already getting a dose of what things are going to be like out in the field," Darren said. "But people are in pain everywhere. And that's when they're ready to invite God into their lives. Some of these guys are going through rough times. A few of them have opened up to me already."

She squeezed his arm. "It's easy to open up to you. You're pretty likable."

"Oh yeah? You think so?"

"Hmmm. Sometimes."

They both laughed as she leaned against him.

"It doesn't seem real," Darren said. "Not yet. It still feels like I'm just imagining that I'm going to be overseas playing soldier."

"I'm sure it won't take long before it becomes very real."

"Yeah."

"And when it does, you're going to be the chaplain people are going to turn to."

He nodded, hoping those words would prove to be true.

9

As she scanned the lawn, camera in hand, Heather spotted Meribeth bouncing in her jumper, her cheeks even rounder with her big grin, loving the sudden ability to maneuver up and down without falling. She zoomed in for a snapshot, then kept walking and guiding their expensive new toy on to the rest of the family. She found Darren pausing for a moment during the game of tag, trying to explain in terms they could understand the news he had delivered to them.

"It's like when we play Fort Bumblefoot and somebody gets hurt," he said to Elie and Sam, while they waited to see if he was going to move to try and tag them. "I'll be there to talk to the soldiers if they need someone to help them feel better."

Then without another beat, Darren raced over and made a lunge at Sam, diving into the thick grass.

"Gotcha!"

Sam scampered away. "No, you missed! You missed!"

"Oh yeah?" Darren looked over at Heather and smiled. She kept taking pictures, knowing these moments would be precious a few months down the road.

Darren sprang up and ran over to Sam, scooping him up in his left arm, then kept running until he reached Elie, grabbing her with his right arm. He spun them around, their arms and legs dangling while their laughter floated by. Darren pretended to lose his balance and stumbled forward, letting the kids drop down onto him while they hollered and laughed. Sam, of course, bolted back up to get away, but Elie remained on her back, sadness suddenly overshadowing her again.

"But Daddy," she said. "What happens now when we need you to cheer us up?"

Darren shifted back onto his legs, but before he could answer, the sound of Elie's familiar wheezing could be heard. She was wincing, her lungs gasping for air.

"Elie, your inhaler," Heather said.

Elie searched her pockets but came up empty. "I don't . . . know."

Heather rushed over to her side. "When did you last have it?"

Elie didn't know and couldn't get any words out anyway. Heather turned and ran back into the house.

"Stay with her," she shouted to Darren. "I'll get a backup. Sam, look in the grass!"

"I've got it! Heather—I found it," her always-calm husband said just as she reached the doorstep.

Darren handed the inhaler to Elie, who squeezed it and took

a long breath in, then slowly began to breathe again. Heather
finally could breathe too, and she walked slowly back over
to them.

"You're okay, sweetie," Darren said as he sat down next to
her. "You're okay."

Elie leaned back on the grass, steadying each breath as she
looked at the sky. Her father did the same, and so did Sam.

"Who's going to find my inhaler when you're gone?" she
asked.

"I think that should be Sam's responsibility," Darren said.
"Sam—do you think you're up for this job?"

"Sure!"

All three of them were now lying back on the grass, looking
up at the blue heavens. Heather picked up the camera and took
a few more pictures.

"I wanna start a countdown, Daddy," Elie said. "When will
you be home?"

The zoom of the lens captured Darren's bittersweet smile.

"Well, probably a few months after your next birthday, Bug."

"Aw, but I just had one," she said.

Heather lowered her camera.

Make this good, Chaplain.

"Well, I promise we're all gonna get through this just fine,"
Daddy said.

"We *know*. It's because 'God is always with us.'"

"Wow. Tough crowd." Darren paused for a moment, still
looking up. "But that's right. Because when He's with us, He's
also there to give us what we need. To protect us. Help us feel

better. Even help us have fun while we wait for something that's hard to wait for."

Well done, Heather thought, knowing it had been hard to utter without becoming overcome with emotion. Mommy and Daddy had to be strong for the children.

"To have fun, like playing tag!"

With that Darren changed the reflective moment, tapping Sam while springing up in the air and helping Elie to her feet.

"You're it, Sam! Elie, run!"

Darren held hands with Elie as they tried to evade Sam. He tagged Elie, and she then chased after her father, all while Meribeth continued bouncing and chomping at her fingers with her gums.

Normally the busyness of life wouldn't allow her to slow down to watch and be mindful of this time, but Heather was totally there, solely focused on the simple fun her family was having.

The simple moments are the ones we're going to miss most.

10

The get-together that Heather and other family members planned to say goodbye to Darren turned into a full-fledged party with a lot more people than he'd expected. Almost every stage of his life was covered, from family members he hadn't seen for years to longtime friends and even teachers and former neighbors. The flow of smiling faces bringing their shared histories with them made him feel both honored and humbled to have so many in his life. All he could say was how blessed he happened to be, and how he gave God the glory.

While playing the role of both the host and the guest of honor, Darren was also showing off his grilling skills. He wouldn't be cooking with his big grill for some time. The hot dogs were already well cooked but he was monitoring the hamburgers and the chicken as he saw a family of four walking across the street toward their lawn.

I can't believe she persuaded him to come.

Their neighbors, the Lewis family, slowly made their way toward Darren while he closed the lid on the grill and went to greet them. They had gotten to know Tonya and the twins, Mia and Nia, a little more since their awkward first encounter after moving in. Yet besides a few customary waves or hollered hellos from their opposite sides of the street, Darren hadn't yet spoken to Michael. Even now, it looked as if Tonya was all but pulling her husband to the yard adorned with streamers and balloons.

"Hey there! Thanks for coming, guys," Darren greeted them, quickly looking back to the house to find the rest of his family. "Heather, kids, look who's here!"

Michael's grip was strong, his expression nothing but serious.

"Darren Turner—*Chaplain* Turner, actually. Nice to meet you."

His neighbor's eyes shifted for a split second. "Major Mike Lewis."

"Good to see you again," Tonya said as she shook his hand.

Heather appeared and greeted their new guests. "Girls, the rest of the kids are in the back by the trampoline."

The twins thanked her and went in search of others to play with.

"They're so pretty," Heather said. "How old are they?"

"Twelve going on twenty," Tonya said, rolling her eyes. "It's so great you guys are doing this. We really should be the ones hosting, since we've been here four years and know the drill."

"We love doing this, but we don't know 'the drill,' so I'm all ears." Heather led Tonya toward the party indoors so the men could talk.

Mike stood there on the grass, wearing the expression of a man in a women's clothing store waiting while his wife tries things on in the dressing room.

"Hope you're hungry, because we have a lot of food," Darren said.

"I already ate. Got a cold one?"

"You kidding? Been icing them down since dawn."

Stepping over to the cooler, Darren dug into the ice and pulled out a drink, tossing it through the air and watching Mike catch it without missing a beat. As his neighbor looked at the square juice box in his hand and then back at Darren, his face said it all.

"Hey," Darren said, "if grape's not your flavor, I have mixed berry and prune. Which the mature crowd seems to like."

Mike didn't even bother to feign a smile. He took off the straw and jabbed it into the box, taking a sip that might have drained it in one big swoop.

"Chaplain, huh?" he said, finishing with another slurp. "So, our occasional fights you've seen—they're not what they look like."

"Hey. All I know, Major, is we all got life goin' on in our houses. And family or not, life's plain hard. Especially, as I can only imagine, for parents of twin girls."

Mike's tense frame appeared to relax just a bit, seeing Darren wasn't going to launch into some kind of lecture or judgment.

"Yeah, twins can be something else. I mean—the family I got in Iraq is one crazy, ugly bunch. But a whole lot easier to deal with than this one."

Darren gave a chuckle that sounded more bleak than amused. "First tour for me, so I'll take any advice you've got."

Just then a volley of laughter fell over them, and they looked to see the twins running with Sam and Elie. Mike's stoic, distant glance didn't change as he looked back at Darren.

"My advice? Just leave your heart at home."

11

There was no way Darren could personally thank every person who came to the party, so instead he left each of them with a note he had written.

> Thank you for coming today. I appreciate your sup-
> port. It's humbling to receive this type of recognition. Many

people making the same sacrifice never get this sort of party. I honor them today as well.

The decision I made three years ago to pursue this ministry has finally panned out. I didn't choose to go to war, but I did choose to be in the army and risk the possibility. Now it's no longer a possibility, and in about three weeks I am going to war. Let me say up front that it is a privilege to be a part of this. I make no apologies for doing it. Men and women are laying their lives on the line every day, and I want to be right there with them as their chaplain.

Please don't grieve for me—grieve for the soldiers and Iraqis who don't know the great salvation of God: "Because God's children are human beings—made of flesh and blood— the Son also became flesh and blood. For only as a human being could he die, and only by dying could he break the power of the devil, who had the power of death. Only in this way could he set free all who have lived their lives as slaves to the fear of dying" (Heb. 2:14–15 NLT). That's the message I will share with soldiers as they are being shot at.

I believe this is God's will for my life. Heather feels the same way. If she didn't feel the same way, I wouldn't be doing this. Since that's the case, I'D RATHER BE WHERE GOD WANTS ME THAN WHERE I THINK IT'S BEST TO BE. My life is His, and I believe this is His plan for us. It feels more "right" than anything I've ever done. I am blessed, because I've found what I was made for!

Heather and the kids . . . they are the true heroes of this story, as are all military spouses and kids. Pray for them!

They will need your love and support on a regular basis. I
will miss them immensely, but I long for the day when I will
get to see them once again and not take for granted their
hugs and kisses.

12

Holding the remaining plates from the barbecue, Darren
walked into the kitchen, where the radio was turned on a little
louder than usual. A slow ballad played as Heather washed
dishes, swaying and humming to a Rascal Flatts song. Darren
stopped and watched her for a moment, a wave of wonder
washing over him.

She really is the very definition of lovely.

Life was often too busy to simply pause and appreciate its
beauty. But for a handful of seconds, Darren looked at the woman
he'd married, knowing how much he wanted and needed her.
Remembering the gift God had blessed him with.

She turned to call out, "Hey, babe! Can you—" and then
noticed Darren standing just across from her.

"Oh, you're here." Suddenly she grew self-conscious. "What?"

"Nothing. Just watching you."

"Oh yeah? I look real cute now." She held up her soapy
hands and then pushed falling strands of hair out of her eyes.

"Come here," he said to her, slipping an arm behind her and
embracing her. "Cute isn't the word I'd use."

For a moment they swayed to the music. Heather couldn't

help laughing as they moved, but as she looked up at him, a realization seemed to fall over her. The same reality that was hitting Darren. They said ten thousand words without uttering a single one, looking at each other with weighted smiles.

"Fifteen months without this face," Darren said.

He leaned down and gave her a gentle kiss, and then he felt her bury her face in his chest. They stopped moving and simply held one another. The world was on pause. For a few more moments. Heather hugged him as if her very life depended on it.

"Hey," she said as she moved to look back up at him. "God's in this, right?"

"I know He is."

"Then you'll be fine. And so will we."

They kissed again and resumed their slow dance. It might be the last one they would have for some time.

13

This is gonna hurt.

Fathers had to be the strong ones. They had to set the example. Perhaps that's where that false belief that "real men don't cry" came from. Darren certainly didn't ascribe to this notion, yet he also knew if he suddenly became an emotional wreck, the rest of his family would follow suit. Well, perhaps Meribeth wouldn't, but she might already be crying because she wanted some more animal crackers.

It was comforting to know everything in their house was in order, with bills paid and the oil changed in the van and a guy hired to mow their lawn. They had even finally gotten a will, and the power of attorney had been done. Sobering tasks, but necessary.

With so much to do these past few days, it was easy to overlook the reality of his actual departure. To forget that he was about to say goodbye to his family not for hours or days but for months. His gut ached knowing he would soon be kissing his wife and kids for the last time.

Hosts of families lined the area just outside the red-roofed hangar at Hunter Army Airfield, bidding their loved ones goodbye before they passed through to board the massive C-17 transport plane waiting on the tarmac. Seeing all his fellow soldiers gave Darren a mixture of strange feelings. He was sad and anxious to leave at the same time. The reality hung in the air, the truth that something bad could and would happen in Iraq. Nobody needed to express it but everyone felt it. Darren knew he was blessed to have this wonderful family to bid goodbye. Not every soldier had one.

He spotted a stoic Michael standing in front of his twins, giving each of them and his wife a quick kiss on the cheek before turning to leave. As he departed, Tonya called out, "I love you!" Michael waved without even turning around.

Maybe he was hiding some tears he was shedding.

Heather bounced Meribeth in her arms, bracing herself for this moment. Kneeling in front of Sam and Elie, Darren put his arms around them. "Okay, bring it in, kiddos. Big hugs!"

As Sam and Elie smothered him, Heather and Meribeth joined them. Then as the two eldest kids finally let him go, Darren held on to his wife and their baby.

"Make sure this little one remembers me," he whispered to Heather.

"Why do you think I made you suffer through all those photos?"

Darren kissed her, first on her lips as a tender husband, then giving her some more kisses on her cheeks, the kind a loving and playful daddy might give to mommy while the kids laughed. With everybody in good spirits, he high-fived Sam and Elie and then grabbed his gear to head to the plane.

Seconds later he heard Elie call out.

"Daddy!"

She ran toward him, past the line where family members could go. Heather called out for her but Elie was too fast, making it to Darren to give him another big bear hug.

"I love you, Daddy."

"I love you too, Bug."

The adoring face looked up at him with those precious eyes so sad. "But Daddy . . . what if you get shot?"

This was a moment to be strong. Darren didn't have to fake it. He felt God giving him strength today. He gave Elie a reassuring smile, then pulled something out of his pocket.

Darren loved the Armor of God coins designed for Christian chaplains serving in the military. With their design recalling the spiritual "armor" described in Ephesians, the coins were meant to be an encouraging reminder of faith.

He handed Elie a coin. "Remember, honey," he said. "I've always got my special armor on."

"I know, Daddy," she said, not exactly sounding as though she meant it.

"You keep this coin safe, okay? Whenever you get scared, or miss me, just hold on to this, and remember who's protecting me."

"Okay."

"And keep saying the Bible verse you've been memorizing. Remember?"

Now Elie just nodded. She had recently memorized Psalm 18:1–3 as part of the homeschooling that Heather did with the kids. The verse was especially fitting today.

Darren wrapped his arms around Elie once more and lifted her up. "I love you like crazy."

"I love you like crazy," she repeated. "Don't forget to send us goofy-face pictures, 'kay?"

"I won't."

Elie ran back to Heather as Darren waved to them one more time and gave them a big confident smile.

14

The words of King David comforted Darren as the plane took off and Heather as she drove the kids back home.

I love You, Lord; / you are my strength. / The Lord is my rock, my fortress, and my savior; / my God is my rock, in whom I find protection. / He is my shield, the power that saves me, / and my place of safety.

They both knew their strength couldn't come from themselves. They needed God to give it to them. They knew He could shield and protect them. They believed He could do the same thing He had done for the psalmist who wrote the following words: *I called on the* LORD, *who is worthy of praise, / and he saved me from my enemies.*

PART 2

DEPLOYMENT

THE FIRST MONTH

1

The words he typed couldn't fully sum up Darren's feelings and thoughts, but they would have to suffice. He and Heather set up a CaringBridge site before he left, as a channel for sharing his news with friends and family and giving them a way to offer encouragement and support in return. His first post after leaving the United States he wrote from Kuwait.

> **May 13, 2007**
>
> Got a few minutes here in Kuwait at the "internet café." Said goodbye Thursday morning to Heather and the kids—the most painful moment of my life so far. I never thought it would sting so bad. Now I am in Kuwait and ready for the mission. I really like being with my soldiers. Watching them get ready for war is getting me ready for it as well. Where we are going is fairly volatile. My guys will be out in it, and I pray they get ready now. I don't want to see anything go wrong.

I can tell their anxiety is going up, as this is for real now.
Continue to pray for them and God's protection, and for me
to be there when they wonder what's next. I have found a
fellow officer who has a strong faith in Christ. I dubbed him
my chaplain. I will get to vent to him as necessary, probably
frequently. Thanks for everyone's encouragement. I am
thankful and privileged to be here, yet longing for home at
the same time. No one prays harder for peace than those of
us in the war!

God bless, Darren

2

The steady blades of the helicopter were broken by the cracks of
gunfire below. Darren looked out the back door to see the fighting on the street below them, only a mile away from the base
he would soon be arriving at. The machine gunner stood by the
opening, ready just in case. As they began to land, the sound of
a large explosion startled him.

Time for training is over.

He climbed out of the helicopter and followed the men to
the group where one of the leaders was waiting.

"Welcome to Baghdad, people," shouted Lt. Col. Jacobsen,
the battalion commander. "Within thirty miles of which 80 per-
cent of all of Iraq's sectarian violence takes place."

As Darren lined up next to the newly arrived soldiers, he felt

the thrill of finally being there at Falcon Base. He knew it wasn't
the worst place they could have sent him, but neither was it the
safest in terms of current threat levels. The young men next to
him were ready, with some having already been to Iraq once or
twice. He listened to the lieutenant colonel continue his official
greetings.

"Here at Forward Operating Base Falcon we are 8.1 miles
south of the Green Zone, but a nine iron from a freeway we are
not allowed to control and neighborhoods full of both people
we are here to protect and those who *will* try and kill us. It's your
job to know the difference."

Darren felt that the longing for adventure and his calling
in life were steps he had taken—that he and Heather had taken
together as a couple—and that now finally after the long journey to get there, he would begin. A quote from *Wild at Heart*
reverberated inside of him: *We don't need accountability groups;
we need fellow warriors, someone to fight alongside, someone to watch
our back.*

Standing in formation, staring with sober eyes at the lieutenant colonel, Darren knew he was next to those fellow warriors,
along with all of the men and women on this base.

Lt. Col. Jacobsen finished welcoming the new soldiers, then
told Darren to follow him. As they walked, he could see the thick
concrete walls surrounding them, walls within walls around a
city of hangars, military vehicles, grounded trailers, and tent formations. As they had flown over Baghdad, they'd seen a sprawl
of sand-colored homes. The freeway they took to get to the base
had nothing on every side except a vast desert expanse. It was a

country of dust, with soldiers dug in on all sides, their machines blowing it into the air.

"Six mortar rounds hit the base earlier today," Jacobsen said while they walked. "No casualties, but you can never know where they'll hit. They usually don't strike buildings or people, but sometimes they do. The good news is we have the ability to strike back quickly, and when we do we usually succeed."

The temperature went from unbearable to simply hot once they stepped inside Jacobsen's humid office. They were greeted by the soldier waiting for them.

"At ease, Major North," the lieutenant said, then gestured to make the introduction. "Chaplain Darren Turner."

"Good to meet you," North said as they shook hands.

Darren noticed the cross on North's uniform.

"Good to meet you, Chaplain," he said.

Chaplain North's role as the base chaplain included receiving incoming chaplains, getting them connected with their units, and keeping track of everyone on base.

As they sat down, North's good-natured smile was more welcoming than the steady and intense look on the lieutenant colonel's face.

"First deployment?" North asked him.

"Yup. Got my M. Div. last year, finished basic training, and moved to Fort Stewart a week before learning I'd be deployed."

Jacobsen opened the file on Darren and scanned it, probably for the first time. "Master of divinity, huh?" he said. "So how's that working out with your kids?"

"Sir?"

"Your kids, son. North here has grand accreditation too, but he'll be the first to tell you, in the real world, much less this one, theories and master's dissertations go out the window. Kinda like at home, with three kids."

Ah, I get it now.

"Well, mine are ten months to eight years, sir, and so far they're on board. But all Heather and I know to do is tell them the truth and trust God with them."

Lt. Col. Jacobsen gave him an affirming nod. "Always a bonus to have a chaplain who's a family man."

Before Darren could reply, the officer reached into a cabinet and pulled out a thick file, plopping it on the desk next to other files and reports.

"Divorces filed in the last three months," he said, gesturing toward the file. "And hey, mine didn't last either, so I'm not judging. But I do know soldiers losing families and having nothing to go home to is not the most stabilizing force we need here."

"To say the least, sir," Darren said.

Jacobsen raised an eyebrow. "This goes for you and yours too."

"Understood, sir. But Heather and I, we're called to this. She's even volunteered for the family support team. It's what it's about for us—"

"The Family Readiness Group, that's great," Chaplain North interrupted. "Takes a special person."

"Which she is, sir," Darren said. "She'll be great. We're thankful for the opportunity."

The lines in Jacobsen's face didn't move. Darren knew he

had heard everything before, but that hadn't stopped him from saying what he did. He just wanted to share the truth with these two men.

"Well, all right, then," the lieutenant colonel said, standing once again. "Welcome to Falcon Base, Chaplain."

After the lieutenant colonel left, Chaplain North pointed to the file that Jacobsen had given to him.

"Deployments strengthen strong marriages and weaken weak ones," North told him. "You'll find guys who just got here who are already mad at their wives. The combat isn't the only trauma these soldiers have to deal with. The hardships on the marital front is why they seek and need comfort."

"I can imagine, sir."

North wiped sweat off his forehead. "So tell me a little more about why you're here."

"I've wanted to be in ministry since I became a believer. I've always wanted to serve people and share the message that helped me, so oddly enough, I'm very excited to be here. I want to be with soldiers when they're going through the crisis of their life."

"Well, remember," North said, "strong families truly make strong soldiers. Come on—let me give you the tour."

Chaplain North headed out of the trailer without waiting for Darren to pick up his large duffel bag, so he had to jog a little with the heavy pack just to keep up. They walked on a service road around the base of the camp. North began to rattle off where everything was, barking while the buzz of the military swelled like the heat around him.

"Gun range is down that road, hospital on the right, chow on the left. The chaplain's tent right over there, with the Falcon lux-amenity package just for you: oscillating fans for A/C, turndown service by resident scorpions, and the blandest food this side of the Tigris."

Darren grinned. "Must be why the price is right."

He followed North down a stone-lined path to pass by his new home. Outside the door, a three-foot stone cross was staked into the ground.

"Got my assistant to make that," Chaplain North said. "Out of some bombed marble our guys borrowed from one of Saddam's castles."

"A room full of preachers could debate that one for a while."

They laughed as they continued, passing by one of the soldiers' tents. A glassy-eyed private who looked barely of legal age to join the army stood waiting.

"Could I speak with you, Chaplain?" he asked North.

"Certainly. Darren, why don't you head over to the range to meet your assistant, Sergeant Peterson? I'll take care of your things."

"Good idea," Darren said.

"Come on inside, son," Chaplain North said.

They didn't even make it inside before the young man began to weep. Darren turned around and saw North consoling the soldier, an arm around him while they entered the tent.

That'll be me soon enough.

He was ready for them to come to him. In many ways, it would be similar to the college students he used to minister to.

Only in this case, the young men coming to him wouldn't be stressed about homework and college bills. They would be anxious to stay alive.

As he walked to the shooting range, he spoke to God the way he always did. To pray without ceasing didn't mean being on your knees in devout communication with the Lord, but talking with Him all day long. Praising God and thanking Him and asking for help and for forgiveness.

"Father, please be with that young man, and give him strength and hope," he said in a soft whisper. "Give Chaplain North the right words to say."

The barrage of gunfire became louder as Darren approached a handful of soldiers at the firing range, shooting at a row of paper targets. A soldier in the middle aimed the M4 carbine and shredded the target with ease. Impressive. He couldn't find anybody who looked like a sergeant, so Darren went up to the range officer pacing behind and watching the shooters.

"Excuse me, Captain," Darren said. "Any idea where I'd find a Sergeant Peterson up here?"

The soldier with the great aim turned to greet them.

"Ya found her, Chaplain," she said, lifting up her Oakley shades and swapping her magazine.

His pause and the embarrassed grin on his face gave away his surprise.

"No offense taken," the sergeant said, before turning to aim her weapon once more. "But if there's a guy here who can keep ya vertical *and* run your office like I can, I'll eat my helmet."

The fellow soldiers beside her laughed, a few of them ribbing her back just as the range officer called out the customary "Ready-Aim-Fire." The lightweight and gas-operated standard issue M4 let go of another barrage of shots. The hanging portions of her target were eviscerated.

She grabbed the empty magazines and placed them on her station table, then she walked up to him to shake hands. She quickly led him back out to the road.

"Any better, you'll embarrass the snipers there," he said to her.

She grabbed the back of his shirt and pulled, keeping him from walking directly out in front of a big truck driving past.

"Six years Atlanta PD," she said as she walked with her M4 comfortably settled in both hands, the barrel pointing down and to the right. "Here by the way of the National Guard."

"Here by the way of Fort Stewart," he stated. "And six years of college campus ministry, which is pretty much the same thing." He chuckled.

Her pretty face shot him a look that didn't require words.

"Hardest day of my life was leaving my wife and kids on that tarmac," Darren told her. "How about you?"

Before she could answer, a piercing whine interrupted and a blast ripped through the base, slamming Darren to the ground. As rocks and debris rained down on him, he opened his eyes to find the woman on top of him.

"Head down!" she ordered, shoving his face into the dirt.

The blast had struck just outside the base, but it had been too close for Darren. The sergeant jumped back up on her small frame, then put a hand out and helped Darren to his feet.

"Name's Shonda. And that's the third blast in four days. One hit munitions last year and killed three hundred soldiers. So if I'm gonna keep you alive, you're gonna listen and follow my lead. And stop asking questions about my family, sir."

He was no longer smiling. "It's a deal. At any price."

3

The clock on the wall said 9:40 a.m., causing Heather to stop for a second to calculate the time for Darren. He was seven hours ahead, making it 4:40 p.m. on the base, which also meant it was almost time for dinner. It had only been a few days, but she already wished he were at home, manning the grill while making the kids laugh.

A knock at the front door broke her reverie. She was surprised to find Tonya and the girls at her doorstep, each of them holding a plate of goodies.

"Oh my goodness," Heather said, honestly surprised to see them. "Hi."

"We made twenty-four cookies," Nia said with a proud smile.

"No, that's how many times you licked the spoon," Mia joked.

"Did not!"

"We figured the kids would love something sweet," Tonya said.

"You figured right," Heather said, urging them to come inside.

Sam and Elie were excited not only to see their neighbors, but to see them bearing cookies. Even though it was midmorning, there was never a bad time for cookies. Heather poured milk for the kids and coffee for the moms. Tonya had brought by some material on the Family Readiness Group, since Heather had told her she wanted to be a part of it.

Enjoying their sugar rush, Sam and Elie ran out to the back with the twins to jump on the trampoline as Meribeth sat in her high chair and decorated her face with still-warm chocolate chips. Tonya opened the big binder she had brought.

"So, let's talk about the FRG," she said as if she was giving a lecture. "The Casualty Response Team is part of Family Readiness, and we, uh . . ." Tonya shook her head and rolled her eyes.

"I'm so sorry," she said. "I can't give this canned speech. They can call it the Family Readiness Group, but it's our third time out, and nobody's ever ready to do this job. Not even close."

"I can imagine," Heather said.

"FRG is a good thing. It's here to make sure all the families get the proper information from command. It helps keep you connected to what's happening. Or, at least, that's what it's supposed to do."

Heather could feel the weight of Tonya's words. They carried history and memory.

"Thank you for being honest," she said. "I really believe I'm called to this, so I'll train and prepare as best I can. And we'll just stick together, okay? I know you have a lot to teach me."

"I don't know about that. But I can show you what to expect. To help you be as prepared as possible."

"I'm so grateful that you're here to show me the ropes."

The kids in the backyard rushed by the kitchen window, laughing and hollering. Tonya seemed far away from the table they sat at.

"I don't want to unload on you," she said. "But, well, every time Michael comes home, he's angrier. More distant."

The two women shared a moment with a single, solitary look. Both remembered the first day they met, how Michael was yelling at Tonya through the front door.

"I have been praying and praying for that man. And maybe I shouldn't ask you this, but . . . do you think you could ask Darren to look out for Michael? To talk to him? We could use all the help we can get."

Heather reached over and squeezed Tonya's hand. "Of course. You're not unloading anything. We don't have to have some official group to be allowed to vent or ask for help. I know Darren would love to get to know Michael. And he's a prayer warrior. We'll begin to pray along with you."

"Thanks," Tonya said.

4

There wasn't much inside this tent. Just two metal desks, some old file cabinets, a set of lockers, and an oscillating fan. And, yes, there was also the world's most out-of-place regal chair sitting dead center in the chaplain's quarters, red velvet stitched with gold trim. Darren had found it amusing, to say the least.

With night setting over the base, he began to unpack his suitcase. The first item he took out had been carefully secured with bubble wrap and tape. It was the small, hand-carved wooden box containing his Armor of God coins. He took one out of the box and slipped it into his shirt pocket, then placed the box on his desk.

Next he found the new leather journal he'd bought for keeping a record of his experiences overseas and opened it for the first time. Inside on the first page were large crayoned words: *WE LOVE YOU! ELIE AND SAM.* The message pinched at his heart, reminding him of the distance and the loss. So did the framed photo of the family that he took out of the bag. He studied it in the silence. Darren knew he was in the hearts and minds and prayers of Heather and the kids, yet it still didn't beat seeing them in person.

He knew it was like that with God, except better. He loved God and prayed to Him all day long and strived to obey Him, yet he had to wait to see Him one day. Until then, he would simply have to carry that hope inside of him, letting it give him strength and encouragement, and hopefully allowing Darren to do the same with the men and women he ministered to.

Somewhere in the distance, the blast of a bomb went off. He could never forget where he was, because even if he did, this place would remind him.

He decided to spend a little time with C. S. Lewis before going to bed, and opened up his copy of *A Grief Observed.* As always, a passage fit in perfectly with this moment in time and the place he was at.

You never know how much you really believe anything until its truth or falsehood becomes a matter of life and death to you. It is easy to say you believe a rope to be strong and sound as long as you are merely using it to cord a box. But suppose you had to hang by that rope over a precipice. Wouldn't you then first discover how much you really trusted it?

Darren knew it was one thing to talk about serving in the army and what he felt God was calling him to do, but it was an entirely different thing to actually be here, miles away from the family. He knew he was hanging over the precipice. He ached to be back home, watching his baby daughter learn to stand and take her first steps, taking Sam and Elie to their first camp. He missed Heather's big hugs and her smile that always made him glad she'd married him.

Only a real risk tests the reality of a belief, Lewis wrote.

Darren knew he was following where he believed God had led him. Like Jonah, he didn't like the destination God had picked, but there was no better place to be than where God calls you to be. He didn't fully understand it all, but then again, that's why it was called faith.

He doesn't ask us to understand Him. Just to follow Him.

5

The seconds drifted away like bubbles floating upward and then popping, never to be seen again. Heather held back her impatience as she listened to Elie and now Sam finally talk to their father on the phone. It seemed like it had been forever since they'd heard from him. There had been blackouts every day of the two weeks he'd been gone, but none were due to his unit. Darren had explained how whenever there was a fatality the entire base would have a communication blackout to avoid rumors or miscommunication while the army notified the family back home.

"And don't forget, Daddy," Sam shouted as he spoke into the phone. "Email us goofy-face photos, okay?"

Heather smiled, knowing Darren would definitely do this. He probably didn't need to be reminded. She moved over and waved for Sam to give her the phone.

"You too," Sam said into the receiver. "Mommy wants her turn now."

As Heather took the phone, Elie gave a swat. "Phone hog!" Elie said. "You hurried me, then you talked forever!"

Heather chuckled. "They were so excited to talk to you."

"It's so great to hear your voice," Darren said.

"No kidding. Two weeks feels like one and one hundred at the same time."

"A hundred? Wow. How are you holding up?"

Where do I begin?

She could have told him about the long hours of playing and taking care of the little ones. Or answering life's important questions including why ants didn't have trampolines. Or Sam coming to her with one of her exercise videos asking if she could do it so he could have a little brother. Or she could have told Darren about the ladies she'd met in the Family Readiness Group, and about Lisa Ainsley, who had stopped by the house to hang out. They had spoken about their spiritual journeys for quite a bit, and Lisa shared that she wanted a relationship with God that was real and practical. Since she didn't understand what the idea of being "saved" meant, Heather suggested they could start doing a Bible study together.

There was all of that and a thousand other things, but Heather simply replied, "Well, I'm enjoying sleeping on your side of the bed. Is that bad?"

His laughter made her smile even bigger.

"Hardly. I've got a one-man cot all to myself. You should live it up too." He let out a wistful groan. "Biggest challenge here is learning all the names and being the first one in after they clean the latrines. But . . . I think I can make a difference here."

"Of course you will," she said, then remembered something she wanted to be sure to tell him. "Oh, by the way, the website's up. And our plan is to add pictures every day so you don't miss a thing."

"Great—" He paused, then let out a sigh. "Ugh. The red light on the phone just flashed. I'm out of time already."

"Wow. Next time the *kids* will have to wait. Hey, what do you think of sending a quick email each night? Just to, you know, say what you had for lunch?"

"Babe, part of me wants to. But I don't want you to worry. Just because our internet's spotty. Or if I'm off base one day and you don't get an email."

"Okay, I get it," she lied. "I get it."

"I love you so much," Darren said.

"I love you too."

The click on the other end of the line felt louder than it usually did. It also seemed to echo even after she put down the cordless phone.

In the background, Sam was yelling that Elie had taken something from him. Somewhere else she could hear Meribeth crying.

Please, God, give me the emotional energy to make it through today.

Heather wanted to be as strong as Darren was being. She didn't want to get to the end of each day feeling as though she had simply survived; she wanted to thrive in this season and one day look back with pride at how God had given her the strength she needed day and night.

I have to labor through with God's power and not my own.

The enemy wanted Heather to feel tired and lonely and ultimately defeated. She kept reminding herself she couldn't do this on her own. But she and the kids weren't on their own, and neither was Darren.

6

Darren sat upright in his fancy red armchair, staring directly into the digital camera. It flashed a yellow button while he scrunched up his nose and opened his mouth and stuck out his tongue—just as someone opened the flaps to his tent. He waited for a second, not changing his expression until he heard the click of the photo being taken.

"Oh, hey, Shonda—Sergeant," he said, correcting himself. "Come in."

"Jacobsen moved up the meet-n-greet, but deliveries from home come first," she said, carrying two boxes over to his desk and then handing him the bigger of the two.

Darren reached for the cutters as Shonda opened her box with her hands. She glanced over at his computer monitor and saw the image of his funny face.

"Official army business there, Chaplain?" she asked with a grin.

"Keep a family together, keep a soldier together. Darn right."

Her expression suddenly changed. Darren knew he had hit a nerve, but he wasn't about to inquire. He'd been warned off.

"Beef jerky," he said with excitement as he saw the massive stash in the box that also included candy and Bibles.

Shonda didn't bother to examine the remaining contents of hers. "Jacobsen's on in ten and we pull out," she told him as she walked back out of the tent.

A moment later Darren walked out to the commons area. He stood next to the senior officers and listened to Lieutenant Colonel Jacobsen addressing the men and women of the 30th Infantry Regiment. The officer stood at a podium, a large and detailed map behind him.

"So while we've made big strides to destroy Al-Qaeda and her offspring to liberate and stabilize this nation, the challenge remains. Hooah?"

The soldiers answered the commander with one roaring "Hooah!" that Darren felt rip through his bones.

"Today, Third and Fourth Platoons are gonna sweep our next-door neighbors again, see if they can slow down the welcome gifts coming over the wall." Jacobsen turned to Darren. "Chaplain Turner? Mind sending them out?"

As he took off his cap, Darren wasn't nervous stepping up to the podium, but he did know this was one of those important moments, a time when many of them would see and hear him for the first time.

"First, it's been an honor to meet such amazing men and women, committed to our country and defending the defenseless here in Iraq. I hope it goes without saying, but my tent's open 24/7. I'd like to meet you all."

He noticed his neighbor, Michael Lewis, joining the group near the back.

"In the interim, as you work hard every day to help the good people here in Iraq, remember your families at home need the same. Takes hard work and courage to love them from here, as best we can, but they need it, so it's courage we gotta have."

A variety of looks could be seen on the soldiers' faces, from wide-eyed attention to indifference to a few rolling their eyes in a scoffing look that seemed to say *Give me a break.* Michael seemed to be in the third camp. Darren closed his eyes and bowed his head.

"Lord, be with these men and women as they go out today. Please protect them and give them the strength they need . . ."

As Darren prayed, he wasn't just praying for those in front of him. He would be going out along with them. He hoped any nerves and anxiety couldn't be detected behind the words of the prayer he lifted up before God.

7

With the seat belt securely strapped over both of his shoulders and around his waist, buckling near his abdomen, Darren sat upright in the MRAP light tactical vehicle as it rode along with the convoy to a patrol base. Every sort of protection for the soldiers was accounted for, from the body armor and helmet he wore to the glasses protecting his eyes. This vehicle itself was the army's next generation of combat vehicles built to counter the enemy's weapon of choice: the deadly IEDs waiting for them.

The MRAP was named for its description as a mine-resistant ambush-protected vehicle. Since so many soldiers were dying in Humvee explosions due to the flatness underneath, the MRAP was designed with a V-shaped hull to offset explosions. Nine feet high and weighing nearly eighteen tons, it could drive twenty to thirty degrees on its side without even rolling over.

The MRAPs were replacing many of the Humvees that were typically used.

The different sort of missions MRAP vehicles would participate in included raids, traffic control, providing convoy security, escorting someone, combat patrol, medical evacuations, and transporting personnel.

With Master Sergeant Russ Carter driving the MRAP and Sergeant Mitchell riding shotgun, Darren sat next to Shonda. Every now and then he would look up at the gunner standing between them, manning the M2 .50-caliber machine gun on top of their vehicle. The remarkable thing about the MRAP was how an eighteen-ton armored vehicle could be so quiet. As they moved across the country, all of them watched the surrounding area outside the small windows as their convoy with other Strykers and Humvees moved steadily along.

The small talk Darren had been making with Shonda hadn't gone anywhere, but he couldn't resist continuing to try. It was either that or being forced to ride alone with his own thoughts.

"So . . . did I sound okay out there today?" he asked.

Her look said, *We have more important things to think about, Chaplain.*

"Sorry," he continued. "I just—I used to be on staff at a church. Now that I'm here, I sure don't want to sound like I'm in a pulpit, or nobody will come around."

"Just leave that box of snacks on your desk. Word will travel and they'll come."

Brilliant suggestion.

He remembered the package she had opened earlier that morning.

"Think I caught a glimpse of your delivery today. Looked familiar."

She smiled and nodded, then pulled the small Bible from her vest, stuffing it back there just as quickly.

"Mom told me to bring it," she said. "Apparently she went into my nightstand to make sure."

"Ahhhh. One of those moms who loves her daughter, huh."

"More like one who thinks getting me back on track is her job, not mine."

Even though he'd only known her for a few days, he already liked the no-nonsense attitude of Sergeant Peterson.

"You? Offtrack? Sure had me fooled."

The sudden steady thumping of rounds bouncing off the vehicle made Darren grab his helmet and duck even though there was no need to do either. He noticed how the two men in the front didn't react, how their expressions remained the same: steady, alert, and unimpressed.

"You on that, Blaylock?" Sergeant Carter bellowed out as he maneuvered the vehicle.

Corporal Scott Blaylock replied by unleashing the .50-caliber rounds, making Darren recoil again from its thundering sound that cut right through him. The gunner moved to hit his target, first firing at their nine o'clock, then their eight and their seven as they quickly moved past the enemy.

Carter looked back for a second, a grin on his lips. "Guess that's a yes."

Blaylock swiveled the gun back to the front of the Stryker as Darren slowly sat back in his seat, his eyes on the narrow slits of light coming from the outside. For a while, none of them spoke, as they moved past the remaining buildings in town and then headed back out into the desert.

8

The heat and the steady motion and the rolling desert berms outside all did their best to lull them asleep, but the soldiers on this convoy needed to remain alert at all times. Darren already appreciated them more now than ever before. As he sat in silence, Shonda's sudden admission surprised him.

"I have a son," she said.

"Wait—what?" Darren tried to hide his look of surprise. "I mean, that's amazing. He must be amazing."

"Yeah? Why's that?" she asked.

"Because . . . they all are."

Every wall she seemed determined to build kept being knocked over by Darren's earnest and open attitude. She let out a sigh, then pulled the small Bible back out and opened it up to find the photo.

"This is Colby," she said as she handed him the snapshot.

"Handsome little guy. You talked to him yet, since—?"

"He's three," she stated without emotion. "Not much of a talker yet."

"At three my Sam wasn't either. Then all of a sudden, complete sentences. And he hasn't stopped talking since."

A thought dawned on him of the reality of his statement.

Colby might start talking and she won't be there to hear it.

Before he could add to it, another barrage of gunfire erupted in the near distance. This time he remained upright and didn't flinch. Darren gave her the photo back.

"So . . . he take after you or his father?"

Shonda chuckled. "You mean the guy who saw the double lines on the pregnancy test, left, and never looked back? That man? No. He doesn't get that title."

So there's where some of this is coming from.

"And no, he wasn't my husband," Shonda quickly added. "So save the lecture. Momma's got you covered."

"I stopped lecturing after working with college students," he half joked, once again trying to soften the tone.

"I can hear my momma preaching at me right now, and she's thousands of miles away."

"Bottom line, Colby is a gift from God. That's all that matters now."

She nodded, then turned to him. "It was long. But you sounded fine."

Darren wasn't following.

"Your prayer," she answered. "You asked how you did. It was long but fine. You sounded like you cared."

He nodded, happy to know the sergeant's thoughts.

Good to see her opening up. Even just a bit.

9

"I posted some new pictures online. Showing off the daily life. You'll see our tents and the blast walls around us."

Heather listened on the telephone as Darren shared about the last couple of days and how it was to have gone out on a patrol, away from their sector. He sounded more animated than usual, so she let him continue without giving him an update on the home front.

"I conducted a memorial ceremony for one of our guys who died back home from cancer. He didn't deploy with us, but we still honored him as a soldier in our unit."

"So you must have done a lot to prepare for it," she said, knowing all that went into something like this, from planning and coordinating to rehearsing and supervising the event.

"It went off without a hitch," Darren told her. "It was incredible to hear what the guys had to say about their lost brother."

She remembered what Darren had once told her about memorials like this, how they had to be flawless. Mistakes could be tolerated in some areas of army life, but not in this. Every soldier deserved the best, and Darren felt honored to be a part of something so sacred.

He shared how they had been getting ready for their upcoming missions, meaning there was a lot of meeting and planning and strategy-making.

"Sometimes I even get to chime in," he said. "About how 'this' might affect 'that.' It's like playing real-life Stratego."

"That's always been one of your favorites."

"So how are things? I've already talked too much. Fill me in."

There was so much to tell and so little time, and suddenly she drew a blank except to say: "Our toilet got backed up again. Took me an hour to unplug it."

A thousand things, and I'm telling him about the clogged commode.

"Do you want to call a plumber?"

"No. Not after I worked on it for that long." She paused and gathered her thoughts. "Elie and Sam can't wait for camp. Sam's been doing 'training exercises' as if he's being sent to boot camp."

"I can't wait to hear how they like it."

"I put some new photos on our website," Heather said. "You'll especially like the one of Meribeth."

"I can't wait to see them. I hope you put some of yourself up as well."

"Yes, I think I've managed a few. Just because I know you're requesting them."

"They won't compare to seeing you in person, but they'll have to do."

She heard the trampling of four feet heading her way and knew their moment was almost finished.

"Be careful," she told him before letting Elie talk to him.

She didn't always need to tell him she loved him. Darren knew.

10

Darren sat alone at the table in the commons area, scrolling through photos on his laptop while wolfing down the plate of chicken and potatoes. Each new picture energized him a little more, filling his exhausted spirit with more life. He could hear Sam giving a loud chopping sound in his karate class, could imagine Elie twirling in her princess costume for her dance recital, could smell Meribeth's skin as she grinned behind a bundle of towels after bath time. There were photos of them laughing on the trampoline and making funny pictures in the kitchen and, yes, there were even some shots of Heather with the kids. But Darren had to pause for a moment and hold back the emotion as he saw the snapshots that Heather had told him he'd especially enjoy.

In one, Meribeth stood, a gleam in her pretty blue eyes, her mouth open as if to say *Aha!* Then in the next, her arms were up in the air as if she was balancing herself. Then he could see it— one foot in front of the next, then another, then her back to the camera as she wobbled ahead. Another shot showed her peeking around, delighted in taking her first few steps. Finally, it showed her toppling over, laughing and overcome with joy.

These were the battle wounds he would be forced to endure. The shots he had to take, realizing the moments like these that he was missing.

There's a reason why I'm missing them. I can never forget that.

As he glanced up to the sky to fight the wave of emotion, he noticed Michael walking toward him with a tray of food. Seeing Darren, he veered off to another table and sat down. Darren decided that Michael wasn't going to get off that easily, so he shut his laptop and took it and his half-eaten dinner over to the major.

"Neighbor," Darren said, nodding his head to greet him. "Mind if I join you?"

Michael gave him the same indifferent look he had offered the day he came over to their party.

"Would it matter if I said yes?"

Darren didn't let it bother him in the least. He paused for a moment, then put his tray next to Michael's.

"Then again, you look hungry," he said. "I didn't touch my potatoes. Enjoy."

The chaplain left Michael behind, only turning around once and noticing him digging into the extra helping. He knew that this wall his neighbor had built didn't always have to be so tall and so fortified. Darren didn't want to tear it down; he simply wanted to build a gate that occasionally would open. One that didn't require a lock and a key.

A couple of hours later, he was surprised to see Michael again. Darren was shooting hoops on the makeshift basketball court. A floodlight lit up the twenty-foot concrete perimeter wall where the backboard rested. It was a good workout, moving and shooting and rebounding as he sweated a few pounds off in the heat.

Just as Michael walked up beside the court to watch him, Darren fired off a three-pointer, drilling it.

"So where'd you play?" Michael asked while Darren went to retrieve the ball.

"Just high school," Darren said as he continued to dribble. "But it's always just been—one of my places." He made another shot. "No matter where you are, there's a hoop just around the corner."

He remembered Michael occasionally bringing the basketball out and shooting hoops himself back home, so he knew the major was itching to play a round—in spite of the man's forced frown.

He really wants to dislike me, but I'm not gonna let him.

"Three for three?" Darren asked, jumping and shooting.

The ball bounced off the metal rim, right toward Michael. He scooped it up, dribbled as naturally as he might breathe, then launched a shot with form and ease. Darren wasn't surprised to see the swish, and ran over to get the rebound.

"So I talked to my family the other day," he said.

"Yeah?" Michael looked more interested in the basketball he dribbled.

"Sounds like mine and yours have been hanging out quite a bit."

"Great."

"You called home yet?"

Echoes of the ball dribbling on the concrete bounced back at them.

"I got the feelin' you already know the answer to that question, Chaps," Michael said, bounce-passing the ball back to him.

Clutching the ball in his hands for the moment, Darren walked closer to Michael.

"Sounds like Tonya would really love to hear from you," he said.

Michael shook his head, a defensive, almost scornful look on his face. "What's your deal, man?"

"What do you mean?"

"Is messin' around in other people's lives part of your job description or something?"

Darren appeared to hesitate and think for a minute, the amusement coloring his face. "I mean, kinda."

"Man, my marriage is none of your business. You don't know a thing about me, or about my family."

No, but God does, brother. God sees it all.

All Darren wanted to do was help Michael and all the others at the camp know that very fact.

The major looked ready to strike any minute. There was such rage inside of him.

Darren had an idea.

"I know your family loves you," he said as he took out his satellite phone and handed it to him. "Most of all, they just wanna hear it back."

"Oh, you know that, do you? Let me ask you something, Chaps. You ever seen fear? In your own kids' eyes? Trust me. They don't want to hear from me."

Darren wiped the sweat from his forehead. "I just don't believe that. I don't."

Michael's laughter mocked him. "Okay," he said and started to walk off.

Then he paused and turned back around, the fight still unable to leave his soul.

"You know what? Let me tell you how it really works, Chaps. See, you haven't been to Iraq before, so you don't know what it's like to come home. You aren't ever going to be the same—and neither will that picture-perfect marriage you probably think you have. Stay outta my business, man."

His long boots began to make their way off the concrete, but Darren moved behind him, refusing to give up. Refusing to let Michael dictate the terms of their relationship.

"Tell you what," he called out. "You call. They hang up? I'll never bother you again."

Michael stopped and turned. "That a promise?"

Warriors like to be challenged. Darren understood this. He'd fallen victim to it many times. The fire inside a man's heart was put there by God, but John Eldredge added something to this fact: *The way we handle the heart is everything.*

Darren nodded as he approached the major, still offering him the phone.

Michael finally took it, looking frustrated to have lost the initial battle. As he dialed, Darren casually picked up the basketball and continued to dribble and shoot. A few moments later, he heard Michael's surprised and softened tone.

"T? . . . It's me . . ."

11

May 21, 2007

I have been away for a few days, joining my guys for some training out in the desert. I can't say enough good about our soldiers! As much as they want to get the bad guys, they also are compassionate for innocent people, particularly kids. They train hard not to hurt the good folks in Iraq. I have been thoroughly impressed with your US Army! They are truly heroes in my book. Tender warriors.

On another note, my time with them during some rough training allowed me to just hang out and get to know them. I've had some fantastic conversations! A couple of guys asked me if God would let them into heaven if they have killed people. Wow! A chaplain's dream question! We talked about King David and the apostle Paul. Both of them had killed, and God saved both in the end after their repentance (not necessarily from killing, but from not having God on the throne of their hearts). War is a tough subject, especially in questions about God and war. I won't elaborate, but God has, and does, sanction war (not all wars, but certainly ones against truly evil people). Another soldier, in his own words, "misses someone who isn't there." He is tired of living just for himself and wants to know how to find a good wife. Another good conversation we had right there in the hot sands.

That's about it for now. Thanks for your continued prayers and support. Homesickness is hitting me now. Hearing the kids on the phone has been great, but not the same as squeezing them on my recliner at home! Yet I'm glad and honored to be here. Please pray for our base in Iraq. There are definitely some bad people around here. God bless you.

Darren

THE SECOND MONTH

1

June 22, 2007

Hey, folks! I'm back at the main base now, having just returned from another visit to the patrol base. I stayed four days this time, and it was again great. We held two church services and had good responses both times. Every day is Sunday here, so it's not a big deal to have church on Tuesday morning at nine or ten and another one Wednesday at nine or ten in the evening. Basically, I look at the "battle rhythm" and find out when most guys will be coming in from patrols. That is the window of time I shoot for, regardless of day or hour.

I had more very significant conversations with some of the guys. One wondered who the woman was in the garden of Eden before Adam and Eve . . . sounds like some New Age stuff, but we really didn't talk about her too much. He was, however, interested in the different theories of the Resurrection. Everything from "it was a look-alike" to "Jesus just fell asleep and didn't really die." Nothing is off limits, so we talk about all kinds of stuff. I always end up pointing them back to Scripture, and challenging them to either find it true or not. Research it, hold it up at all kinds of angles and look at it, read it, read about it, do what you must—but you have to decide, is it real or not? That's the bottom line. If it's not, then I am most foolish of all to believe and to come to combat on a false pretense. What a waste. But if it is true, and of course I believe it is, then all the horrors and the bombs in the world can't take away the fact of the gospel, and the hope it offers for all who choose to believe and follow.

It is getting better around here. We are capturing or killing a lot of bad guys, and "peace" is slowly becoming more of a reality. We're not done by a long shot, but there are fewer attacks by the bad guys, and neighborhoods seem to be growing more safe. I hope it's really working and not just a lull for the bad guys to regroup . . .

Darren

2

Freedom Park on a sunny day was the ideal setting for taking family portraits. The hills were dotted with trees and the grounds were well kept, the grass always thick and green. Heather was glad they were able to enjoy the park as a family before Darren left for Iraq. Now she came here often, either to bring the kids outside to play, or sometimes to work at her part-time job as a professional photographer. Today she was doing both.

As Sam and Elie entertained Meribeth nearby on a blanket, Heather gave directions for poses to the Collers, a cute young family of four. Luke practiced in family medicine, while Marci was a very busy mother with their three-year-old daughter and year-old son. Avery already had mastered her toddler smile, while Ben looked at Heather in wide-eyed wonder while his parents took turns holding him. They wore combinations of white and blue that matched the sky and clouds above them. As Heather took multiple shots, she already knew there were some definite keepers.

"So how's he sleeping?" she asked while adjusting the large lens and snapping a few shots.

The couple looked at each other and smiled.

"We're having to let him cry it out," Luke said.

"At least we're *trying* to," Marci said, adding, "but sometimes Daddy can't help checking on him."

"Avery was so much easier," he said.

"That's 'cause I'm a girl," Avery shouted, getting all of them to laugh as Heather kept collecting digital pics.

Ooh, those are gonna be good ones.

There was just nothing as beautiful as an authentic smile, whether on a baby wrapped in blankets or an elderly woman in a wheelchair. A smile shared a person's soul while warming the heart of those who saw it. This was why Heather loved taking pictures, not just of her own family members but of others. Years ago she had been encouraged by a middle school teacher to keep taking photos, that she had "quite an eye." Though it had always been a hobby, even through college, she came to realize it could be more than that once she began getting requests to take photos for families and couples.

The Collers understood her situation, with Darren serving overseas, so they were gracious and patient in allowing her to have her three children nearby. They compared notes on parenting as she photographed them. When it was time to leave and everybody said their goodbyes, Marci handed her a check, even though Heather had told them she would bill them later.

"I can't wait to see the pictures and send them to you," she said before they left.

Heather looked at her watch and saw that it was only a little after four in the afternoon. She glanced at the kids: Sam was trying to do a cartwheel, and Meribeth was crawling over Elie.

"Hey, guys. Guess what? I have my camera and it's not dinnertime yet. And it's a beautiful day. So . . ."

Sam and Elie beamed, knowing what she was going to say.

"It's Turner Time!"

She grabbed the tripod near the blanket and fit the camera onto it. The kids were used to this by now, taking regular photos for Daddy to see at his base. For the first handful, she got them all to pose just as the Collers had, sitting together on the blanket, arms around one another.

"Smile for Daddy," she told them.

Sam and Elie soon morphed from grins to goofy expressions, tongues hanging out and mouths opened wide, laughing and dancing and trying to share as much joy as possible with their father. Meribeth hadn't yet figured out how to look any different from one shot to the next.

"Well done, Team Turner!" Heather said, giving her two eldest high fives.

The kids wanted to see the pictures right away, but Heather told them they had to wait. She slipped the camera into its case, then began to pick up some of Meribeth's toys that were scattered around the grass. In the distance, they heard another baby crying. Heather turned to scan the park, and spotted a young mother sitting on a bench near the pond, a stroller next to her.

"Watch your sister," she told Elie and Sam. "I'll just be a minute."

The closer she got to the young woman, the louder the high-pitched rattle of the newborn's crying became. The young mother didn't even seem to hear it, staring out to the water instead.

"Amanda?" Heather called out.

The woman turned her head quickly, startled. Then she wiped the tears off her cheeks and stood to lift her baby from the stroller.

"Heather Turner. We met at the base when our husbands deployed."

Amanda Bradley looked like a girl still in high school, lost and unsure of what to do as she bounced the baby in her arms.

"Yeah, I remember, I think," she said in a thick southern

accent. The baby continued to cry. "I'm sorry. She just won't stop crying. She doesn't want to nurse and she won't take her pacifier and I think it's because she knows her daddy's gone. She didn't sleep last night, so I didn't sleep either, and I had to take the day off work, which we cannot afford, and I just—"

"Amanda," Heather said, putting a hand on her arm. "This is by far the hardest thing I've ever done. It's okay. It's okay to have rough days."

I've had a few myself since Darren's been gone.

Heather stroked the baby's curly dark hair, speaking just above a whisper to help soothe her. "Hello, beautiful girl. How are you?"

The smile and soft voice seemed to do the trick.

"What's her name?" Heather asked.

"Alexis," her mother said, relaxing a little and not jouncing the child as much.

"What a lovely name." Heather smiled at Amanda, trying to give her any sort of affirmation she would accept. "Look— you're not the only one who feels this way, I promise. I think we just have to reach out to each other, you know? My number's on the Readiness Group contact sheet, so please, any time you need something—"

"I'm pregnant."

The two words stunned Heather for a moment, and she knew her expression reflected her surprise.

"I haven't told my husband yet. I don't know how to. We already were surprised when Alexis came. We just—we got married out of high school and just wanted to have fun, you know?

We wanted to save up to travel and see the world and then suddenly all of that stopped. And now—"

The tears began to show up again. Heather looked over to make sure her children were okay, then sat down on the bench and patted the space beside her, inviting Amanda to sit back down.

"We moved into a double-wide when we got married. Our folks didn't want us to get married, but they didn't want us living together either, and we were going to do one or the other. My husband—Lance—he's a daredevil. Drives a motorcycle. He's a thrill seeker. Got me to go parachuting with him. Hang gliding too. Can you believe it? That I went parachuting and hang gliding?"

"Of course I can," Heather said. "But nothing's as awesome and scary as giving birth."

The encouragement didn't seem to do its job as Amanda continued to wipe fresh tears away from her eyes.

"After he joined the army, we got the news that he was going to be deployed. He had just come out of basic training."

"Sounds like Darren, my husband. I know the feeling."

"I knew instantly that we'd have to move back in with my mom and her husband," Amanda said. "But Lance told me to relax, that it'd be fine. He said I could stay right here near the base, near the other wives and kids. But I explained to him I couldn't make it alone. Not with work and Alexis and nobody else—"

"But you are making it," Heather said.

"'One day at a time, Sweet Cakes.' That's what Lance likes

to tell me. 'One day at a time, we'll make it.' But he's not up at night with a colicky baby. And he's not trying to figure out this breastfeeding thing."

"That's why God lets us women do that," Heather joked. "It's because men wouldn't be strong enough to figure it out."

"I'm not strong enough either. And now . . . I didn't know. We didn't know. We weren't thinking that it could happen again so quickly, but it did. I just can't be pregnant. Not with him gone. Not while I'm on my own."

Heather studied the pretty young woman, her face flawless even with barely any makeup on. Amanda's eyes searched for something she couldn't see.

"You and your children are not alone," Heather said. "Come on—I have a pot of spaghetti sauce I made that can serve a dozen. There are some other moms I want you to meet."

"No, really, that's kind of you, but I can't."

"Listen, Sweet Cakes, I'm not taking no for an answer," Heather said in her best deep country drawl.

Amanda let out an unexpected laugh, surprising even herself.

3

Darren sat next to Lt. Col. Jacobsen and Michael at the conference table along with several ranking officers, all of them listening to Sergeant Carter as he stood and spoke about their latest objectives in the war. They had congregated in the Tactical Operations Center. The wall in front of them was decorated with a variety of maps, with the center revealing a WANTED poster of Osama bin Laden.

"Despite the sweeps, intel says Al-Qaeda still owns too much dirt in Sadr City," Carter told them. "So the marines are moving in for door-to-doors tomorrow, and we're backing them with two platoons."

Lt. Col. Jacobsen leaned forward in his chair. "When exactly do we get them back?"

"Six weeks. Maybe seven."

"Tough duty," Jacobsen admitted. "So Chaplain Turner, in about three how'd you like to go for a visit? They'll no doubt have something to talk about by then."

"Of course, sir. Just say the word."

The door opened and a private stepped inside.

"Excuse me, sirs. We have soldiers arriving . . . It's not good."

Everybody rushed outside, where the throb of low-flying Black Hawks forced them to scream in order to be heard. Officers and medics crowded near the road as vehicles from a convoy began to arrive. The first out of the lead Humvee was Cpl. Blaylock, who wiped the blood and sweat off his face as he approached them.

"That your blood, Corporal?" Jacobsen barked out.

"They hit us with two RPGs, sir. First grenade missed, but the second one hit Cosgrove's vehicle, and we—"

"Who exactly is injured, Corporal?"

Blaylock breathed in for a moment, his eyes wide and unblinking. "Mitchell, Cosgrove, and—"

A high-pitched scream from a young girl interrupted him. They turned to see the rear gate of Transport-1 open and figures appear from the back of the truck. Darren froze, a brief second of sheer panic locking him in place until he willed it away. A soldier cradled a young Iraqi girl in his arms. She couldn't have been more than six years old.

Dear God please no . . .

"Abdomen wound," the soldier yelled out. "Get her down!"

Behind them came another focused soldier, a woman, who leapt down onto the dirt road and then helped a distraught Iraqi man down as well. Both of them were covered in blood.

"Hurry! Hurry!" the man said in a thick accent, his eyes red and watery and wrecked.

"His two daughters, sir," Corporal Blaylock explained.

As medics took the wounded girl, she gave another ragged cry of pain. The father followed, his desperate prayers audible even in the chaos of the incoming soldiers. Darren watched them, hurting with them as they disappeared into the tent.

"Hey—who's gonna take this one?"

He turned around to see the same soldier at the back of the truck holding another girl, this one even younger. He rushed to the back to take her, to carry her to her sister and father and the medical team. But as he saw the pretty face with closed eyes and felt her lightweight body in his arms, Darren already knew. The voice above him only confirmed it.

"We couldn't save her, Chaplain."

So small, so beautiful, so soon. Darren stood for a moment, just looking down at her, the body resting in his arms just like Elie might, just the way she used to do when she pretended she was sleeping, arms hanging down and her head to the side, so he would carry her. But each time he placed Elie onto her bed and then kissed her good night, she would bounce back up and wrap her arms around his head.

This little girl is never going to bounce back up and give her daddy a kiss good night. Never ever again.

"Guess you should just . . . Do what it is you do."

The words from the soldier with the thick southern accent snapped Darren back to reality, back to this place where he needed to act and move just like everyone else. He nodded as the young soldier climbed off the truck and stood in front of him, his face looking as harrowing as his own probably did.

"Specialist," Darren said. "What's your name?"

"Bradley. Lance Bradley."

"I'm sure you did all you could," Darren said, with all the pride and admiration he could muster.

The young soldier simply nodded, his face not believing the words. Then he walked away, vanishing around the truck. Darren turned slowly toward the medical unit.

There was no need to rush.

4

The bright light of day disappears as Darren steps into the medical tent. The movement around him blurs, while the voices all sound like static noise. He forces each step, the body in his arms feeling fake, feeling too slight and thin.

"Listen to my prayer, O God. / Do not ignore my cry for help!"

At least he can pray now. At least he can cry out for help, unlike the dead girl in his arms.

"Please listen and answer me, / for I am overwhelmed by my troubles. / My enemies shout at me, / making loud and wicked threats. / They bring trouble on me / and angrily hunt me down."

Darren looks into the first treatment room, unsure where to take this sweet burden. A group of medics and physicians surround a soldier, desperately working to save him. He keeps moving, walking past three soldiers who kneel with their weapons at their sides, praying for their comrade.

This is it. This is real. This is the fight. The battle. The guts it's going to take to get through. Just to keep breathing.

"My heart pounds in my chest. / The terror of death assaults me. / Fear and trembling overwhelm me, / and I can't stop shaking."

King David's words haunt and heal at the same time, whispering in his memory like ancient melodies.

He stops and looks into another treatment room, sees a couple of medics pull a sheet over the face of a soldier on a stretcher.

"Oh, that I had wings like a dove; / then I would fly away and rest! / I would fly far away / to the quiet of the wilderness."

He blinks, his eyes stinging, and then spots the Iraqi down the hallway, locking eyes with him for a brief moment. The man stands beside a stretcher holding his other daughter, demanding answers in Arabic while a translator tries to communicate to the surgical team. An oxygen mask covers the young girl's face, and an IV is stuck into her arm.

"Tell him we're putting her to sleep and taking her to surgery!" the physician says. "He can't come!"

The translator explains to the irrational father that they must operate on her this instant. And that he cannot accompany them. The father protests in vain as they wheel her away.

Darren watches, holding the girl's dead sister in his arms.

"But I will call on God, / and the Lord will rescue me. / Morning, noon, and night / I cry out in my distress, / and the Lord hears my voice."

The Iraqi is left alone in the hallway, and then he begins to walk toward Darren. The father's eyes widen as he gets closer, a scream erupting from the depths of his soul.

Rescue this man, Lord. Please, Lord, hear my voice. Help this man. And help me.

5

Heather scrolled through the photos of the Coller family on her computer monitor, marking her favorites for editing. The news channel on the television behind her remained on, a steady sort of white noise that had become the background to her days. The only time she ever really heard it was when someone reported news from Iraq, as the reporter on TV started to do now.

"Tragically, officials confirm two soldiers from Fort Stewart were killed by Iraqi insurgents today . . ."

She spun in her seat and saw a newsperson dressed in khaki pants, a button-down shirt, and a vest, holding a mike in the middle of the desert. As she focused on the screen, Heather forced her eyes to remain open to see if any names scrolled in the feed.

For several moments she braced herself for impact, for a reality she had refused to dwell on for longer than a few fleeting seconds every now and then.

For a few minutes the reporter gave details of the insurgents and what the army was doing, but Heather only focused on whether or not she would hear or see the name Darren Turner.

A pounding knock on her door jolted her.

No no no no. Please God no . . .

She swallowed a gasp of air and then held her breath, her eyes wide and worried as she looked at her front door.

She couldn't move. She began to shake as a hundred thoughts went through her mind. She knew what happened when the worst news became true. A Casualty Notification Officer would arrive along with a chaplain, both prepared to share the unthinkable and then hope and pray to somehow help the shocked widow.

That word . . .

Widow.

The knocking continued, and she stood up and slowly began to walk toward it.

She kept moving, knowing that was all she could do, knowing that's what Darren would do and what he would encourage her to do now. As she turned the handle and pulled back the door, she watched Tonya's slight smile vanish as her friend realized what Heather had been thinking.

"Oh my gosh," Tonya said, rushing to put her hand on Heather's arm. "I am so sorry. I wasn't thinking. I should have called."

Breathing in and out, trying to slow down her racing heart, Heather said, "Yeah, you should've."

They were on the same team—they knew the gravity of the situation.

"I just wanted to let you know—the notifying chaplain and casualty officer are at the wife's house now, so we're next. Till family arrives."

Heather nodded as she scanned the front lawn, noticing how the grass needed cutting.

Family arriving. What a terrible thought.

"Heather. Our husbands are okay."

"Which makes me feel even worse," she said.

"Someone's on the way from Base Family Services now," Tonya told her. "I'll bring my girls here to keep an eye on your kids till they get here."

The children were in the backyard, playing without a care in the world. Sometimes it seemed like the trampoline could keep out all the bad news this world had to offer them. If only that were really the case.

Heather continued to breathe slowly and steadily, the way she did when all three of the kids were born.

"I can't believe I just did that to you," Tonya said, shaking her head. "Even after three tours, I still feel the floor disappear every time there's a knock at the door. When he's gone, I can't even order pizza."

Heather laughed, releasing some of the terror that had built inside of her. She wiped slight tears from her eyes as she hugged her friend.

God didn't want people to go through trials alone. Darren had his comrades-in-arms out in the desert, and Heather had hers on the home front.

"Dear Lord, we have to do this well," she said, more to herself than anyone else.

Tonya gave her a knowing nod. She had been down this road before, so she knew what to expect.

Not knowing what was coming was the worst thing about all of this.

6

The page was blank and empty, ready for Darren to pour out his heart and share his thoughts. Yet all he could do was watch his hand as it shook, the pen barely held in his grip. He wiped the sweat off his forehead and turned toward the floor, thinking about everything that had happened. The spinning sensation inside of him hadn't completely ceased.

Once again he pictured the little girl he had carried, so light and lifeless. He saw the other soldiers, wounded and weary, continuing to fight by helping others or by being strong with their injuries. What haunted him the most was the face of the father, wrecked and desperate, so lost.

Closing his eyes, Darren saw Elie's sweet smile and round cheeks. For a moment, a terrible and twisted moment in his imagination, he saw the dead girl jumping on their trampoline, laughing, and himself carrying Elie into the tent.

He opened his eyes and closed the journal, then placed it down along with the pen. He grabbed the sat phone and stabbed in the numbers as fast as he could.

Fear was not going to consume him. The enemy had won a victory today, but Darren still planned to fight in any way possible.

The line rang once, then twice, then started a third time when it was interrupted by a familiar and delicate "Hello?" from Elie.

"Hey, Bug. It's Daddy."

"Daddy!"

Her shout calmed him far more than writing in the journal could have. The only voice that could encourage him even more was Heather's.

"It's so good to hear your voice," he told Elie. "I miss you so much."

In ways you don't know and hopefully never will.

"I miss you too. Is everything okay? Mommy looked worried when she left with Miss Tonya, and you sound—"

"Yes, I'm okay. I promise."

She waited for more, but he didn't—he couldn't—tell Elie everything.

"Daddy?"

"Yes, honey."

"Are you wearing your armor?"

His eyes burned with tears as he stared at the photo of his daughter on the screen saver of his laptop.

"I sure am," he said. "Are you?"

"Every day. When I remember."

Her voice felt like water on a patch of dry grass in the middle of a desert.

"Give everyone a great big hug for me. Bye, baby."

"Bye, Daddy."

Daddy. Her sweet voice said the word with such intimacy and adoration.

Sometimes that simple word was enough to keep going.

Sometimes it had to be.

7

"You okay, Chaplain?"

The officer's words jolted Darren out of the daze of thoughts surrounding him in the middle of the sweltering day. He sat on the sandbags outside the office, his gaze facing the buzz of activity on the base but his mind elsewhere. Far elsewhere, away from this country and this fight. He stood as Jacobsen approached.

"Yes, sir."

His voice masked every bit of pain and question his heart held.

"Good. 'Cuz some folks around here could probably use a visit about now." Jacobsen handed him a thick file. "Some info on our lost warriors."

As Jacobsen began to move toward the barracks tents, Darren followed him from behind, trying to shake the cobwebs of confusion from his thoughts. He imagined Heather back home, walking up to the soldier's house with her friend, knocking on the door and waiting. Waiting for it to open. Waiting for the pain to invite her to come in.

He knew her warm and inviting presence would be comforting to the women who were suddenly dealing with the news. Yet he also knew how hard her job was.

He stood for a moment in front of the entrance to the tent, unable to go inside. He wiped the sweat off his forehead, then did the same for the back of his neck. His mouth was dry, his back ached, and his uniform felt gritty against the rest of his body.

He felt like he was waiting to reload his rifle, but he couldn't find any rounds to fill the magazine with.

"Turner?"

"Sorry, sir," Darren said with a wry chuckle. "Standing here, in this moment—I guess I'm not exactly sure what to say."

"Well, I'm no expert in your line of work, Chaplain. But I bet you'll leave that master's of divinity back in your tent and just give a few boys your heart. It'll probably go a long way."

The commander's no-nonsense attitude never wavered. Disciplined. Decided. Undaunted.

"Thank you, sir," Darren said as he entered the tent.

8

Later that evening, having made the rounds that afternoon and talked to a variety of men on the base, Darren still needed to meet with a few more from the platoon of the soldiers who'd died in order to do a Critical Incident Stress Debriefing (CISD)—which basically meant helping them talk through what happened. To ask what they thought during and afterward, to talk about how they felt now and how they could cope in the days ahead. Darren knew it would be tough to get the guys talking at first, but once someone really shared, conversation could take off. This was vital in helping them deal with their loss and ultimately get back in the fight. Otherwise, they could become paralyzed with grief and think they were the only ones feeling this way. It also brought the platoon together even closer, which was good in combat for sure.

When he entered Alpha tent after dinner, Darren found half a dozen soldiers sitting and resting on the line of cots inside the tent.

"Third platoon, Alpha?" he asked.

Some of the men looked curious, while others appeared indifferent or didn't even bother looking at him.

Corporal Blaylock nodded and urged Darren to enter. "You found it, Chaplain. Come on in."

The smell of sweat and cologne hovered in the air. Darren spotted a folding chair along the wall, grabbed it, and pulled it near Blaylock to sit down. He noticed one of the soldiers staring at the floor, a grim and hopeless look covering his face.

"Sorry to interrupt, guys, but I could use some help. This will be my first memorial for guys we've lost out here."

A couple of them sighed; others dropped their heads. Nobody wanted to open up and expose their feelings. That's not what men did, especially strong men like these guys. But they were still wounded and hurting, and Darren needed to find some way to attend to the wounds.

"I would love to know a little more about your friends," he said.

For a while the silence stretched out like a knife cutting the skin. Then Corporal Blaylock finally spoke.

"Civis were all around us as we came off the last bridge. Two blasts, one after the other behind us, and we ran back, pulled Mitchell outta the fire, but he was already gone. And Cosgrove was already inside, getting those two girls out. The flames just took him."

Darren waited for more, but Blaylock stopped, as if considering the gravity of what he had just shared. Two men, perishing in two blinks. With two breaths, they were suddenly gone.

A soldier named Diego looked up at the chaplain. "Mitchell was engaged. And Cosgrove's wife is pregnant."

The words swirled around them like quicksand.

"I've been with both of 'em since basic. And when my fiancée decided military life just wasn't for her, those two guys didn't leave my side till we shipped out. Probably kept me from—"

"What'd you do with the little girl?" another voice interrupted.

Darren turned to spot a soldier lying by himself in the dim light at the end of another row of cots.

"Bradley, right?" Darren asked.

The soldier nodded.

"Medics finally took her," Darren told him. "And her father. To make arrangements."

"So did you bring us some Bible verse explaining why a little girl had her life taken away before it began?"

The cynicism wasn't lost on Darren.

"No, I didn't. Bring a Bible verse, that is. But I do have a daughter. Her name's Elie. The thought of losing her is beyond what I can imagine."

A few more soldiers looked over at Darren.

"Yeah, I got a daughter too. So what? You're peddling a God who'll take mine tomorrow. Maybe yours the next day."

Normally when he was challenged, Darren would run toward it, unflinching and ready to battle. But this wasn't a competition or a game of one-on-one. This was real life. This was the reason he was in Iraq in the first place.

He moved closer to Bradley to talk.

"You're angry. I get it. I mean, we all rage at death, right?" He looked around the room to address the others as well. "I think there's a reason for that. I think it's because we were made for life. And I believe in a God who came to rescue us from death and bring us into life. Who gives us all life to begin with. For a specific time and purpose. Until He chooses to take us home with Him. Forever."

Lance Bradley shifted and sat on his cot, adrenaline pumping fury inside his veins. "You know what that little girl told me when we first picked her up? She told me through the translator—she just wanted to stay alive to do two things. She wanted to fly in an airplane, and she wanted to climb a mountain. To be closer to God. Little innocent girl didn't do anything to deserve to die. She wanted to be closer to God. And the God she believed in didn't stop it. Who needs that?"

Darren dropped his head, feeling the weight of the soldier's grief tugging him down. He let out a sigh, then stood up.

Grief didn't like to listen, especially when the enemy had it weighted down with hate and bitterness.

There's nothing more I can say to him. Not now.

"I hear you. I do. Sorry about your friends." Then he faced the young soldier who had initially opened up about his life. "And I'm sorry about your fiancée."

Diego nodded. "Thank you."

Darren walked toward the door, then turned around to look at all of the young men, sitting and lying there as if they had just lost a championship match and had nothing left inside of them.

"If anyone wants to talk, I'll be in my tent. Eating beef jerky."

9

The base slept under a humid blanket of black, but Darren couldn't. He kept replaying what had happened, thinking of Heather and the kids back home, of all the things he needed to say to them. Of everything they would need to hear if the unthinkable ever happened.

He knew he couldn't wait. He had to do this.

Setting up the camera on a tripod on his desk, Darren pressed record, then sat upright, smiling at the camera.

"Hi, babe. Man, I hope there's never a reason for you to see this video—"

A mortar blast nearby interrupted him, causing him to cringe in his chair. He reached over and paused the camera, considering whether to rewind and start over. Instead he pressed record and kept going.

"But if you are watching this, I guess there's no use in covering up things like bomb blasts. It just feels so wrong, not sharing everything going on over here, like we do at home. Even the small stuff. I realize now what a luxury that is."

For a few moments he poured out his thoughts, saying things he always avoided telling her when they had those few precious moments on the phone. Heather didn't need to hear about the soldiers filing for divorce or, worse, about the ones they had lost. He didn't want to fill her mind with thoughts about how dangerous it was around the base, about how evil their enemy really was. She didn't need to learn specifics about IEDs, about their KIAs and WIAs.

Tonight, however, he didn't edit himself. He shared how intense things had been. Then he shifted and began to remind her of the important things.

"Heather, please . . . know how much I love you. And have since the day we met. And yes, I know I ruined those flowers you were taking pictures of." He gave a sober chuckle, thinking of the fond memory. "Chrysanthemums, right? Who the heck names flowers anyway?"

He looked into the camera as if he were staring at his wife.

I can see her now, those gentle and caring eyes looking up at me, knowing how much she loves me.

"I miss you more than you can imagine. And love you just the same."

It was enough. Darren stopped recording, then took the tape out and slipped it into the top drawer of his desk.

Please, God, don't let anybody ever see this tape. Let me bring it back to Heather so I can throw it away.

10

Darren turned to his CaringBridge blog to update his family and friends back home on life.

> In the last three days I have counseled and talked with about fifty soldiers. Some were very close to those who died, and some are just plain scared. As I get a chance, I encourage them to consider Christ as their ONLY hope. He's the only one who proved hope after death by coming back from the grave. All others are just talk and wishful thinking. He is the One we can trust and put our hope in. The guys who embrace this, really embrace this, find that their fears subside and their courage rises again. If we know our life is in His hands, then we don't worry so much about our body armor being perfectly positioned. He ultimately is in control! The gospel truly does make better soldiers. "If He is for us, who can be against us?"
>
> I am back at Falcon planning for these ceremonies and talking with the soldiers who are getting a quick break before going back out. The pace is insane right now. Once

the ceremonies are complete, I will most likely go back out and stay at the combat outpost (COP) for a few days at a time. The soldiers need serious care and attention as they come back in from the fight each day and night. The things they've seen, heard, and smelled . . . They are truly heroes!

I ask you to continue to pray for me and our soldiers to remain out of harm's way in the middle of harm's way. Make sense? I can't believe I'm doing what I'm doing . . . finally. I/ we (my family) have prepared for this for so long it seems, and now I'm in the middle of some of the most intense fighting of this long war. It's an honor to be here. There is a sense of urgency, that we're in a window of opportunity to take this NOW. God bless you all.

Darren

THE THIRD MONTH

1

July 3, 2007

"The only thing necessary for the triumph of evil is for good
men to do nothing."—Edmund Burke

On this day before our great nation's birthday, I've been
thinking about our freedoms. That quote above really
is true. If you remove people who honor and respect
righteousness and goodness, the void is quickly filled with
evil. It comes, uninvited. Some areas of Iraq that our forces
once occupied but now have left (for reasons that are too
strategic and lengthy to be discussed here) are once again
refilled with bad guys planning and plotting evil. But before
you jump to condemn the Iraqis, it is true in our own land as
well. Remove good ol' God-fearing people from the scene,
and bad things quickly rush in. So back to the quote. It is

true, regardless of geography. Evil is constantly looking for the absence of righteousness, and where it succeeds, it flourishes. I believe that is true both in the physical world and the spiritual.

God, help us to guard, to stand firm on Your truth and to stand against the tide of evil both in this world and . . . in our own hearts!

This Fourth of July, I ask you to pause and try to imagine life without our freedoms. We can rest at night without the threat of death squads bursting into our homes . . . We can eat at restaurants without a fear of suicide bombers . . . We can go anywhere to worship without fear . . . And on and on the list goes.

This place is very dangerous, and our freedoms are foreign here. But our troops are great! They are part of a long line of men and women who have served to protect our freedoms. Regardless of the politics of the current situation here, your sons and daughters, husbands and wives, moms and dads who are fighting here are true heroes! Celebrate our freedoms, and pause to honor those who put their lives on the line to preserve them for me and you. God has graciously given our nation freedom and protection because we have a history of honoring Him. These men and women are part of that great history. It's my honor to be here in the middle of them.

Tomorrow I will go to the COP and stay for a couple of
days. We will have a Fourth of July celebration—a hot
meal with ice cream instead of MREs (prepacked military
rations). I hope there won't be any "fireworks!" Pray for my
safe travel to and fro.

Once again, thanks to all of you for the amazing comments
and encouragement. It makes me swell with pride to know
you are thinking of us and praying for us. God bless. (Oh
yeah, new pictures are available.)

Darren

2

As Darren wrote down notes for yet another memorial ceremony, he thought of all the men he had spoken with in the last
few days. A young warrior had stepped on a buried roadside
bomb while out on patrol, and even though he never saw it
coming, his friends witnessed everything. Those men were still
reeling when Darren first spoke to them. He decided to stay a
few days longer than he had planned, simply to meet with them
and counsel them through what they were experiencing. This
meant being out of touch with Heather and the family, but he
couldn't do anything about it.

Those men . . . their emotions ran the gamut, from angry to
sad to confused to crushed. His job had mostly been to be there

and to listen. Even though their friend had perished, there were acts of heroism to be reported. Even while there was tragic loss, there was tremendous victory as well.

The paradox of the war.

Darren knew already that he had grown to love these guys, and that love was a risk. He would hurt like they did when they lost a buddy. He continued to hope and pray that they wouldn't come close again to losing another soldier. Yet he also realized he'd only been out there for two months, and that he had thirteen more to go. This was war, and bad men wanted to kill them. They were always thinking of new ways to try and get them, but so were the soldiers—always thinking of protecting the innocent and the oppressed.

He heard the door open and footsteps enter his tent. Lance Bradley walked over to his desk, scanning the shelf of candy and beef jerky.

"Hey. These free?"

"Twenty bucks a pop," Darren joked.

"Smart man. Or I'd clean you out."

The young soldier's glance shifted down to the desk, then his hand whipped to his side, pulling a knife out and lunging toward Darren so quickly that the chaplain didn't even have a chance to react.

The blade sliced into the wood desktop, slicing a scorpion that had been skittering across it. For a moment, all Darren could do was look at the weapon and the creature cut down by it. He swallowed, then nodded to the candy.

"Well, for doing that, the candy's free," he said.

For a second I thought that knife was coming at me.

After seeing the trauma these men carried, and hearing all the stories not just on the battlefront but about their lives back home, Darren knew anything could happen. He knew every soldier had a different way of dealing with grief and wounds, and he had to be on guard every moment.

Taking his knife and what was left of the dead scorpion, Lance then grabbed a handful of beef jerky and some sweets before sitting down in front of Darren.

"I was a bit hard on you the other week," Lance said as he chewed on the jerky. "Sorry about that."

"Don't worry about it. It goes with the territory." Darren saw the young man studying the framed photo of the family on his desk. "That's Sam, who's six. Elie is eight. And Heather with Meribeth, who's all of eleven months."

The soldier grinned, then took out a picture from his shirt pocket and handed it to Darren.

"Daughter's Alexis. And that's my wife, Amanda." Lance shook his head, looking at the ceiling for a moment and laughing in a bewildered sort of way.

"What is it?" Darren asked.

"She just told me five minutes ago that we gotta come up with another name! And money to pay for it too. How about that?" Lance let out a sigh, then tore into another piece of jerky.

So that's why you came in to talk.

"Well, congratulations. That's great news."

"I'll tell Amanda you said so. I'll even give her your number."

Popping back up to his feet, Lance began to pace in front of the treats again, obviously lost in thought. Then he began to walk toward the door, looking as if he thought it had been a mistake to come in. Darren let him debate with himself, not saying anything for a few minutes. Finally Lance glanced over at him.

"Something on your mind, Bradley?"

"You said something the other day."

"Yeah?"

"Something about how God gives us life for a specific time and purpose, then takes us home safe."

Darren shifted in his chair, nodding at the younger man, recalling the rage on his face when Darren had uttered those words.

"Yes," he said. "Home safe in heaven. But that's not a guarantee of safety here."

Lance shuffled back over toward him.

"See, that's the part that got me. So let's say I buy it here, right? And something happens to me and I go 'home safe' to heaven. Where does that leave my wife and kids?"

He slid back onto the seat facing Darren, for a moment searching his thoughts and confusion, trying to make sense of the questions he wanted to ask.

"I mean, what happens to them? Do they go off the rails without their dad? Does Amanda lose it and let some drunk loser move in and hurt all three of them, making their lives a living hell while I sit up in heaven all safe and warm? Is that what you think oughta make me or anyone else feel better?"

This wasn't some hypothetical question the bright-eyed soldier was asking.

This is his own life he's talking about.

"Lance, I'm sorry."

"I don't care if you're sorry! Tell me He is! And tell me my kids won't *ever* go through what I did! Can you tell me that, Chaplain? Can you?"

The shouting clearly could be heard yards around the tent, yet Darren didn't mind. He understood. He knew it was the kind of release men like this needed.

The blue eyes stared at Darren, so desperate and so ready for an answer.

"When my father left us, I knew he wasn't coming back," Darren said. "Ever. Said he stopped loving my mom. But it felt clear as day he stopped loving me too."

"This is not helping, man."

Darren hadn't talked to many men about his father, especially not like this. But the time was right and he knew he needed to be open. Sharing his heart didn't mean to spout out a bunch of things he'd learned in seminary. It meant opening up about the wounds his heart had experienced.

"I didn't have my dad, but I did have—still have—another Father. Who has never let me down. Who has never abandoned me. Who won't abandon you or Amanda or Alexis or that new little one, no matter what comes."

He took one of the Bibles he had for the soldiers and slid it across the desk. Lance simply eyed it, then stood up again and headed out.

But then he turned around, walked back to Darren's desk, and picked up the Bible.

"Don't get any ideas," he said with the charming smile that had surely attracted Amanda to him when they first met. "I just like free stuff."

3

They had walked through Freedom Park for a while, just the two of them, mothers taking a break from their children to talk. Heather had been there from the moment Anna Cosgrove learned about her husband's death, and since then had been staying in touch and making a point to see her. This morning Heather had scheduled a time to have their kids babysat while they got outside to take in the midsummer day. With Anna in her third trimester, she needed to sit and rest for a while after the short stroll.

There were so many things Heather wanted to say to Anna, but most of what she was doing was listening. Anna admitted her hormones were racing as she shared her frustration and fears.

"I know what they say, how they tell you to accept the reality of your loss, how you can't be in denial. But part of me is still thinking they made a big mistake, that Dirk's going to call me up and say there was one huge misunderstanding."

Sometimes Anna would wipe away tears, then would find herself laughing so hard she had to wipe away more. Then sometimes the wave of emotion would seem to drift back out to the

ocean, leaving her staring out in wonder, her hands resting on
the little life growing inside of her.

"I'm still trying to figure out how I'm supposed to raise a
baby on my own," she said.

"You can't do it on your own. And you don't have to."

"Are you signing up for babysitting services?" Anna half
joked.

"You have a support system here. That includes me and a
lot of others."

The pregnant woman gazed at a pair of ducks flying together
above them.

"I know that. Everybody keeps giving me information and
showing me resources that are going to help. But eventually it's
just going to be me and my baby. And what then? There are
lots of other folks who are going to need help. And I'm—I'm just
really scared."

A passage from the Bible came to mind, and so did a couple
of groups that Anna could become a part of. But instead of giving her more advice or wisdom or resources, Heather just put
her arm around the younger woman and stayed by her side.

Sometimes that was all anybody could do.

4

The sound of footsteps woke Darren up, not with a slight nudge
but more of a violent jolt. As he jerked in his chair, he scattered
papers and CDs on the desk he'd been slumped over. Sleep was

nothing like it used to be. Now it was hard to find and too easy to leave behind.

Shonda looked surprised to find him at his desk.

"Oh, hey," Darren said. "Sorry, Sergeant." The alarm on his watch began to chirp. He swatted it silent. "Wow. Couldn't sleep last night, then apparently couldn't stop . . ."

Shonda seemed to understand all too well. "The amazing power of anticipating a mortar blast. Then doing whatever you can to forget about it. It can be a vicious cycle."

As she walked over to help him pick up the pages that had scattered onto the floor, she noticed the emails on the computer monitor.

"So, just checking, but did you want me to protect you from all kinds of trouble? Or just bullets and bombs?" She stood, waiting for him to respond. "That's lots of emails from your wife, Chaplain. Better answer at least one of them."

Darren glanced at the inbox displayed on his screen. There were multiple unopened emails from Heather with subjects like *Are you okay?* and *Please write back!* and even *Darren?*

He sighed, knowing he needed to, remembering he had started to yesterday but hadn't been able to figure out what to say or what *not* to say. He had told himself he would just talk to her on the phone, but that hadn't happened yet.

That has to wait. I have a job to do.

"I'm late," Darren said as he began to get his materials ready for the morning service. "Mind cross-checking those CDs with the service run while I check setup?"

He had been checking a few albums for music that could

be used for the memorial service. Many times, like now, there wasn't a bugler or trumpet player around to play taps, so they used a CD player instead.

"No problem," Shonda said, picking up a CD to begin looking through them.

Once again, there would be a memorial ceremony for another man killed yesterday. Darren now knew a little more what to expect. The guys who were closest to the deceased would be hit the hardest. Big infantry warriors would be crying hard tears. But that was good. They needed to do that now, and then get ready for the next mission coming up. If they kept the grief inside, or delayed it, they would be a liability on the battlefield.

5

July 15, 2007

I share this not to freak out anyone, but to be real. The courage and bravery I've already seen here are phenomenal. Soldiers continue to go in and out of our gates, patrolling the area we're in and trying to do the right thing. War is confusing, but our guys are doing the best they can to secure this place, which will in turn get us home. That's the goal. And they are doing a great job, with minimal mistakes. They have joined the fight and hit the streets, knowing it might not always turn out well. I've promised my guys that I and lots of people behind me are praying for them and their safe return each and every

day. There are times that I have to go out as well. No lie, it's
not an easy place here. But my guys would have it no other
way. If they would've wanted a safer existence, they would
have done something else. They are true heroes! Pray for
God's supernatural protection—bullets missed, bombs not
exploding, bad guys' plans thwarted. God bless you all.

Darren

6

The image on the computer monitor showed Elie by her countdown calendar, with three of the fifteen months each marked
out with a big X. Heather studied it from the table full of photos
and possible mattes for framing. Those empty boxes on the calendar seemed bigger than ever.

Twelve more months. A whole year.

The busyness Heather used to fight against now was an
unusual ally in her battle against missing her husband. The photography helped, and so did parenting the kids, and so did all of
her involvement with the community of army wives and families. Yet everything could potentially remind her of Darren.
And when she hadn't heard from him for a while, like lately,
those reminders could linger for longer than they should. They
could sting too.

Today the reverse happened when the phone rang, breaking
the silent questions in her heart. Heather felt an overflowing

relief to hear Darren's voice. She didn't expect an apology for his lack of contact, but it was the first thing he said, saying how busy the last couple of weeks had been. Never talking specifics, but revealing more through his tone than any word he might say.

Darren sounded not just tired but worn down. His voice didn't match the last set of pictures he had shared last month that showed him laughing and being goofy like his normal self. She wasn't going to tell him that, however. He surely knew how he sounded.

"I can't wait to send you the latest pictures," she said. "The kids made a cake for our anniversary."

Darren sighed. She could picture him on the other line shaking his head.

"They remembered, and I didn't?" he asked. "Did you eat it all?"

"Don't worry. I boxed up a piece for your next care package."

"I can't believe I forgot." He paused for a moment. "I miss you guys."

"Believe me, we all miss you too."

In more ways than you'll ever begin to know.

As usual, there were too many things to tell him, too many stories to choose from. But she quickly tried to share a few stories about the children, at least telling him something notable about each one.

"Meribeth is eating everything in sight. The other day Elie suggested we take her to the doctor to make sure she has a taste bud since she loves vegetables!"

Darren's laugh felt good to hear.

"Sam was so proud that he earned his green belt in karate—"
Darren interrupted. "Already?"

"Yeah. I posted the pics two weeks ago."

"Aw—right. Shoot. I gotta look more."

Once again, she could hear it surrounding his words, almost smothering them. That depleted feeling. A tone that Darren rarely spoke in, but one he couldn't disguise today.

"Did you get the recent packages we sent?" she asked.

"Yes. Those items and goodies from Buffington Baptist and the Creekview High School ROTC were incredible," Darren said. "I'm going to put all the items in a big box and take it out to the COP for the soldiers. They don't have anything out there, so these things will be a huge blessing to them. Especially since they don't even know the people it's coming from."

"That's great to hear."

"And hey—this may be a wild idea, but any chance you're up for coordinating Christmas stockings for the soldiers? You could fill them with gifts and snacks like you've been sending me."

Heather looked around the house that needed cleaning, among other things. Yes, she wanted to keep busy, but she didn't want to suddenly be drowning in work.

"Well, sure," she said. "How many do you need?"

"Give or take a thousand."

It was a good thing he couldn't see her eyes popping. "O-kay. I'm going to need some reinforcements then. I suppose I can ask a few wives."

Her mind began to start seeing it. Suddenly it didn't seem daunting; the project felt like it could be inspirational.

"We can even make it a community thing," she continued. "Get a few churches and schools in on it."

Heather shared some ideas with Darren, but she didn't get much excitement or energy coming back on the line. She decided she didn't want to let him go without asking. Who knew how long it would be until they would talk again.

"Babe? Are you okay? You just . . . you sound different."

"Nah, I'm fine. Sorry. Really, it's a lot like faith for people at home, I guess. Slow and hard. Maybe harder here than I expected."

7

July 28, 2007

I have found that there are two options to mental survival over here: one is to constantly be on edge because, really, at any moment there could be some sort of attack and people could die. The other is to go numb to the threat and live as normally as possible. I think I am choosing to go numb because the once-scary "incoming" sirens are no longer that scary. I just hit the ground and get back up a few minutes later, hoping nobody got hit. Not sure if that's the best way to cope, but it's how I'm getting through the days. Remember the first time you drove a car? I do. I was scared, thinking I could crash and die at any moment in that huge piece of moving metal. Then I got used to the threat and just drove. Kinda the same thing here.

Tomorrow is Meribeth's first birthday. I'm sad that I'll miss
the party. I so want to be home with Heather and my kids.
That ache comes and goes in waves. It's definitely here
now, in light of her special day. It's times like these that I
question what in the world am I doing over here. I know why
I am here, but like Jonah, I want to run away at times. But
just as God wouldn't let Jonah, He won't let me. Pray for my
cooperation in the midst of being here.

Happy birthday, Meribeth!! I love you so much, and I can't
believe you are already one year old. Enjoy your party.

Love,
Daddy

THE FOURTH MONTH

1

August 5, 2007

Hey, friends and family! Hope you and yours are doing well. I want to share a couple of quotes from some kids in a Norfolk, Virginia, Sunday school class who sent me some encouraging letters. I will quote their original spelling as well.

Dear Chaplin Turner, I hope that you will try not to die and be happy.

Dear Chaplain Turner, thank you for helping are country. Do you know my Dad? My Dad is not thar because he chaped his anckale.

Dear Chaplain Turner, I just want you to know I'm praying . . . so have a good battle.

And finally,

Dear Chaplain Turner, I am praying that the Iraqeys don't have machinge guns and canyons. I pray you kill all the jermans and Iraqis.

I'm sure he means well! Thanks, Norfolk First Baptist. Those letters brightened my day.

Good news story at a patrol base I went to. I held a service on the roof and shared a passage from the Gospel of John, chapter 20, about "doubting Thomas" and how his doubt actually turned out good because Christ came to him in his sincere questioning. Doubt is good if it causes us to seek the truth more. Then, once Thomas met the risen Lord, he called him "my Lord and my God." The first one to use that phrase.

After the service, a young soldier came up to me and asked if I "had known about that verse." I asked him what he meant. He said he thought his sergeant had told me about their conversation previously. He's been to church three times, including one of my services, in the last year, and each time, the ministers have preached from that same passage . . . Wow.

He thought I knew about it and planned it for him. Once he figured out I didn't, he was a bit freaked out. I said, "What are you waiting for?" After we talked for a little longer, he decided it was time to become a believer. We prayed right there, with his buddies watching, and he sincerely

asked the Lord into his life. It was great. He's no longer a

"doubting Thomas."

Darren

2

The basketball felt as comfortable in Darren's hands as the Bible did. Underneath the scorching midday sun, he dribbled the ball, ready to set the attack. Michael jogged underneath the basket, then to the outside edge of the court. As they played a sweaty game of two-on-two alongside the tall walls that protected them, they were a unified team. Jacobsen was not their commanding officer but their enemy, along with Lance. For twenty minutes, four men in drenched army-issue T-shirts and shorts battled each other as hard as possible, as Shonda and Master Sergeant Russ Carter provided commentary and banter from the courtside picnic bench.

Just beyond their game, over the wall and out in the field, a group of Iraqi kids kicked around a soccer ball as joyfully as the men playing inside. The only difference was the danger of the ground they played on, and the violence that could rip it apart at any moment on any given day.

By now Darren had picked up Michael's strengths, knew the rhythm of his movements. Seeing Michael jogging to the half-court line, Darren began to move toward the basket with the ball. Without even looking toward him, he passed the ball to his teammate, then stood still, setting the pick against Jacobsen. As the lieutenant colonel slammed against him, Michael swooped past and easily bounced in a lay-up.

"Good job," Darren said as they gave each other a high five.

"Eighteen to seventeen," Shonda called out.

Darren wiped the sweat off his forehead, then readied himself against their formidable opponents. Lance never stopped moving and never seemed to tire, while the older Jacobsen conserved his energy but was still machinelike in his shooting. The two of them dribbled and passed the ball back and forth, with Jacobsen beginning the attack by driving toward the middle. Darren spun around him to tap out the dribble, taking it away to midcourt.

Michael was already sprinting to the basket, ready for the pass.

"Open! I'm open!"

With no one near on the outside, Darren didn't hesitate, but pulled up and shot. The basketball didn't touch an inch of the rim as it dropped through. Michael grinned as he jogged back to Darren.

"Aw, man, I was open," he teased.

"We didn't need two points, boss. We needed three for twenty-one."

"Yeah, whatever. Lucky shot. Or ya got help." Michael nodded at the sky.

Darren chuckled and waved him off.

"All right, gentlemen, that's game," Sergeant Carter said behind them. "Shower up, we move out in thirty."

"Next time I got the chaplain," Jacobsen said with a big grin underneath his black shades.

Michael gave Darren a fist bump. "Good game, man."

With the base alive with action, the two soldiers caught their breath and grabbed water bottles to chug. Darren knew this would be as good of a chance as any to give Michael the gift.

"Hey, before you head out, I've been meaning to give this to you."

The God's Armor coin shimmered as he offered it to Michael.

"Nah, dude. I'm good. I don't do lucky charms."

"It's not about luck or the coin," Darren said. "It's a reminder of who to rely on—"

"If it ain't gonna stop a bullet or defuse a bomb, I don't need it." He paused, noticing Darren was still holding the coin. "But if it makes you feel any better, I been talkin' to Tonya."

Darren gave him an affirming nod. "Good to hear."

"Yeah, yeah—don't get too excited. I don't know what that wife of yours has her thinking you're gonna do for me, but she keeps pushing me to talk to you. So—you know. Good talk today."

As Michael walked away, Darren slipped the coin back into his pocket.

3

For a moment, the coffee cup made her stop. It was Darren's favorite, one Elie enjoyed using for hot cocoa. As Heather held the wet mug with ARMY emblazoned on the side, the morning sun bursting through the window above the sink, she wondered what Darren was doing. She prayed and asked God for His protection over her husband.

At the same moment, Darren was speaking to thirty soldiers sitting on the ground or in folding chairs at Camp Bucca. The place was a detention facility for Iraqis and consisted of cinder block housing units, tent compounds, and a military hospital. This afternoon Darren was giving Communion to the soldiers who wanted to participate, and even though he had given the same message earlier that morning, he still spoke with urgency and passion.

"So my kids love to play battle," he told the watchful faces. "My son Sam has this whole outfit he puts on—the helmet, the chest plate, shield, and sword. He goes all out, but to him it's still a game. My daughter, Elie, however—she's an old soul. She sensed the danger ahead."

As he spoke, Darren could see Michael and Lance in the back listening. The sound of gunfire cracked in the distance, forcing everyone's attention to look to their left for a moment.

"So before I left, I sat Elie down and reminded her. I told her about something everyone who believes in a good and mighty God knows, or at least senses, but something that's also easy to forget. I said I have an armor unlike any other protecting me."

Darren didn't know that at the same moment, Elie was reading about a group of young warriors in *The Lion, the Witch and the Wardrobe*. In its pages, she imagined herself as being as brave as Lucy.

"This armor has the power to conquer all my fear because it guarantees life beyond the grave," Darren shared. "The power to flood my soul with peace even in the most terrifying circumstances, because I trust in a God who promises never to leave us."

He didn't need to try to get these guys' attention. They had chosen to be there, and all of them were in the same boat. Their fears were real and had become part of the routine of life. Some of the faces nodded understanding as Darren spoke, while others tried to make sense of what he was explaining.

This was a typical field service, consisting of some prayer requests shared, a song or two, a short sermon like this one, and Communion. Out in this place, Communion meant so much; it was a great picture of all of them receiving Christ and His presence with them, a very welcome thing in the savage spaces in which they lived. The informal and laid-back services were only thirty minutes long. Anything more would be too much for the attention span of tired soldiers.

"So I told my Elie I'd be safe. But I also told her that by trusting God, that same armor will keep her safe too. As it will your family. Yes, we're in a form of hell right now. But by trusting in the promises of His armor, we can find peace."

While Darren spoke, Sam sat on the couch at home, coloring a picture of a soldier wearing armor, putting an extra coat of gold crayon over it just to make sure he colored in every inch.

The short message Darren gave concluded with a line of soldiers receiving Communion. With each individual, he held up the cracker in one hand and the miniature cup in the other.

"The body of our Lord broken for you. The blood of our Lord shed for you."

4

The lone figure sitting on the picnic table near the perimeter wall hadn't escaped his attention as he spoke. After all the men had taken Communion and gone on their way, Darren walked over to sit beside the soldier he already knew well. Her rifle rested in her lap.

"Long day?" he asked.

Her thin, uneasy smile and silent nod reminded him of the first few times he'd ever spoken with her, of how guarded she had been. By now he knew something was bothering her, and he would have bet it had nothing to do with the army.

"You're doing a great job, Shonda. You know that, right?"

"Does it really matter? If I'm a failure as a mom?"

She paused, looking the other way as if hating herself for admitting this. Darren waited, feeling no rush to respond.

Help often came in the waiting and the listening.

"It's true," she continued. "A few months after Colby was born, I started finding excuses to not be home. Acting like it was to provide for him, but . . . I got so used to it, I don't think he'd remember being with me if I—"

"Hey, I got news for you. It's not too late to fix that. So let's just do it."

"But how, when I'm here and he's there? It's too late."

Thick tears pooled in her eyes, refusing to spill out.

"It's never too late," Darren said. "You'll be surprised to know all the things your kids might remember. All we're asked to do is try. To keep loving them no matter what."

"Here I have training. I know what I'm doing. But nobody ever taught me how to be a good mother, a good parent."

Darren only laughed. "A thousand books all say something different. You learn by doing it."

"But I can't parent, not from out here," she said.

"You absolutely can—"

Before he could continue that thought, they heard Sergeant Carter's familiar call. "Let's go! We're movin' out!"

They stood and started to walk toward the convoy. Darren made sure he pressed pause on the conversation instead of trying to wrap it up.

"We'll talk about this later. But trust me, God's got a thing about letting us think it's too late."

5

Heather heard the footsteps rushing into a bedroom, then couldn't hear another sound. With the kitchen cleaned up for the time being at least, she walked down the hallway to see what the kids were up to. As she stood in the doorway to Elie's bedroom, she saw both Elie and her brother kneeling beside the bed.

"Right now, God, please protect Daddy, wherever he might

be," Elie said as she rubbed the coin her father had given to her. "Watch over him and keep Daddy safe from the enemy."

Sam knelt beside her, a pair of Darren's combat boots on the floor beside him.

"Kids?"

Sam looked up and then jumped to grab her arm, pulling her to the bed.

"Mommy, hurry," he said.

Heather wasn't going to question their prayers. Instead, she knelt beside them and closed her eyes while Elie continued to pray.

"And bring Daddy home safe, Jesus. And Mia and Nia's daddy too."

After Heather prayed for Darren, Sam stood up and gave a confident "In Jesus' name. Amen." Then he gave a series of karate kicks and chops in the air. "Kiii—yaaa!"

Now that was a way to end a prayer. Heather knew God listened to their prayers, and that He watched over her husband. Perhaps the children somehow knew or felt something. Perhaps the Holy Spirit was leading them in the mysterious way He moved.

Be with him, Lord.

6

The prayers were heard, and indeed, were necessary. Only moments after standing to prepare to leave, a piercing blast ripped through the outside perimeter wall. Debris rained down on

Darren and Shonda as they were thrown to the ground. Darren noticed his Bible had fallen out of his jacket and landed several feet away from him in the dirt. He began to crawl toward it.

"Let's go! Now!" Shonda said, yanking him by the shirt and then leading him away.

Darren knew he had other Bibles. He had only one life.

They ran to a nearby cement wall that was under construction. Shonda dived behind it with Darren following, while all around them soldiers scattered for cover.

The next mortar landed inside the compound, louder and shaking the ground. It was followed by one even closer, an explosion obliterating the picnic table where they had just been sitting. Darren looked in horror at the gaping hole filling the space where they had been moments before. Rapid cracks of gunfire resounded outside camp.

"This is Oscar 2. We are pinned down on the northeast corner!"

Shonda was next to him, barking into the radio. More gunfire popped nearby as the attack siren in the camp began to whine. The large, sporadic roar of the .50-caliber came from the nearby tower above them.

"Head for the bunker!" the voice on the radio told them.

That's Michael's voice.

Shonda looked around. "Where? I don't see a bunker. Repeat. Over!"

The radio was silent as sets of gunfire sounded from different areas.

"Chaplain! When I move, you move!"

There was no time to reply, to think, to even comprehend. Darren just acted and reacted, standing and sprinting after Shonda. He swallowed but his throat felt dry, the taste of sand and acid on his tongue. Above the scattered gunfire, a high-pitched whine sounded, getting louder and closer as they—

The wall exploded, sending bits of concrete everywhere. Darren stumbled, blacked out for a second, then opened his eyes, unsure where he really was. The ringing in his ears prevented him from hearing any of the soldiers shouting at him nearby.

His body shaking, Darren sat up, dizzy and still not sure what had just happened. Shonda appeared over him, as if she was acting as a shield to any more incoming mortar. Then he could see Michael and three other soldiers running.

They're desperate to get someone.

"Get up!" Michael yelled at him. "Come on, get up! We gotta move."

Darren realized the men had come for him.

"Chaplain, let's go!" Shonda ordered.

He couldn't balance himself, and for a moment Darren thought he might tumble back over. The world spun around and his head ached.

Have I been hit?

"Chaplain! Get up!" Michael shouted, grabbing his hand and then yanking him up.

Suddenly they were moving fast, with Michael's arm around his neck, basically pulling Darren along.

"Jackson, we're coming to you," Michael shouted into the radio as he led the way.

By the time they made it to the bunker, Shonda was helping lead Darren past the door. Soon they were all inside with the door safely shut. Michael carefully lowered him against a wall as Darren sucked in air and tried to have a straight thought once again.

"Hey, you're gonna be okay," Michael said. "Neighbor, you're gonna be okay."

Darren could only look up at him but couldn't answer. He couldn't do a thing but just breathe.

"Props for the help, Major," Shonda said.

Michael simply gave her a nod, then went back out the door to see who else he could help. Shonda knelt beside Darren, offering him a water bottle and then helping him lift it to his lips.

7

With the kids all fed and outside, Heather and Tonya were finally able to sit down and eat. The August day was sweltering, so the sprinkler set up for the children to play around was more refreshing than fun. The mothers could hear the laughter outside as they talked, with Meribeth still in her high chair playing with the remnants of her animal crackers. Heather told her friend how the kids had suddenly stopped what they were doing earlier that morning and prayed.

"I've never seen Elie pray like that before. It was intense, like she sensed something very specific was happening."

Tonya reached over and grabbed her arm, her eyes wide open.

"What? What is it?"

"I'm going to give that girl a list of things to pray for, that's what," Tonya said.

"Why? What have you heard?"

It was a question all the wives carried around with them every single day as they waited and listened and hoped.

"There was a mortar attack," Tonya said.

Heather stood up. "What? When? Are they okay?"

Tonya nodded, pulling on Heather's arm and speaking in a calm tone. "They were visiting other bases for officer meetings."

"Tonya. *Are they okay?*"

"Yes, they're okay."

"My gosh." Heather sat down, breathing and gaining control over her emotions. "Why didn't he call and tell me?"

"Girl, something like that happens, your man is busy."

"I know, but—I mean . . . Ugh, I know." Heather sighed, realizing this was still so new, that she was still learning as she went. It had only been a little over three months. "Still, I just feel like something more is happening between Darren and me."

"Between you two?" Tonya said. "Honey, trust me. It's not between you two. It's between you two and that war."

8

August 21, 2007

Hey, friends and family. This isn't going be a very pleasant journal entry. Friday a mortar attack at one of the bases we were visiting resulted in the loss of a couple of guys. As they always do, the attack came out of nowhere and it was harrowing, hard stuff to deal with. I'm exhausted. Everyone is. Been counseling since then for the last four days since it happened, and I'm not done. Many tears, hugs, and long silences. Words fail. Just being there with them and hurting with them.

The memorial ceremony is tomorrow night. Please pray for me to be strong and courageous. The ceremonies are supposed to be more patriotic than religious in nature, but I have a good rapport with my guys. I want/need to be bold with the true hope of the gospel, not preachy but real with them. "In this world you will have trouble. But take heart! I have overcome the world"—Jesus (John 16:33). They so desperately want out of the trouble, but it's my challenge to help them through it. God rarely rescues us out of the trouble, but promises to be with us in it. Through the pain and loss. God can be found by those who choose to look for Him. That's all I have. That's what they need. Slick advice and clichés are empty, hollow.

One of the men who died was married and had kids. The other's father-in-law is here. He's in the National Guard and deployed to Iraq, and since getting word Friday about the tragedy, he made his way down to base. I met him today. He broke down as we talked. He simply had to be at the ceremony, so we will have a very special guest. Wow.

We just want to come home. We're trying to be patient while the local government gets its act together. But our patience is thin, if it even exists at all. In times like these, it seems senseless. I know we're making a difference, just not a lasting one. You can lead a horse to water, but . . . God help!

I hope I didn't bring you down, but this is our reality. As I've said before, take extra special care of these warriors when they get home. They need it. Just listen. Be patient. Don't talk about yourself. And let them get the weight off their chest that's been pressing on them for months. War is hell.

Because of His great mercy,
Darren

The Fifth Month

1

September 2, 2007

Homesickness . . . it has set in deeply around here. The honeymoon of the initial deployment is definitely over, and we're staring at the calendar moaning about how long we still have left. I can't wait to see Heather and the kids in the airport and just hold them again!

0True, we are accomplishing some military successes, but that's only a temporary fix—like getting rid of a fire ant hill in south Georgia, only to look around and see the other billions of ants! Until they want a better existence, and put people in place to make it happen, there won't be any lasting benefit. Reconciliations, apologies, repentance, humility, desire for safety for families, etc. All of these things need to happen. We have given them time, now it needs to happen.

I ask you to pray that our leaders not dance to a political tune, but call an ace an ace and not linger in indefiniteness. For Iraq's sake, and our own morale, we need some concrete answers and goals. I remember when I had to start doing things on my own as a kid—wash clothes, pay for gas, etc. It made me step up and do it, or it wouldn't get done. It's time for them to step up and take over so we can move out of the way. Sorry for the rant . . .

I have loaded some new pics. These are some random shots of life around the main base, not the patrol bases. Here at the main base, life is very different. The pace is actually more hectic here, with meetings and coordinations, etc. Out at the patrol base, there are two speeds: either on a mission or hanging out/sleeping. I will stay at the patrol base to hang out with the guys, have a few counseling sessions and a service or two, play chess, and, of course, restock the care package goodies table. I'll mingle with the guards on the roof as well as the guys hanging out in their tanks. It's really a lot of fun, when things are going well. When crisis hits, I run to it. The "hanging out" with the guys prior to a crisis prepares them to receive me when it hits. And that can happen literally any moment.

Finally, I do have hope despite the previous ramblings. In the middle of all of this, God is still very much at work. I have talked with and counseled numerous guys who are desperately in need of something bigger and better than

this. For reasons we don't fully understand, God has brought
us here to the desert and is bringing soldiers to Himself. It
is a privilege to watch them come to the end of themselves,
and finally reach out to the Lord! He is there, waiting—
just as the prodigal finally gave up his waywardness and
returned to the waiting Father (Luke 15). So many troops are
doing the same. In light of that, it's all worth it! God bless.

Darren

2

Once again, as the morning was still waking up, Darren sat in his
quarters at his desk, facing the camera and recording a message.

"I still can't believe how close the mortar attack came. Even
a couple of weeks after it happened, I can't help thinking about
it, remembering what was going through my mind. All I could
think of was, would I ever see you again? And I have months
left before I do."

For a moment Darren imagined Heather standing in place
of the camera, looking over at him with her beautiful and reassuring grin.

"I walked onto that plane last May confident. Certain our
lives were in God's hands. But today, all I felt was fear. Just
desperate to get back to you. To the kids. Afraid of either of us
losing the other."

He blinked, noticing the red light on the camera. Heather was gone and he was alone.

Once again Darren had the now-familiar thought. This time he spoke it out loud before shutting off the recorder.

"I really hope you never see this."

3

The church gymnasium was unusually active for Friday noon-time. Several lines of long tables filled the space, with parents and kids standing alongside to assemble Christmas stockings for the soldiers. Even though Christmas was four months away, it wasn't too early to be working on these, nor to be enjoying festive tunes while doing so.

Heather and Tonya were running the operation, filling the assembly lines with the necessary items. The plan as Darren had shared with them was to be able to hand each soldier a stocking full of goodies on Christmas Eve.

The women asked for help, and help had certainly arrived. More than fifty volunteers had shown up today to help pack. They made the contents of each stocking the same to avoid one soldier getting something better or worse than his buddy. The main gift in each was a thirty-minute calling card; a variety of hard and soft candy and a couple of candy canes sweetened the deal.

The women had set the end of September as a deadline for commitments to the stockings, with November 1 as the mailing date so Darren would receive them by the beginning of December. He planned on going to different locations with the stockings in order to have a little party with Christmas music and the sharing of the Christmas story.

"Looks like somebody just brought another set of stockings," Tonya said as she carried a large box over toward Heather.

"How many are there?"

Tonya set them down on the floor and made a quick assessment. "It looks like there might be close to a hundred!"

"We're going to need them," Heather said as she scanned the nearest assembly line. "We already have over five hundred committed, but we need double that amount."

Tonya opened a bag of assorted lollipops and laughed. "There's something kinda funny about sending a bunch of soldiers suckers."

"They can't melt on the way over, right?" Heather said. "It'll be like Halloween. Except, of course, they'll be hearing the message of Christmas."

"If it helps them even just a little to find some joy and hope over there, it'll absolutely be worth it."

Heather watched her friend carry the bag of candy to an assembly line, knowing that Tonya had been through this before. The soldiers weren't the only ones who would need some joy and hope around Christmastime. Day by day, Heather was learning how to live without her husband by her side. In his place came the specter of death, the always-present reality that at any minute, she could hear news that he was gone.

Candy couldn't cover the fears and the grief soldiers carried inside, but it could be a sweet little reminder of loved ones back home who were helping them carry the cruel things that war could bring.

4

"Hey, Chaplain. Got a story you can share on your blog."

Darren was surprised not only to see Michael peering into his tent, but to hear that he knew about the online journal he had been keeping to share with family and friends.

"I didn't know you were reading it," Darren said.

"Nah, Tonya told me about it. Listen, we were out on patrol today. Local father ran up to our vehicle carrying this little girl. She looked gone, like what happened a couple of months ago. She couldn't have been more than two. Our translator said she'd fallen into a canal and was underwater for something like five minutes! The medics went to work, and they revived her! They've checked in with the family since, and she's doing well."

"Praise God," Darren said as he gave an affirming nod.

"Yeah, I'm sure something like this won't make the news. It's way too hopeful. Some folks in Washington don't want to hear good news."

Darren nodded, knowing how much was happening in the capital right now that would determine the future of this war.

"I know the army doesn't pay me for my opinion, but I hope and pray some resolution comes from everything," Darren said.

"Not knowing is the worst. I just want to get back home."

Darren knew there was no simple answer. Yes, they had been making progress, but there was so much more they could be doing. Should they stay and finish, or should they all simply head back home? Could Iraq stand on its own, and if not, what exactly was the role the United States should have?

"We just have to stay focused," Darren told his friend. "The bad guys exploit any opportunity when we're unfocused. We can't afford any more casualties."

"Yeah, well . . . Ramadan starts September 13."

Ramadan was Muslim holy month, when the devout believed all their actions had more of a significant value to Allah . . . including attacking US soldiers.

"Every little piece of good news counts," Darren said. "Thanks for telling me this."

Before Michael could slip back outside, Darren added one more thing. "And thanks for reading my blog!" he joked.

"Next time tell them how valuable I am to your two-on-two game," Michael said, and disappeared.

Later that night, right before heading to sleep, Darren began to write another blog entry, telling readers about the young girl who had been saved. Before he could post it, he got an email from Brian, a friend back in Athens, Georgia. With September 11 approaching, Brian was sharing some thoughts about that day and about the world they lived in currently.

Darren . . . I tend to believe we are doing the right
thing, despite the words and actions of those who
try so hard to have us think otherwise. So much is
being made of our losses (and every single life lost
is terrible), but the very same evil and hatred that
brought about 9/11, and would love nothing more
than to bring about much larger acts of terror, is
what we as a people are up against. Our struggle in
Iraq is not as much about Iraq as it is about standing
against an ideology and an extremist belief system
that wants nothing less than total world domination. It
doesn't believe in coexistence with other religions—it
demands conversion, subjugation, or death.

On the surface much of this has become simply
political for most Americans, but deep down there
is, in fact, a major spiritual element. We hope and
pray for a quick resolution over there, but I'm afraid
that we are in for a long battle—either there or
somewhere else—until those who declared war on
us are defeated, or we are. I know that's not very
comforting, but I fear it's true.

Darren decided to share this along with the story about the
young Iraqi girl whose life had been saved. It was good to have
reminders of the struggle and battle—and also reminders that
hope could always be found in the middle of them.

5

September 14, 2007

Hi all from Heather!

I wanted to give you an update from this side of the war,
to share what happens when the wives and families are
notified of casualties from the front. This evening we, the
commander's wife and FRG leaders, will host a grief and
support gathering for the families of our unit. Many of
the women coming include those who've just found out
about their loss. It's always incredibly painful. Wives will
ask questions about the condition of their husband's body
and if they are going to be able to see him before burial.
Others have children who are trying to process the loss.
Once after a nine-year-old girl found out about her dad,
she ran and hid in his closet. When they found her, she was
wearing her dad's army boots and hat, clutching her dad's
clothes. It's painful to watch others go through this, but I
remain thankful to be there for them.

I was overwhelmed seeing this for the first time, but
watching the other wives who have been there before has
been amazing. Even though they also are terribly sad, I see
them bravely rising to the occasion to comfort those who
will one day be able to comfort others. Darren has often

described the soldiers as "tender warriors." I must say that
these women are tender warriors themselves. Tender to
comfort the hurting and care for their families; warriors
to stand in the face of fear, sorrow, loss, loneliness, and
exhaustion. Please pray for the wives of the soldiers. It
doesn't make sense, but there is nowhere I would rather be
right now. In this place there is nowhere to go to get comfort
and peace other than Christ. Pray that we all run to Him.

Heather

6

A mother never clocks in and out, and neither does an army chaplain.

She can watch out and be wary, yet her son can still come through the front door with a bleeding gash in his knee after hitting a pothole and falling off his bike.

He can be strong and solid, yet see soldiers coming back from a routine mission that suddenly erupted when an IED went off and killed one of their group.

A mother always needs to be ready to console and comfort, and so does a chaplain. Yet as much as a mother can mend the wounds of a scraped-up knee, a chaplain can only strive to do the same to the damages of a scarred soul.

Exhaustion for a mother comes from dealing with tantrums and impatience and questions and distractions, while for a chaplain it comes from dealing with the sadness and grief facing soldiers who have lost a comrade.

Neither job is more important than the other. Both are necessary roles that oversee valuable lives.

A mother will never stop caring. She can't. And as for a chaplain, he can't stop either.

7

September 27, 2007

. . . Finally, I'll conclude with what has become my prayer

every time we roll out the gate. I pray for us, our vehicles,

our eyes to see things that don't look right, God's protection

and wisdom on where to drive or not to drive. Most of

this prayer comes straight from the Scriptures, both Old

Testament and New.

"Lord Jesus, You are above all spiritual rule and authority.

Everything is subject to You. I pray for Your protection today.

You said no weapon formed against us should prosper.

Make it so. Disarm any roadside bombs meant for us. You

said You would command Your angels concerning us. I ask

You to do that now, Lord God. And You said not to fear man

who can only kill the body, but fear Him who has the power

of heaven and hell. Give me the courage to do that. In Jesus'

name. Amen!"

So far, God has not only protected our convoys, but has given me real courage when we roll out. I'm not gonna lie, I was very afraid initially, but He has given me faith and courage. For your "battles" today, I pray He does the same. God bless.

Darren

The Sixth Month

1

October 1, 2007

Good morning from South Baghdad! Hope you all are doing well. We're fine here today, and three days ago the temperature finally dipped below 100 degrees! Cause for celebration. It's so much more bearable now. Evenings are dropping into the upper sixties. The morale in our battalion is on an upswing. After a very tough summer, we're beginning to see gains in security and safety in our area. Less and less enemy activity, compared with early and midsummer. We've killed or captured lots of bad guys, combined with many local citizens choosing to help us secure their neighborhoods. It is working! And we've just set up yet another patrol base. It is called PB Hawkes. One of our companies has just taken ownership of it, and they are building it to their liking. It doesn't have a preexisting structure on it; it's just a field full of our stuff surrounded by protective walls. That is the same company that has taken heavy casualties. They are excited about this, a place to call their own. They needed something to look forward to, and this is it. I saw many smiles when I went there this past week, something I haven't seen in them for a long time. I've included some pics from the new PB.

The Christmas stocking project has reached its goal! We have received commitments for 1000 stockings as of a few days ago. I'm excited about this, getting to have Christmas with these guys over here. We have a party planned at each PB: some Christmas songs (I'll play guitar and they'll sing), handing out the stockings, our commander dressed as Santa, and coffee with dessert from the dining facility on the main base. I know this will bring some good times to them during this hard-to-be-away-from-home time. And they will get to call home during this time thanks to you and the calling cards! Thanks to all of you who have committed to the stockings project.

Now that the Christmas project is finalized, those of you who still want to send care packages are welcome to do that as well. Many guys are now receiving packages from their friends and family, but the stuff I bring to them from your care packages always seems to be the "right" stuff. For example, one care package had a random sewing kit in it. I put it out on the table at the PB, and a soldier walked

up and said, "Yes! I needed one of these." Who would
have thunk . . . One item in particular that seems to be
in short supply over here is good deodorant. Everyone's
personal stock that they brought over in our initial
deployment is running dry, mine included. The deo that
they sell on the main base is no good. Most of the guys like
the Old Spice deodorant-only stuff (Red Zone, I think it's
called, in a red container). The antiperspirant/deo combo
irritates a lot of armpits. Anyway, for what it's worth. Jerky
is always popular as well (beef and turkey). And, now that
it's cooling down, chocolatey things won't melt. I'm getting
hungry . . .

Finally, prayer is more real to me than ever. I'm sure it's
the bullets and bombs, and missing my family immensely,
but the sense of urgency in prayer that I feel is growing.
When our guys roll out of the gate, my heart grows heavy
for them. I ask the Lord to watch over them with almost a
boldness, like Moses in Exodus 33 when he asked God to
go with them, or not send them at all. And God agreed!
Wow! And for my family, that our kids would be a blessing
to Heather, and she to them. And that is happening also.
So much could go wrong with three munchkins, but so
far so good. Heather is the true champ of our family. For
that I am simply grateful. The Lord is so good, if we just
give Him room in our lives. "Now to him who is able to do
immeasurably more than all we ask or imagine, according
to his power that is at work within us, to him be glory in the

church and in Christ Jesus throughout all generations, for
ever and ever! Amen" (Eph. 3:20–21).

Because of His great mercy,

Darren

2

The war might physically be in Iraq, yet it was being lived out
all the way to the Turners' home in Richmond Hill, Georgia.

Every day Heather strived to "fight the good fight." She
understood what this familiar term meant now, since it was so
easy to fight a bad fight, or to not bother fighting in the first place.

She had a list of all the wives she had met and their children.
She noted all those who had lost their husbands, and she kept a
long list of prayer requests that she tried to look over regularly
and pray about.

She had attended far too many memorials and shared far too
many tears with those who had lost so much.

Heather's unit were all the women who were waiting and
wondering and hoping and praying every single day. And she
told them something over and over again: "We wear combat
patches too. But ours hang from our hearts."

Whether it was filling a bowl of cereal or doing a load of
laundry, the work around the house was endless. She balanced
that with the kids' homeschooling, with specific times in the

morning and afternoon blocked off to sit down and help them read, write, and figure out problems. Elie and Sam were both involved in tennis lessons, and Meribeth was into everything, so the children kept her busy.

There were occasional photography jobs, but the big projects like the Christmas stockings took up more time than she initially realized. She would never tell Darren that, because she wanted and needed to help him in any way she could. Nothing she did could compare to what the soldiers were going through. But Heather reminded herself that her work was just as important.

Every day, she hoped not to hear the worst. She also hoped to hear from Darren.

3

The letters brightened Darren's day and warmed his soul. A school in New York had mailed in letters from seventh graders, and so many of their comments made him laugh.

Dear Chaplin, I have no pets (don't ask why), I've gone to Myrtle beach several times, and 3 people in my family are left-handed.

Dear Chaplain, This Halloween I might be an old man and my friend is going to be my wife, the old woman. My life isn't all that exciting.

Dear Battalion I have a flour baby. Her name is Adagal. I think my Sience teacher hates me! Today we had a half day for NO reson.

And finally,

Dear Chaplain, Tomorrow we have a test. My brother skipped

*school. Haha! I laughed. My mom thought someone broke into the house
today. She's crazy. Okay. Bye.*

Humor and laughter were some of the many things he had
often taken for granted back home. With October there, he
couldn't help thinking about life back home during this time
of year, his personal favorite. The cooling temps and changing
colors of the leaves . . . Friday night football and the faint thumping of the high school marching band warming up . . . The smell
of burning leaves and finding his favorite sweatshirt that smelled
musty from its long summer sleep on the shelf.

Thinking about these things made Darren think about all the
things he would never be able to get back. Meribeth's first words
and steps and vegetables. Sam's karate lessons and learning his kicks
that he thought he could beat him up with. Elie's transition from
little girl to bigger girl and her learning to love reading and art.

The level of heartache, homesickness, and frustration was
truly indescribable, at least when he tried to sum it up on his
CaringBridge site. He now truly understood why guys returning
from the war went through what they did. They didn't want to
be called heroes. They just wanted to be called, but not too often.
They wanted to be reintegrated to their life after the fog of war,
and it always took time.

How long will it take me?

These men needed a new mission, something they could be
a part of apart from battle. For believers, they needed a mission
from God.

So many guys joined the military to be a part of something
bigger than themselves, but many soon realized that being in

the army didn't scratch their itch. The guys Darren knew who
were true believers had a distinctively lower amount of stress and
negativity than those who didn't share that faith.

In light of eternity, all of this is but a grain of sand on the seashore.

Yet some days he had to force himself to gain that perspective.

Darren knew that no matter what happened in Iraq, or on
this earth, in the end God would win. Being on His team made
the middle part not so bad, because he knew the ultimate turnout.

Darren shared this belief publicly and privately with the soldiers he met and interacted with. This was the hope he held out
to them, day after day. Sorrow may last through the night, but
joy comes in the morning!

So Darren continued to choose joy, every morning, noon,
and night.

4

As another morning of stuffing Christmas stockings was nearly
completed in the church gym, Heather noticed a pregnant
woman step foot into the building, then look around and start
to leave.

"Amanda," Heather called out as she rushed over to her.

She hadn't spoken to the young mother in a few weeks, and
she'd wondered how things were going. Amanda was already
five months pregnant.

"Oh, hey, you're here," Amanda said, sounding relieved to
see her. "I hoped you would be, but I didn't see you. I heard you

still needed help with the Christmas stockings. I tried to get out here earlier—"

"Don't you think your plate is already full?"

"I know. I just—I—Honestly, I just wanted to have a conversation about something other than Elmo."

Heather laughed. "I hear you, girl! C'mon. I want you to meet someone."

She was glad to finally introduce Tonya and Amanda to each other. The former's been-there-done-that sort of attitude combined with her sense of humor was a nice change of pace for the latter's uncertain and worn-down season of life. The three women soon found themselves talking around a table as they opened up bags of candy and separated them.

"I don't know how I'm going to manage when this one comes," Amanda said as she put her hands on the bulge she carried on her slight frame. "I'm barely hanging on right now with Alexis. She's been taking her diaper off in the middle of the night. Then she pees herself, gets all wet, and wakes up crying. I got up to change her sheets three times last night. On top of getting up to pee two times myself!"

"Meribeth does the same thing! Put her in some footie jammies. She'll never get to the diaper."

Amanda shook her head and smiled. "Tried that. She's like Houdini."

"All I can say is I'm glad those days are behind me," Tonya said with exaggerated eyes wide open. "I had nightmares my first year with the twins. I tried to nurse them at the same time and, well, let's just say that I'm definitely no Houdini."

"I'm sorry," Amanda said. "Here I am complaining and you two already have more than me."

Heather put her arm around the younger woman. "It's not a competition, sweetie. Not a thing about this is easy, and as a single parent? It's a whole new world of hard, and you're getting it done."

"That's right," Tonya confirmed with a knowing nod.

For a while they worked around the table in silence. Then Amanda said, "I miss his toes. Touching me under the covers at night."

Tonya shook her head. "I *don't* miss that. I got a thing about feet, girl."

They laughed.

"I miss his laugh," Amanda said.

Heather glanced over at Tonya, who gave her a knowing look back as she said, "Yeah. Yeah, I know."

5

October 24, 2007

I was out there the other day and couldn't wait to write about this. Let me set the scene: Okay . . . first of all, these are infantry guys. If you don't fully understand what that means, they are the "boots on the ground" of our military. As they say, "You're either infantry, or you support infantry." Ultimately, the infantry guys are the ones patrolling, arresting, or shooting bad guys, and giving candy out to kids—all in the same day.

With this in mind, understand that they are very tired when they return from a mission and often forget (better yet, neglect) basic hygiene. Having worn an extra fifty pounds or so of body armor and patrolling for several hours and miles, you can imagine the number of calories they burn. There are times when I can count multiple sweat rings on their T-shirts. Like rings in a tree trunk, you can tell how many days an infantryman has had that shirt on by the number of dried, salt-white sweat rings. And the smell of that house when they get back from an all-day sweaty mission . . . it will untwist your DNA! They come in, laugh about it, and wipe their muddy sweat on each other and everything they touch. Often times I greet them coming in and get slimed once or twice. I'm just glad to see them all make it back safe. That alone is worth it.

Ah yes . . . this is my church, my congregation! As an army chaplain, this is my flock. And these are your sons, daughters, dads, brothers, sisters, nieces, nephews . . . I can't imagine anyone else being with these guys at this time. I would be jealous.

God bless!
Darren

THE SEVENTH MONTH

1

November 4, 2007

Hey, folks! Another fine day here in Iraq. Cool evenings, down into the lower fifties. Highs during the day are mideighties. I never thought it'd come. I'm currently at another location for a few days, at a chaplains' retreat. The units in-country that have had a tough time, unit ministry teams were invited to this retreat. It's a time to get away, relax, pray, and fellowship with other guys in the same boat.

I had no idea how many people know of our battalion. When I told them I was from 1–30th Infantry Battalion, they were like, "Oh, wow. We've heard of you guys. Y'all have had a tough time." It was an awkward reverence, kind of a hushed respect. It was humbling, but I was reminded just how fierce of a summer it has been for us.

Man, it's nice here . . . It's at one of the "super FOBs" in-country (very large base with lots of amenities). I had Taco Bell last night for dinner . . . with sweet tea! They also have a Pizza Hut, an indoor pool, and a huge movie theater. My room has a double bed and a TV. I watched NFL all night last night. Very surreal. It's a former Iraqi air base. Saddam used to come here to watch his military in action. Oh yeah, and if you messed up while he was here, bye-bye (in the worst kind of way)! But they had nice facilities, and when we took over, we kept them nice. It's a totally different existence here. I almost feel embarrassed, as our base and patrol bases are so far removed from this kind of living. Here they rarely get mortared or shot at on patrols. I'm trying not to be judgmental when I hear conversations in the dining facility about he said, she said—knowing others would give their left toe to live like this. But . . . I count it a blessing just to get to spend a few days here and live almost like a king. I probably won't tell my guys too much about it, though. I think they'd be a little angry.

My guys are doing well as a whole. Our sector is still doing amazingly well on the battlefield, but there are pockets of trouble on another front. We've been here almost six months now. More than a few guys will be getting their divorces finalized after going home. Home-front issues are really becoming a problem for many. A chaplain friend of mine told me once that deployments strengthen strong marriages and weaken weak ones. That is so true. The long

deployments affect much more than just the soldier. And
the kids involved . . . It hurts to hear these guys talk about a
family falling apart. I try to encourage them and challenge
them to do the right thing, especially for their kids, and to
ultimately look in the mirror and stop blaming everyone else.
Pray for our families. They are hurting and suffering too. Pray
also for reconciliation between disgruntled soldiers and
their lonely spouses, tasked with being both mom and dad.
There's almost two wars going on: here and there.

Because of His great mercy,
Darren

2

The latest photos on their family website were from Halloween,
though it was now two weeks later. Darren hadn't seen them
until now, so it was a reminder he needed to get online to
see the photos more than he did. He smiled seeing Sam in his
armor, holding a sword and ready to attack, and Elie posing so
pretty as an angel. Then in his mind he saw the closed eyes of
the dead girl in his arms, lifeless and unmoving, and beautiful at
the same time.

Whoa. Shake it off.

The image wouldn't leave him alone. He forced himself to

continue looking at the pictures, seeing Meribeth in her pink camouflage onesie, with so much hair already. Underneath her picture was the following caption: *Kids dress up for Dad— praying for U!*

Elie posed by her countdown, with five months Xed out but so many more left to go. Darren groaned, looking away from the computer monitor.

A truck drove by in the distance, and images battered him again, surrounding and smothering with their memories. Lance shouting from the truck and handing him the deceased girl. The father pleading for help, seeing his daughter in Darren's arms.

Those cries. Those awful cries.

The bomb blasts late at night and the dirt raining on Shonda and him in the base. Those soldiers coming in, stinking and dirty and tired and needing some kind of hope. The faces absent of any emotion, just empty. Fear wasn't the worst thing out here. It was apathy.

The sound of footsteps nearby broke his wandering thoughts.

"Starting to see a pattern here, Chaplain," Shonda said, noticing the pictures on his laptop. "I leave, you either make silly photos or you look at them in silence, and so it goes."

"Yeah," Darren said, coming back down to reality. "Man, how much can you miss someone? Times three?"

"Don't look now, but the chaplain might need a pep talk of his own right now. Whose job is that?"

Good question.

It was one he hadn't figured out quite yet.

"Maybe later. Right now, the seat's yours."

Darren stood up and moved the video camera on its tripod so it faced a chair he had positioned by the side of his desk. He'd been waiting for Shonda to show up today.

"What do you mean? What's up?"

"Special assignment," Darren said as he handed her a kid's book.

She looked at the copy of *I Love You This Much* in disbelief. "How'd you get this?"

"Who cares? You said it's Colby's favorite."

She opened the book and began thumbing through it, turning each page as gently as though she was holding her son's hand. Darren could tell she remembered the story fondly.

"I'll upload it so your mom can play it for him, but right now I'm headed out," Darren said. "Just hit record on the remote and read to your boy."

"I don't know what to say," Shonda said, sitting down on the chair as if she were light-headed and needed a moment.

"Just take it from one who's done it badly," he said. "Don't just read; pretend he's sitting right there in your lap. 'Cuz to him, when your mom plays it, he'll feel like he is."

He left Shonda alone, then stood outside the door and waited until she finally began to start talking to the camera.

"Hi, Colby! Momma misses you so much, my boy. And I love you more than anything in the whole wide world . . . So I want to read you a story. It's one we both know."

There was a pause, and Darren knew Shonda was composing herself, probably holding back the tears.

"'When you arise . . . with sleepy eyes, my smiling face you see . . .'"

As he walked away, Darren imagined what it would be like for Colby to see his momma on the television reading to him. He imagined the boy jumping up and down and talking to the screen, telling his mother he loved her.

It was a good reminder that he needed to tell a few people he loved them too.

3

Heather was having one of those days. Perhaps there was a full moon tonight, or maybe the kids had gotten into some treats without her knowing. But all day long, she had been putting out little fires. And she knew the primary cause of death from indoor fires wasn't the flames themselves, but the smoke inhalation. She felt like she was choking on it as she made dinner and the telephone rang.

Lord, please don't let it be him.

The thought wasn't a selfish one. She wanted to talk to Darren, but now wasn't a good time. Meribeth sat in her high chair, half of her baby food covering her bib while the rest of it hung on her face and in her hair. She usually liked applesauce, but tonight she acted as if it was a new toy they just got at the store. Since Tonya and the girls were coming over in half an hour—actually, more like twenty minutes—and she had decided to make her homemade meatballs and spaghetti sauce, she had both burners on the stove going full blast while a loaf of cut-up garlic bread heated in the oven.

"Hello?" she said as she slipped the cordless between her ear and shoulder.

"Hey, babe. How's it going?"

"Oh, good. It's crazy. Tonya and the twins are coming over for dinner tonight, so—I'm glad you're calling."

There was a slight pause, as if he was waiting for her to say something. Or maybe thinking about what to say. She checked the bread just to make sure it wasn't burning.

"I was checking out our site," Darren said. "I noticed you hadn't updated photos lately."

She made a puzzled expression, as if he were there in person to see it. "Well, it didn't seem like you had time to look at them, so . . ."

In one of the pots, the sauce for the meatballs began bubbling and splattering, making Heather duck for cover as she reached for the knob to turn down the heat. Red sauce speckled the stovetop and the wall behind it. In the other room, she could hear Elie and Sam screaming and laughing.

"You there?" Darren asked.

"Yeah, sorry, just making a mess in the kitchen. And the kids are in a mood."

Another pause, then Darren said, "Just before calling—I got word we lost three more soldiers today."

What is this? Some sort of who's-having-the-worst-day competition?

As Meribeth began to fuss, wanting to come out of her seat,

something fell in the living room. Heather couldn't help thinking of what needed to happen next after the casualties.

"Means Tonya and I have three more widows to convince to go on living," she said.

"Mom! Sam's using your camera!" Elie called.

The last thing she needed was a broken camera. "Sam, put it down!"

Now Meribeth wasn't just fussing; she was full-on crying, ready to be set free.

"I'm taking pictures for Daddy!" Sam yelled.

"Sorry, I didn't mean anything by it," Darren said on the other line. "I think you heard me wrong."

"I couldn't hear," she said. "I did what wrong?"

As she grabbed a rag to wipe the mushy sauce off Meribeth's face and hair, she heard Sam and Elie getting even louder in the other room.

Every time I need to talk on this phone, they do this.

"Kids, quiet! I can't hear your dad!" She sighed as she unfastened Meribeth and then let her sit on the floor playing with a spatula. "Did the Christmas stockings arrive?"

She had developed a to-do list when it came to Darren. She couldn't help it—this was their life—so she wanted to make sure she could at least cross that one off the list.

"Oh yeah. They're amazing. I can't wait till Christmas. They're gonna love them. Thank you so much."

She needed to stir the sauce, but she didn't know where the . . . Heather grabbed the spatula from Meribeth and quickly dipped it into the pot.

"It was actually great," she said. "We had over a hundred people helping at different times. I still can't believe you won't be here for Christmas. My parents are coming."

Now the other pot of meatballs began gurgling over, so she turned the switch, accidentally lighting another burner. She turned all of them off.

"Mom!" Elie screamed in the other room. "Sam's taking pictures of Meribeth's boogies."

She spun around and her side caught the spoon on the counter, sending it to the floor and causing another explosion of red sauce. The smell of something burning drifted from the oven, and she opened it to see the pieces of garlic bread resembling blackened chicken. As she looked for the oven mitt she had just put down, the fire alarm began to join in the cacophony. Heather felt like screaming.

"Honey, I'm sorry . . . ," she said as she pulled out the charred pieces of bread.

"It's okay," Darren said, his disappointment obvious in his tone. "I get it. Bad timing. Love you too. Bye."

She barely got in her goodbye before the line cut off.

Heather didn't have time to feel bad about the call. At least at that moment, as Darren hung up the phone, he wasn't dealing with chaos there at the base like she was right this instant. Yes, they were on two very different battlefields, but on hers, the troops didn't follow orders very well, nor did they understand anything about rank or order.

With the pan of burnt bread dumped into the sink, the alarm above her still going off, and the kids in the living room still screaming, Heather stood there trying to figure out which problem to fix first. So naturally, the doorbell rang.

Tonya and the girls were early. Of course they were early. But this was good news.

The reinforcements are here.

4

"So, we'll be transporting former Sunni insurgents fighting with us now to stop Al-Qaeda, and we're not the only ones who know," Lt. Col. Jacobsen said to the officers around the meeting table. He pointed to a map. "At Al Sakhar Province, here, Bravo will neutralize opposition out front for Alpha running escort to get these civilian forces in for training at PB Hawkes, here. Questions?"

As the rest of the men all shook their heads, Darren raised his hand slightly toward the commander. "Sir . . . before we, uh . . . can I?" He was surprised at how nervous his voice sounded.

"Knock it out of the park, son," Jacobsen told him.

All of the men closed their eyes as Darren began to pray. Every day, the prayers seemed to grow more intense, with the men understanding their significance.

Moments later, with a convoy of Humvees and Strykers rumbling as they waited to head out, Darren sought out Lance. Finding the soldier standing next to his designated vehicle, he pulled out some jerky from one of his pockets and tossed it to him.

"Fuel for the road," Darren said as Lance swiftly caught it.

"Hey, thanks . . . And thanks for what you're doing here. It's helpful. To me, anyway."

"Of course."

Lance pulled out a Bible from his vest and proudly waved it. "Been takin' this on all our trips out of Falcon. It's a big book, and I don't understand some of it."

"I can help you out with that," Darren said.

"Bradley, one!" Sergeant Carter shouted as he passed them by. "Turner, two with me!"

Before following Carter, Darren pulled out one more thing.

"Hey, Lance. Hang on to this, will ya?" He offered his Armor of God coin to the young man.

Lance looked at Darren and shook his head. "Man, you're a closer."

"It's a reminder. That you don't have to be afraid. That God has your back."

"All right, we're moving out," Carter shouted as he climbed into the MRAP.

Lance slapped Darren's palm, taking the coin in his hand and giving him a wink. "Told you before. I just like free stuff."

Darren chuckled as Sergeant Carter barked at them one more time to go.

Just another day and another trip down a winding desert road and another chance for any of them to die.

The ritual of risking their lives had, strangely, become routine. Yet for Darren and many of the other men, so had relying on the Lord.

5

November 20, 2007

Happy Birthday, Heather!! On November 22 it's my wife's twenty-fifth birthday. Just kidding, she's thirtysomething. I love you and miss you, baby!

And Happy Thanksgiving to everyone else. I can't believe the holidays are already here. Wow. Where did time go? We're gearing up for a whirlwind tour of Thanksgiving meals and services here at the main base and out at the PBs. We have a total of five meals/services in two days. Thanksgiving in the military is a big deal. It's a time when special guests come, high-ranking officers show up to serve meals, and everyone else gets nervous about the special guests and high-ranking officers showing up. Somewhat of a photo op, but I understand their desire. They want the troops to be appreciated, and they show that with a good meal and important people serving the food. For me, I will be there to pray for the meal, then have a service afterward for anyone wanting to attend.

Thanks to all the groups and individuals who have sent care packages and Christmas stockings recently. In the past two weeks, I've had no fewer than seventy-five boxes come in for me and our great troops. That has been no small job, but it's worth it. You all have equipped me to be a huge

blessing to these guys. I thank you for that. I would list all
the contributors, but that would take a lot of space. I hope
my sincere thanks will suffice.

Once again, Happy Thanksgiving! "I will give you thanks,
for you answered me; / you have become my salvation"
(Ps. 118:21).

Darren

THE EIGHTH MONTH

1

December 2, 2007

Guess what? It rained last night! With thunder and lightning. Our first rain. It was so stormy early this morning, I thought we were getting mortared. I haven't heard those sounds in eight months. It was weird. It's also very chilly at night now. It's been in the midforties lately, and is supposed to dip into the upper thirties soon. Related to that, our three patrol bases finally got hot water. It's a pretty basic setup: big containers of water with pipes going into a couple of upright hot water heaters attached to a small water pump that pushes the water into "shower sheds." That has greatly increased morale at the PBs! Amazing what a hot shower can accomplish. Since it has gotten cooler, soldiers have been heating water bottles next to generators to get them warm and taking water bottle showers. Now with the hot showers, it's like home . . . well, almost.

Good news story: a woman who was injured in the war back in 2005 is about to get long-awaited help. Basically, her colon was removed due to a gunshot wound, and she's been using a bag on her side. She is now lined up to go to the big US hospital in Baghdad and have surgery by our doctors to correct this! Many of our soldiers met her and her family, and they are so happy and ready to be normal again. That will happen soon. Also, tomorrow our medics are having another MEDOP (a medical operation) where they will go set up a small "office" in the streets of our area and help anyone who walks up. Relationship building and helping the locals.

We continue to see improvements in our area. Six months ago, no one would have dared do this. Now it's a reality. And our Concerned Citizens (CC) also continue to help provide security. In one of my new photos, you will see a crazy picture! One of the CCs pointed out to our guys an IED that he knew was planted recently in a dirt road. We watched it in the TOC using a high-tech camera that can zoom out pretty far. I couldn't believe he actually went and dug it up, knowing it could blow at any moment. But it didn't. One more bomb off the battlefield that could possibly have hit us. They regularly turn in, or point out, all sorts of weapons that we confiscate and remove from the fight. The bad guys have weapons caches all around, but they are shrinking.

I'm excited that my favorite time of year is near. Christmas, true Christmas. The Invasion of God! "O Holy Night . . . the night of our dear Savior's birth . . . He appeared and the soul

felt its worth (my favorite line) . . . FAALLLL on your knees!

O hear the angel voices . . . O night divine, O night when

Christ was born!"

God knows the pain of deployments. He came here, from

heaven. Now that's a deployment! He knows. May you be

filled with awe as you ponder the Invasion of God!

Darren

2

Darren no longer thought about the weight of all his gear and the steady motion of the MRAP as they sped down the desert road to Al Sakhar Province. Now all he kept thinking about was being surprised by an explosion, hearing the wailing sound before feeling the impact on their vehicle. His mouth felt dry and his breaths felt heavy.

Once again their mission was to provide an armed escort for the civilian forces that were training at their patrol base. The empty desert land outside no longer looked ominous to him, and he was as familiar with riding in this armored vehicle as he was with driving his own kids to the store. The scary part consisted of wondering what kind of carnage could suddenly start raining down on them at any given moment.

Sergeant Whitsett's voice crackled over the radio as he

steered the Humvee in front of them, with Diego riding shotgun and Lance standing up through the hole and manning the
.50-cal gun.

"Roger that, Atlas 7–2," Sergeant Carter called out.

Once again, he drove them while Michael sat next to him
and Shonda and Darren sat in the back. The MRAP hit a giant
pothole, sending Darren and Shonda lurching forward.

"Man, Stevie Wonder drives better than you, Carter,"
Michael joked.

"Turner, doesn't the Good Book say 'Be kind to your neighbor'?" the sergeant shouted back at Darren. "I'm sittin' next to
you, Major. That makes me your neighbor."

Darren gave a halfhearted laugh as he balled his hand into
a fist to stop it from shaking. He was trying to do everything
possible to not let any of them know how nervous he felt.

"Oh, man! Tell me I didn't do it."

In the passenger seat, Michael began searching his pockets,
almost frantic. Then he looked over to Carter.

"Dude, I forgot my ChapStick." Michael slapped his palm
on the windshield in front of him. "I gotta bum yours, Stevie."

Sergeant Carter shook his head. "Oh, no. Nobody bums
ChapStick!"

"Aw, come on, man. You just said be kind to your neighbor.
I'll pay for it, but my lips are cracking bad."

The younger sergeant smiled, seeing a chance to give
Michael a hard time.

"How about I make you a deal?" he said. "If we pass a
Walmart, I'll stop. Okay?"

Darren and Shonda looked at each other and laughed. Any sort of amusement was welcomed out here. Darren looked back down at his hands and made sure they were still clenched and out of Shonda's view. The trip would be over soon enough.

3

One minute the kids were playing with goats at a petting zoo, the next minute they were climbing up the steps of an inflatable slide and whipping down it. Sam and Elie loved to play with Mia and Nia, and it seemed the twins enjoyed playing with them, too, despite the age difference. Heather was happy to see this, knowing how close the two families were becoming. She wondered if Darren and Michael were developing any sort of relationship as well. She loved picturing the future, seeing the two families barbecuing on a hot summer day, spending the evening laughing while the sun drifted far away into the west.

The farm was alive with families this late morning, mostly mothers with their children. Every year the army held a Thanksgiving harvest festival, where there were carnival rides and food vendors and even a warrior maze kids could go through. As the foursome of children ran from one attraction to the next, Heather, Tonya, and Amanda sat in the grass nearby, keeping Alexis and Meribeth entertained. Soon Mia ran back to them.

"Can we take Sam and Elie through the maze, Mom?"

Heather glanced over to the entrance of the maze, then gave Tonya a nod.

"Okay," Tonya said. "We'll wait at the entrance. By the funnel cake booth!"

Heather laughed. "God help us. Stay together, please!"

Sam and Elie followed the twins into the maze as Heather turned back to Meribeth. She was learning that there was a big difference between two children with both parents present as a team and three active children with only one parent. She didn't have the time or energy to be monitoring every kid every moment. That was another reason she was so happy that Tia and Mia enjoyed playing with the children. They served as quasi-babysitters.

"We have got to get us some of that funnel cake," Tonya said to the other women.

It didn't sound too appetizing to Amanda, who made a face and held her pregnant belly.

"We haven't even had lunch yet," Heather said.

Tonya looked through her purse to get her wallet. "There is nothing wrong with having funnel cakes for lunch. Or having your dessert first. Remember—this is a Thanksgiving festival!"

4

As the convoy arrived at the village of Al Sakhar Province just on the outskirts of Baghdad, the drivers slowed their vehicles. While maneuvering through the half-blasted stone walls and houses, they passed a group of men in long-sleeved robes, with scarves called *kaffiyehs* on their heads. The men gave them suspicious looks while several women wearing long black cloaks and scarves covering their heads and faces ran away from the Americans.

"So how much we payin' these goat herders to fight with us anyway?" Sergeant Carter asked Michael.

"I think they're just fightin' for what's theirs. Right, Sergeant?"

"Or what's left of it."

Carter was young, brash, and cocky, a perfect combo for his ranking. The enthusiasm and energy from young men like him filled Darren with a similar sort of fuel, one that he desperately needed to combat the wear and tear this place was taking on his soul.

"Looks like our objective, gents," Sergeant Whitsett said on the radio. "Eleven o'clock. I got one male. Repeat, one male."

Every individual they passed, whether man, woman, or child, posed a potential threat. That was why they were always on alert and ready for anything once they entered a village like this one.

An Iraqi man waved to them alongside a city street.

"That's our escort," Michael radioed back.

Every parked car and every barren window carried potential danger. The soldiers scanned their surroundings, the walls and the buildings and the balls the children were playing with. Nothing could be taken for granted in this place.

"We're looking for a twelve-pax bus," Michael continued to say on the radio. "Bradley, whatcha see up top?"

Lance's voice came in loud and clear over the radio. "Lookin' good. Roofs are all clear. Wait . . ."

Just like that, they began to slow as Lance continued. "Ho! I got two on a roof at one o'clock! One's on a cell! One o'clock!"

Slow and steady. That's how Darren breathed as the convoy slowly weaved through the narrow streets following their escort. They all knew the obvious. They were sitting ducks in this current position. Above in the Humvee, Lance swiveled the .50-caliber gun at the two men above their group of vehicles.

"Come on!" Lance called out on the radio. "Faster! Let's go!"

Sergeant Whitsett's voice cut in. "No sign of a twelve-pax, gentlemen. I think we got a problem."

Michael looked out the side of his window and then forward once again. "Stay alert. Bradley—update?"

"Bogeys are gone. And I see the bus."

Sitting between two war-torn buildings, the rusted-out squat bus blocked their way. Broken glass and a missing door didn't exactly give any of them confidence.

"Roger that," Whitsett said. "Looks empty from here."

"Here we go, gentlemen," Sergeant Carter called out as they pulled to a stop.

Michael blurted, "Hey . . . where'd our escort go?"

Darren looked out and then back as Michael and Carter checked all sides of their MRAP. Lance's voice over on the radio gave Darren a terrifying ache in his gut.

"Dude . . . he's gone."

"I'm telling you, I don't like this," Sergeant Whitsett said.

As Darren looked over at Shonda, she just shook her head. "Believe me. It happens every—"

Rapid gunfire pelting their vehicles interrupted her.

"Get outta here!" Michael shouted. "Now! Move!"

Darren caught a brief glimpse of two figures standing in the bus, firing at them with their AK-47s. The echoes inside the bus and the walls lining the narrow city streets seemed to make the gunshots even louder than usual.

"Stay down!" Shonda ordered Darren.

He couldn't move in his seat, so Shonda shoved him down and shielded him. It felt like they had entered some kind of maze and were now stuck at a dead end. The problem was they couldn't easily back up and get back out.

"My gun's jammed," Lance shouted over the radio.

There was a blast and rattling in the front of their vehicle as another steady stream of bullets caused Carter to hit his steering wheel in anger.

"We got serious damage on one!" he said.

"Just move!" Michael told him.

Finally the sound of Lance's machine gun roared to life, his swivel clanking as he moved into place, shredding the bus and tearing it wide open with blasts of eight and ten rounds at a clip. The incoming gunfire stopped. Darren knew the M2 had taken care of the men on the bus.

Michael's voice rose once more. "Move! Move! Move!"

5

Inside the maze, as Elie laughs and runs away from Sam and the twins, following the twists and turns, the dust from the hay on the ground suddenly gets to her. She coughs and has to stop. Where are the others? She coughs again, and this time she can't get a deep breath. Rushing back to where she came from, she turns a corner and realizes she's run back into a dead end. She turns around and sprints back, her heart racing as she tries unsuccessfully to catch her breath.

"Sam? Sam!"

Her voice is but a whimper now. "Sam?" She has to sit down, trying to breathe but wheezing and gasping.

And she's lost her inhaler.

6

The vehicles turn around and race through the walls of the crumbling village, trying to reach the safety of the desert. For a moment, Darren can breathe a little more easily, but then another set of loud pops sends them on the defensive again. Bullets bite into the metal sides of the MRAP, ricocheting and causing Darren to tighten his body and lean down as much as he can.

"He's in the window up there!" Lance shouts, adding, "We got multiple shooters."

"Whit, get us outta here!" Michael yells as the driver ahead of them floors the pedal and the vehicle swerves left to race down another street.

We're trapped like a bunch of sitting ducks.

Everything inside of Darren surges just like the roaring engine of the MRAP. His eyes are wide open, scanning every inch of ground he can see from his limited viewpoint. Shonda is next to him doing the same, preparing for a possible evacuation from the vehicle. The gunfire continues, cracking and careening off the protective armor. The insurgents seem to be everywhere, on street corners and standing on rooftops and peeking out from slightly open doors.

Looking ahead of them at Whitsett's Humvee, Darren can see the back of Lance as he fires the .50-caliber like some kind of animal. The gun drowns all the other shots around them.

"Push through!" Michael orders them. "Just push through!"

The two vehicles turn right and rush down another narrow street, flanked by two buildings several stories high. The Humvee veers to the right a bit as it suddenly slows down.

"On the stairway! Heading to the roof!" Whitsett calls out on the radio.

Only seconds later, Lance yells out the deadly word a couple of times. "RPG! RPG!"

"Right turn! Up ahead!" Diego cries.

Lance swivels as the machine gun sucks up ammunition on its metallic link-belt and spits it out just as quickly. The Humvee is moving at its top speed now, trying to make the turn and then violently veering right, while Lance continues to launch a barrage of rounds at the enemy above them.

Darren holds on while their MRAP swings right as well, just as a grenade from the RPG explodes into a chunk of wall they just passed.

"Bradley, my man!" Michael booms out on the radio.

The Humvee in front of them turns another corner, then plows into a wooden produce cart before making it to the edge of the town and bursting out to the open space of the desert.

7

As soon as Heather sees Sam, she knows there's a problem. She's standing in the funnel cake line with Tonya while Amanda watches over the little ones. Sam is sprinting toward her, yelling something.

"Sam—what is it?"

He's white as a ghost with round, frantic eyes. "She can't breathe!"

That's all Heather needs to hear. She rushes back into the maze, following Sam, calling back to Tonya as she runs.

"Call a medic! Now!"

Heather runs after Sam, taking one turn after another, all while clinging to the hope that he knows where he's going. Then they turn right and she sees Elie, lying limp and unconscious on the ground. Heather rushes to her, scooping her up and then running back as she cradles her daughter.

But running back where? She has no idea which direction to take. Mia and Nia suddenly appear.

"Which way? Girls, lead us out!"

Now she follows the twins, winding back and forth through the maze as passing kids give them terrified looks. It's taking too long, they're obviously going the wrong way. They reach one long path only to have it come to a dead end.

"This way!" Mia says, sounding certain.

Heather clutches her little girl, saying, *Lord help us, Lord help us* over and over in her heart all the while. The path narrows and she's sure they've arrived at another dead end, when the wall opens up and they're back out of the maze.

Blinking for a few seconds, still moving as fast as she can, Heather sees Tonya running toward her, a medic at her side.

"Elie, it's going to be okay. Come on, Elie, you're going to be fine."

Inside the ambulance, Elie rests on a stretcher, breathing with a respirator, while Heather sits next to her, caressing her head. The siren blasts above them as the ambulance races back to the hospital.

"It's gonna be okay," Heather says again, brushing Elie's soft hair.

8

The convoy left a wall of dust and sand as they tore down the road back to base. Darren felt pinned down and unable to move. The world circled up and down, and the blasts wouldn't stop going off inside his head.

For a moment he thought about how close geographically they were to the Holy Land, to the birthplace of the Messiah. How incredible was it that God came down to this very place and became flesh and blood. He came down to this hot, barren place to the people He created, yet the people didn't recognize Him. Some eventually came to know Jesus as their Savior, but it took some time.

Darren identified with that. He had always heard about God and Jesus, but the moment finally came when he took a hard look at his life and finally believed to the point of action. He surrendered the rest of his days to the One who came for him, to rescue and save Darren and the rest of the world.

Curiosity transformed into commitment.

The Good News of Christmas. The gospel he spoke about every day. This was why Darren was over here. Because he had been changed and wanted to do what was right with his life. That's why he was in this place, why he was serving with these men and women.

"Chappy, you can relax now." Michael's voice seemed to be coming from far away. "*Chaplain.*"

Darren's shaking, blurry vision was finally starting to get better as he felt the pressure against him ease up. Shonda had been keeping him down with her elbow . . . protecting him maybe?

Perhaps protecting me from myself?

"Shonda," he said. "I'm good."

She moved, letting Darren get back up into his seat. As he sat there trying to unrattle his scrambled brain, he saw a ChapStick rolling on the floor.

"Hey, Major . . . look what I found."

"Chappy! You're the man!" Michael reached back and took the ChapStick out of Darren's weak hands. "Mmm, mmm," the major said as he rubbed the ChapStick back and forth over his lips. "Almost got shot with cracked lips. That ain't right."

They all laughed except Darren. All he could do was force a smile and try to not think about how they had almost died back there in that small village.

9

She finally got hold of Darren on her sixth try. By the time she heard his distant and muffled voice on the other end, Heather's anxiety and anger had reached boiling point. Her hand tightened over the receiver as she stood just outside the curtain surrounding Elie's hospital bed.

"Darren—what took you so long?"

"Sorry, babe. We were off base and . . . they couldn't reach us."

She could tell he was outside by the sound of the noise in the background.

"Couldn't reach you?" she yelled. "I thought the military could—Never mind. It was just so horrible. Our little Elie—"

"*Elie?* What happened? Is she okay?"

Heather's heart was still racing and she knew she needed to slow everything down. "Yes, she's fine now. Stable, thank God."

"Heather, what happened?"

"We were at the Fall Festival today and the kids went in the maze. I can't believe I didn't think about the hay!"

The anger she held inside was mostly directed at herself for being so stupid and not realizing the potential danger.

"Oh no. Where was her inhaler?"

"I don't know. And I can't ask her right now."

"Never mind. I'm sorry. She's okay, that's all that matters."
He paused for a minute, then asked what seemed to be more of
an afterthought. "What about you?"

"I'm not . . . very okay," she mumbled. "I can't stop shaking.
I just—I thought we'd lost her."

"But we didn't lose her. She's okay."

Knowing Elie was indeed okay in the hospital bed next to
her, while Darren was talking on the phone with her, Heather
finally felt safe enough to let the tears start falling.

"I know. I know." Her voice sounded hoarse and half there.
"But this was the hardest day yet. Not to have you here—"

"Sounds brutal, babe. Is Tonya there with you?"

"Yes. Thank God. But . . . she's not you. Not Elie's daddy,
for Elie—"

"I understand," Darren said sharply, cutting her off.

She waited for more, for anything more from him. But there
was nothing.

I just need a little help here. Just a little.

"I'm sorry," she said. "I'm just feeling so alone in this right
now. I miss—"

"Babe, I get it! Okay?"

His words felt like a slap in the face. "Whoa, whoa . . . what
was that? I'm just trying to tell you that—"

"And if you knew what I went through today—if you had
any idea—"

"Then give me an idea for once," she shouted back, not caring who might hear. "Please! I'm all ears."

Another slap, this one in the form of silence. The brutal divide between them felt endless and overwhelming.

"How can I possibly know what you're going through if you won't even tell me?" she said.

He sighed, pausing for another moment, before he said, "I've gotta go."

"What? Really? Are you serious?"

"Heather, I'm sorry . . . ," Darren said, his voice trailing off, sounding completely defeated.

What is going on with him?

Her body shook again as more tears filled her eyes. She wanted to say something more, anything more. Just to try to grasp some piece of him, something that could stay with her.

"Yeah, okay. I've got to get back to Elie anyway."

"Okay," he said, his voice lacking any emotion or encouragement. "Keep me posted. I lo—"

She hung up before she could hear the rest. Her body felt numb as she stood there in the corner of the silent room. Her insides felt like they were clamoring to crawl out of her, to escape this prison she felt she was living inside. A solitary confinement for a parent, where the only person she could rely on was herself. The tears tore out of her in a flood, but she fought them and tried to pull herself together. She needed to think of her daughter now, so that was what she did.

Pulling the curtain back, Heather looked at the peaceful

face of her little sleeping beauty. Then she spotted Elie's closed fist. What was in her hand?

She turned the little girl's hand over . . . and found Darren's Armor of God coin clenched tightly within.

10

The Falcon Christmas party was in full swing, with hundreds of soldiers laughing and yelling and in good spirits. Sergeant Carter stood on the stage in the commons area, his Santa hat drooping to one side while he read to the soldiers from the large, colorful book in his hands.

"Lieutenant Colonel Jacobsen sprang to his sleigh and unloaded a few rounds from his M249 SAW . . ."

The crowd roared with approval as Carter grinned and continued his Christmas tale.

"And the insurgents ran away from his Yuletide shock and awe. But I heard him exclaim as he drove out of sight, 'Merry Christmas to all, and to all a good night!'"

The soldiers clapped and cheered as the sergeant took a proud bow. Shonda and Lance joined in the applause, but Darren just stood, taking a sip of his water. He was glad everything was going so well today.

Carter signaled toward the Humvee pulling up beside the building. The vehicle was decorated with garlands and blaring "Here Comes Santa Claus." Two soldiers opened the back to reveal the presents on board:

A thousand stockings all tied and ready to be distributed.

Darren couldn't help letting out a somber chuckle. It was great to see all those stockings, but it made him think about Heather and the kids.

The door to the Humvee opened and Santa Claus himself stepped out of the vehicle, giving all of them a loud "Ho! Ho! Ho! Merry Christmas!" Then, as he walked to the back of the Humvee, his beard began to detach on one side, dangling off one ear to reveal Lt. Col. Jacobsen. He was either unaware of his wardrobe malfunction or just didn't care; regardless, he began to pick up the stockings and toss them out to the nearby soldiers. Then he took the microphone from Carter.

"Thank you for your hard work, your sacrifice, and your service to our great country. Come and get it!"

A swarm of soldiers engulfed the commander while Darren stood at the back of the commons area, viewing the celebration with a sense of relief. A whole lot of exhaustion too.

He wished Heather were standing next to him, holding his hand, grinning up at him and knowing they'd accomplished what they set out to do.

We're a good team. Even if we're 6,700 miles away from each other.

With Christmas almost here and the new year soon to follow, Darren knew he only had seven more months.

He pictured the kids sitting around the Christmas tree back home while Heather and her parents watched them open presents. Like so many images and memories, the thought pierced through him.

Eight months stationed in this blistering and bleak part of

the world. He'd made it past the halfway mark, he realized. But he realized something else, something Heather and the kids didn't know. Those eight months were leaving marks on him that might never go away.

11

There were many things he could write about in his online journal for December 25, 2007, but Darren kept his Christmas post positive and in the spirit of the holiday. It wasn't that he didn't believe the sentiments he shared, but he held back on some of the deep-rooted feelings stirring inside of his soul. Those were ones he couldn't even share with Heather. She had enough on her plate, and there were things she didn't want or need to know. The realities of the battlefield, the raw stuff of life that only soldiers could truly understand.

So after he wrote about some good news on the war front, Darren shared his thanks and appreciation for the Christmas stockings and the successful parties that had taken place. Then he ended his entry with some Christmas greetings.

> Merry Christmas to you and yours, and God bless you all during this season! As you gather with family and friends for your parties, and you eat all those munchies, and you open gift after gift—all without fear of being murdered by Sunni or Shia extremists—think of us. Not out of pity, but with pride. Your safe parties and scented candles are possible

because good men and women are standing in the face of evil and saying no! Rest assured, there are many who would love to take that privilege away from us and export the evil to our homes, but we say no! It's for you and yours to enjoy! Merry Christmas!

Darren

THE NINTH &
TENTH MONTHS

1

January 3, 2008

. . . Remember a couple of journal postings ago, when we
had a mission into a neighborhood where Al-Qaeda had
infiltrated, but we kicked them out? We went there, and this
pic is in the heart of that village! The Concerned Citizens are
now helping us guard the area, and helping us identify and
root out the bad guys . . .

January 7, 2008

. . . More than a handful of soldiers are in the middle of
ugly family situations, divorces, etc. It seems the stress of
deployment hits here and home equally hard. I've been
counseling with many of these guys, and it's hard to watch
them feeling totally helpless over here while things are
going bad at home. They can't focus here, and they can't

do much for their marriages back home. Well, they can, but many don't want to. They are just too exhausted. I challenge them to fight for their families regardless. Some do, some don't. This is what I've come to expect lately when someone wants to meet with the chaplain . . .

January 27, 2008

. . . The soldier and I talked for a while, and he was broken. Life and war have beaten him down, and he wondered if God really, I mean really, cared about him. I shared some other verses with him, not pressuring him at all to believe. I left that up to him. But the Truth did its work and caused him to want to follow Christ! We prayed, and he told the Lord he wanted to truly believe and follow Him. Another diamond in the rough, a trophy of God's grace! Pray for him and his newfound faith. I will continue to follow up with him and help as needed. I am going to have a baptism at each patrol base this month, and he wants to be baptized. That will be a day I won't soon forget! Baptizing soldiers in the land of the garden of Eden, of Abraham's travels, of Babylon, of Nineveh (Jonah and the whale), and more. Not sure how we're going to do it—maybe dig a hole, line it with a tarp, and use water bottles to fill it up! Maybe. We won't do it in the Tigris, it's way too nasty and dangerous . . .

February 4, 2008

. . . It's so hard fighting an enemy you can't see, but when there are tangible results of authentic justice, it is gratifying.

Yet another story you will never hear about, what your great American soldiers are doing over here for the people of Iraq. It has yet to be seen whether the Iraqis will run with this opportunity of peace and freedom. It's up to them. We've done the hard part, now they have to step up.

February 14, 2008

Today on this Valentine's Day, I'm gonna brag on my wife. Excuse me while I don't even think about Iraq or soldiers or Baghdad for this post. I've been wanting to say this for some time here, so this day is a great excuse.

To my Heather:

You are amazing. I can't even begin to tell you how happy I am that you said yes to me eight and a half years ago. Now, that amount of time and three kids later, I love you even more. I shudder to think where I would be in life had you not come into it. You are my best friend, and have been my rock during this deployment. The way you've handled our family, and the way you've handled me when I've gotten out of line, have only made me love you more. Thank you for your grace and elegance.

I know a marriage is a dance, a give-and-take. But I think you have given way more than I have. Being a single parent for a fifteen-month period is difficult enough, but you live every day with the crippling fear that someone from the army may knock on the front door with the worst news imaginable. You, not me, are the true hero in this family!

Aside from everything you do to keep our family and marriage alive and well, you are amazing. I have to boast on this V-day that you are simply beautiful! More than beautiful, you are . . . stunning! I remember seeing you for the very first time in Athens, and it was like somebody kicked me in the gut. You walked up and took my breath away. I was speechless, like a deaf and mute little boy. I couldn't hear or say anything, only look. I knew I was in the presence of someone special. I think I heard "Dream Weaver" in the background! ☺

You were so polished, and I felt so clumsy in comparison. I knew it was much deeper than your skin. I thought there was no way I had a chance with you, that you were far out of my league. I still do. Forgive me for the times I've taken you/us for granted and treated you in less than the way you deserve to be treated. I'm sorry to say that it will probably happen again. I'm dumb that way. But you are bigger than that, and I'm grateful. I wish there were another set of words that trumped "I love you." If so, that's what I'd say.

Darren

THE ELEVENTH MONTH

1

March 14, 2008

. . . It's time for me to submit what I want to do in the future—stay in the army or get out in February of 2010. That sounds far away, but once we get back to Fort Stewart, it will only be a year and a half away, and the army likes to plan well ahead of any changes. Pray for us. I honestly don't know what we're going to do. I love soldiers, but I can't stand being away from my family. I want to go home and stay home. That thought of coming back here anytime soon makes me nauseous. I believe God called us to do this, but for how long? That is the million-dollar question. I need His guidance. I know what I want to do, but I also know He will lead me if I submit to Him.

Darren

2

"Hey, buddy. Mommy told me you got your orange belt in karate! Way to go!"

"Thanks, Daddy!"

Heather hoped Darren could hear the smile hanging like a bright half moon on Sam's face. She had told him how well he was doing in karate class, how he was the best student, and sure, she might be a *little* biased, but that didn't matter.

"I'm really proud of you," Darren said over the speaker-phone. "Mommy also was bragging about how well you've been doing at listening and obeying. And especially being tough."

"Yeah," the six-year-old said, bashful at all the compliments.

After Darren and Sam spoke for a little while longer, with Daddy doing most of the talking, Heather took him off the speaker and talked to him again.

"It's so great he has that outlet," Darren said.

"He needs it, since he's the only male in a house full of ladies."

Darren had already spoken with Elie, hearing about how well piano lessons were going for both her and for Mommy. Heather had even played him a song on the piano as he listened.

"Meribeth knows now what 'Mommy' means. She's calling after me now."

"Which is a good thing and a bad thing," Darren commented.

"Tonya says she's been talking to Michael more on the phone," Heather said.

"Maybe he's actually paying more attention to me than I realize."

"We've enjoyed seeing Amanda and the new baby. They came over for dinner the other night."

"I miss you," Darren said.

"We all miss you too. Elie already marked off the twelfth month, even if it's not officially over."

"Let's all imagine it is. I only have a few more months left."

"I can't wait."

"Me either, babe. Me either."

3

As Darren worked on notes for his Easter messages, he could hear someone stepping into the doorway. Lance stood there, holding a gift bag.

"This a good time, Chaplain?" he asked.

"Hey, Lance. Come on in."

Darren stood to greet him, first shaking his hand and then pulling him in for a big hug.

Lance handed Darren the present. "For your generosity. I hear it was your wife who set me up with all the pictures of Elijah. Man, I can't wait to see my boy in person."

"Won't be long now, brother."

Digging into the gift bag, Darren couldn't help but laugh. He pulled out two pieces of beef jerky, handing one to Lance.

"Had to resist the whole way over," Lance said. He started

chomping on the jerky while looking over Darren's shoulder at his desk. "Easter service, huh? Whatcha got planned?"

"You gonna be there, man?"

"You kidding? You are looking at a genuine, bona fide believer, brother. I'm all in. 'Course I'll be there."

"All in, huh?" Darren said, nodding. "Well, I'm coming up short on the orchestra. Got any ideas?"

Just then a deep voice spoke out, surprising both of them.

"Ah, man, I didn't need to see your ugly face today," Michael said, stepping into the tent and then pretending to walk out before reaching over to give Darren a hug.

"Wow. This is new. Major Lewis in the chaplain's office?"

Michael didn't answer, instead trying to snatch a piece of the jerky.

Lance pushed it out of reach. "Get your own," he joked before tossing Michael a piece.

Then Shonda arrived, making the silent room suddenly a party. She beamed at Lance. "Hey—I hear congrats are in order."

"Right on," Lance said. "A son this time!"

They shared a fist bump.

"I got it on good authority, sons are pretty awesome," Shonda said.

"Hey now, don't be dissin' my girls," Michael teased.

"Hello. What am I?"

"Man, we gotta get 'em all together when we're back. I mean it."

Everybody gave Lance a *hear hear* and a nod. Darren was grateful that all these months out here had produced solid friendships such as these. God had put these folks in his life, just as He had put the women in Heather's life.

He wouldn't be alone in celebrating the joy of Easter.

4

"Far more than I, you men and women *know* what it is to offer up your life for the good of others."

The sun warmed the soldiers on this cool midmorning at Falcon Base. Over three hundred sat in the recreation area listening to Chaplain Turner share his Easter message in front of one of the concrete walls. In his comfortable gray army T-shirt and shorts, Darren looked as though he could just as easily be playing ball, but he was doing something he enjoyed even more.

"One of the many challenges, here and at home, is that unless you've done it, actually *lived* it, it's hard to appreciate what it's like to make that sacrifice."

He saw a handful of confirming nods and even heard a few *amens*.

"Well, you know who else actually lived it? Who willingly sacrificed His life so that others could live? Jesus. He came, laid it down, and rose again for me, for you . . . so you and I can live."

A chorus of more *amens* sang out.

"Out here we put our confidence and hope in a lot of things, and in each other. But if that act isn't cause for hope and confidence in a Gód who loves you and would do anything for you, I don't know what is."

He paused for a moment to look over all these faces, so many he knew personally, many who had come to him to share about the problems they were having. About the fears and struggles of being in Iraq, and about the turmoil and struggles along the home front.

"That's what this day, what Easter, is all about. *Hope.* For all of us."

Darren stepped toward the water barrel they had placed at the base of a lone oak tree.

"If I've learned anything from you about what it takes to be a soldier, it's that you know how to go all in."

He gave Lance a quick glance, then climbed up the rickety wood steps and lowered himself into the waist-deep water.

"And there's no better day than Easter to go all in for Jesus," he told them.

For a few moments, Darren stood in the water alone, just waiting. He wasn't worried if nobody came. All he wanted was to offer this opportunity, to share the blessing Jesus demonstrated when He asked John to baptize Him.

When Lance slowly stood up, Darren felt a burst of joy. He couldn't help smiling as the uncertain soldier stepped into the water and stood, not knowing what exactly he was supposed to do. Darren put his arms around him.

"Army Specialist Lance Bradley, I baptize you in the name of the Father, the Son, and the Holy Spirit."

Darren lowered Lance into the water, and the soldier came bursting back up slapping the water with satisfaction.

"Whoo-ee!" Lance called out in his joyous southern way.

Everybody liked Lance, and his animated spirit was contagious as everybody applauded. Darren looked out and saw Michael clapping too, an unashamed broad smile on his face. The chaplain breathed in deep, soaking all of this in and silently thanking God for this moment.

5

March 26, 2008

Easter was great (see new pics)! Four Easter services over a period of a few days, two different baptisms for five soldiers, and continued mortar attacks made it one for the memory books. We traveled to all of our PBs and had a Communion service at each one. The turnout was good, grabbing a lot of those guys who go to church once or twice a year. ☺ The message was about what Christ did FOR US on the Cross (broken for us, as Communion vividly reminds us), and the resulting resurrection as proof of His divinity. I reminded our guys to stay focused not on the cross, but on the empty tomb! He's not on the cross anymore, nor in the tomb. The resurrection was the single most significant—and controversial—event in human history. If it's true, it changes everything. If not, then I am chief of fools. I believe it to be true, and there is ample evidence historically for its validity. Not blind faith, but informed faith. He was indeed the Savior, King of Kings,

Lord of Lords. We are left with a choice: yes or no. Take care in making that choice. It is of utmost importance.

That was our Easter . . . hope amid chaos, life among death, light in darkness. The baptisms were powerful, as the guys each shared their testimony of faith in Christ to their eagerly listening buddies. I was humbled to be there with them in this time of their lives. It was truly a privilege. Tough warriors brought to tears because of their realization of God's grace in their lives. Stories of marriages being restored, stress and anxiety being relieved, and finding God in combat. Pray for these five soldiers, that their faith won't be just a quick, convenient decision—but that they would grow deep, lasting roots into God's Word, love, and salvation.

As you may have noticed recently, mortar attacks have picked up. *Duck-and-cover* is once again in our vocabulary. Several different factors seem to be contributing to this, but regardless, it's no fun. Counseling has also picked up as our soldiers once again are confronted with a real enemy bent on their destruction. Our time of ease for the last several months has been interrupted, and it's causing significant stress. Hopefully this is just a spurt of activity and not a sustained pattern. We are after the bad dudes, hounds of righteousness on the trail of seething wickedness. Just a matter of time till we get them, one way or another. It's amazing to watch our guys do what they do.

Hope you and yours are doing well. Thanks once again for the encouragement and comments you write. We are on the homestretch, light at the end of the tunnel. God willing, we'll all make it home safe and sound. As always, continue praying for our safety and God's protection over us. Thank you! God bless you and yours,

Darren

The Twelfth, Thirteenth, and Fourteenth Months

1

April 10, 2008

. . . The mild days and cool evenings are quickly turning
to hot days and warm nights. Soon it will reach over
100 degrees daily and get to 120s and 130s by July and
August, with a balmy 100 at night. But by then, we will be
out of here! Man . . . I can't even begin to imagine how
exciting that's going to be, to get on the planes out of
here, go through Kuwait for a few days, and head home to
Savannah. As it stands now, most of us will be home by mid-
July, with a few remaining to close up shop here, inventory
equipment, etc.

Tomorrow, on Friday, April 11, my son Sam will turn five. I
have now missed everyone's birthday. It's tough. I guess I'm
just homesick . . .

April 14, 2008

. . . It's been a roller coaster lately. Two days after my last post, we lost a soldier in an IED blast. Another tough day, night, next day . . . It was his platoon's first loss, and they took it hard. He was part of the Route Clearance Team, a platoon that goes first in a convoy in special vehicles to find and eliminate IEDs. Most times they find nothing and the route is clear, meaning the bad dudes didn't set one that day or night. Sometimes they do find IEDs before they blow and "clear" them (either blow up in place or call another team to come and cut the wires to dismantle). And then there are those times when the IED finds them rather than the other way around. Even then, most of the time the soldiers are okay. But that rare time that it hits just right, soldiers die. It was painful . . .

April 21, 2008

. . . One of our Bradleys (armored fighting vehicle, looks like a tank) hit an EFP IED and caught on fire. Nine guys inside, all got out with burns and shrapnel, but all got out! Trust me, that truly is a miracle . . .

April 25, 2008

Another powerful story. Buckle up for this one. One evening last week, while I was out at a patrol base, we got a call from a local Iraqi leader. He said a ten-year-old girl had been kidnapped by three men and was being held in a house near the PB, possibly being raped. The girl's family was poor and couldn't defend themselves, so they called us and asked us to intervene. We got a platoon of soldiers ready, briefed them on the situation, and sent them out to see what was up. They got there, and first called the occupants of the house out using a bullhorn and an interpreter. Nothing. They did it again, and noticed some movement in the house. They got ready, not knowing that was about to happen. Finally, someone came out like nothing was going on. Looked fishy. Our guys went in, over the man's objection, and found the girl tied up. They also found the three men, along with a couple of older women (why weren't they helping her, was my question). Our guys separated all of them and started asking questions. At first the girl defended them, saying they were family. Then one of our guys said, "Listen, we have these guys. They will never hurt you again if you tell us the truth." She unloaded the whole story. I'll spare you the details, but it was bad. Those guys were handed over to the Iraqi police, which is not a good place to end up. There is no telling if they're alive or not at this point. But really, we don't care. Our guys were absolutely overjoyed. True righteousness! I talked with them after they returned and they were pumped.

May 4, 2008

. . . I personally am tired. The long deployment, the heat rising, the soldiers I talk/counsel with and the issues, our base still getting hit and mortared on occasion—it's all taking its toll. I'm not complaining, just being honest. I knew what I was signing up for, but am ready for it to be over. We

can't get home fast enough. What keeps me going is The
Picture . . . the picture I have on my wall of Heather and the
kids and me sitting in a park in Savannah last spring before
I deployed. It's my oasis in the desert. I love my family more
now than I ever have before! I hope and pray not to take
them for granted ever again . . .

May 7, 2008
Happy Mother's Day!! To all moms, thanks! Especially to my
mom—thanks and I love you! I can't imagine how it must be
to have a son in combat. I salute you!

I want to wish my wife a very special Mother's Day!

Heather, you are a great mom to our babies! They love you
so much, and I love watching you with them. I'm so glad the
Lord has given us the privilege of you staying at home to
raise our kids. I'd want no one else to have the influence on
them that you do. You honor and cherish them, encouraging
them to be the persons God created them to be. You think
about what's best for each of them. That is a gift I stand in
awe of. When you tell me what you learn about each one,
and what God has shown you about each one's heart and
character, I rejoice. That is definitely the gift of a mom! That
is why I celebrate you today!

I've enjoyed watching you blossom this year, Heather. In
a few more weeks you will enter your first triathlon. You

have worked hard to get there, and it's been a dream of yours for a long time. How you've done it in the midst of everything else in a given day of family life, I haven't a clue. Also, you'll be leading a wives' prayer breakfast at Fort Stewart soon. It's been good for me to watch you enjoy being in the army and being with soldiers' spouses. I know you're going to do well leading that. And you're learning to play the piano, which I've heard, and it sounds great! I can't wait to get back and play guitar with you as you tickle the keys!

I have a song for us: "Maybe I'm amazed at the way you love me all the time . . ." Paul McCartney took the words right out of my mouth.

Here is a passage from the Song of Songs in the Old Testament. Yes, this is straight out of God's Word. It's literally about King Solomon with his bride, but also speaks of God and His way with us. He is a lover, and knows the anticipation of wanting to be with His bride—those of us who believe! But it's also a model, an example, of how a husband is to be with his wife. For that, I'm very glad!

"How beautiful you are, my darling! Oh, how beautiful! Your eyes . . . Your lips . . . Your neck . . . (And some other body parts, read it yourself!) . . . You have stolen my heart . . . my bride; you have stolen my heart with one glance of your eyes" (Song 4:1–9). Time to pull the blinds now!

Once again, Happy Mother's Day! I'm sure I speak for our three little ones. You deserve it. And best of all . . . you are mine! I'm counting the days, hours, minutes till I'm home and together with you again. All my love,

Your husband

May 14, 2008

. . . As chaplain we have several different classes we have to teach to every soldier—usually to platoon-size groups—before we go home. We had training to show us the content and some ideas on how to keep it interesting and engaging. It is extremely boring if you just do it by the book. But that's not my plan . . . ☺ I can't stand boring lectures, so I will spice it up a bit with some video clips, jokes, role playing, etc. It is serious content (suicide prevention, family reintegration, don't be a soldier at home with your wife and kids, etc.), but it doesn't have to be too heavy. Those classes will start soon . . .

June 17, 2008

We are getting closer and closer, but sooo slowly, every day inching by like Savannah honey in January. I'm beginning to look at my watch way too much. Our homecoming at Fort Stewart is only weeks away. I stand in awe of this year and this deployment with these guys. I will never again take for granted our military personnel all around us, especially ones who have deployed before. It's funny, I'm almost sad

to leave. Can't believe I just said that. Wow . . . but it's true.
I can't explain what it's like to have been through a combat
tour like this with these guys. I know some of them better
than their families do. I have had times of extreme heartache
and vulnerability with them, more than once wondering if we
were really going to get out of a situation. Surrendering to
the possibility of breathing your last breath at any moment
is a sobering experience. Doing business with God and
your life and everything in between . . . It's actually very
healthy! Until you're ready to die, you're not really alive. Only
then can you look any given day in the face and say "Here I
come!" And God willing, make it through . . .

June 23, 2008
. . . I ask you to continue praying for us, not only for our
safety, but for our upcoming reunion with our families. That's
not always a good thing for some soldiers. Some have been
stabbed in the back and taken for all they're worth. Others
have big decisions to make. Still others don't know what to
expect. It's a huge transition, from here back to there. I also
have some decisions to make about our future. I'm nervous,
but excited. Thanks again for your thoughts and prayers.
I hope this journal has given you a good look into what a
combat tour is like through my eyes these past fourteen
months . . .

Darren

THE FINAL MONTH

1

July 1, 2008

Hello, everyone! Man, is it good to be alive . . . and headed home soon! Unless you've deployed to a combat zone before, you can't even imagine how giddy everybody is around here. Most of the guys are joking, doing stupid guy stuff, and generally having a ball right now. It's blazing hot, but who cares? It has to get hotter before we leave, so bring it on! This will probably be my last update for a while, possibly until I get back home. We're packing and things are getting busy . . .

2

Lance was loading boxes of ammunition into the back of a Humvee when Darren arrived on the scene. He could smell the exhaust from the running engines and knew they were heading out soon.

"Gather 'round, let's go!" Michael's voice shouted out nearby.

Darren looked around and found the major walking to the front of another vehicle. When Michael saw him, Darren flipped an Armor of God coin toward him. Michael swiftly caught it, gave Darren a playful *You shouldn't have done that* stare, and tossed the coin right back—except Darren didn't move and only watched it land in the dirt.

Michael simply shrugged.

"Putting a coin in your pocket doesn't mean you believe," Darren said. "But who knows. Might help you consider when it matters."

Michael ignored the chaplain's comment, focusing instead on the soldiers who were gathering around him. It seemed that in the major's eyes faith was something you could talk about off the clock, when you just wanted to kill time. For now, his concern was with final checks on M4s and handguns and knives and scopes, and making sure the armor was in place and everybody had enough ammunition and PowerBars.

"All right. So, eyes alert," Michael told the men around him. "Scan the rooftops, windows. Watch the road, grandmothers, kids, livestock, and bumps in a field. Follow our ROE and *stay alive*. Got it?"

The soldiers confirmed they got it, and Michael turned to look back at Darren.

"Chaplain . . . Do what you do."

Darren pulled out his small, tattered Bible. Many of the

soldiers bowed their heads, and several even took a knee. Lance was one who knelt while Darren read the prayer for the day, then paraphrased an assortment of Bible passages he'd marked.

"The proud have laid their snares, and along the path they have set traps to catch me. But you are my strong deliverer. You shield my head in the day of battle. Do not grant the wicked their desires, Lord. Do not let their plans succeed. Amen."

As Darren opened his eyes, he saw Michael's hand slipping the coin into his pocket as he boarded his Humvee.

"Chaplain! You not comin'?"

Darren turned to see Lance, sweaty and grinning.

"Not today. Got some meetings, and they want me to start packing up. But hey—you don't need me, Bradley." Darren gave a nod to the sky. "You got something way better. See you tonight."

Another routine convoy, another set of vehicles moving out, the soldiers armed and ready. Darren walked back to his quarters, knowing the moment was finally here. He was packing to head home.

3

The words felt like shrapnel stuck in his leg or arm, lodged so deep inside he couldn't see them but knew they were there. Darren could feel their numbing pain as he glanced over his journal—not the online journal where he censored his most raw and real emotions, but the leather notebook where he had been scribing thoughts and feelings since his arrival in Iraq.

Shonda walked in and found him lost in those dark and sometimes hopeless words. "Bit too real?" she asked as she saw the look on his face.

He nodded, closing the journal and tossing it into his big backpack. "Yeah, even for me. I didn't want to sugarcoat things out here, but this'll have to wait a few years. Or ten, before Sam reads it."

As he loaded his video recorder and all the mini DV tapes into his bag, he added, "I'm glad Heather's never going to have to watch these."

"You certainly have a lot of them," Shonda said, partly teasing him about all those silly videos and pictures he had taken over the year.

"I almost feel like I can breathe again," he said.

That motherly look Shonda just couldn't help giving him appeared once again. "Good to hear, Chaplain. Been worried about you lately." She gave him a thin smile. "And before I forget, thank you. Your being here made a big difference. In where I'm headed when I get back."

This was news to Darren. "As in?"

"Oh, I don't know," she said. "I'm thinking maybe I won't be a half-bad mom when I get back. And probably won't fight my own mom so much."

Slipping his desk drawer open, Darren pulled out a coin. "So does that mean you wouldn't mind carrying one of these?"

"You and your coins," she said with a smile as she took it. "I'm gonna miss you, Chaplain."

"You too, Sergeant Shonda. But I still have a few weeks left.

You aren't rid of me yet. So you hungry? I'm in the mood for a nice soy burger."

4

One moment. Just like that.

A switch flipped on. A bulb burning out. An engine starting. A door slamming.

In one single moment, the world can suddenly turn upside down.

Even though Darren knew this all too well, he hadn't yet seen it up close and personal. But the moment he saw Lt. Col. Jacobsen walking toward him with that look on his face, Darren knew. Jacobsen was about to flip a switch and shatter the light and deliver some dreadful news.

"We need to take a walk, Chaplain," Jacobsen told him without a greeting and without acknowledging Shonda, who was by his side. She headed another direction as Darren followed the officer to the wall at one side of the base.

"Just got the call. Alpha and Bravo were on their final transitional patrol and hit an IED."

Darren nodded. "With due respect, sir. Get to the point, sir."

The lieutenant colonel's eyes weren't behind shades like usual, yet seeing them didn't offer Darren any warmth or connection.

Jacobsen spoke without emotion. "I'm sorry. I know he was a friend . . . We lost Lance Bradley."

Darren couldn't even begin to process the information. He nodded, his body feeling stiff and sweaty, and then followed Jacobsen back to the commons area.

"Anyone else?" he asked, trying to look calm and controlled. Trying to be a good soldier. Dealing with injuries and deaths came with the territory. Especially if your territory happened to be out there.

"Man nearest the blast site went to pull Lance out of the wreckage when another went off." Jacobsen cursed and shook his head, then stopped and looked at Darren. "Michael Lewis. From what I'm told, he'll make it. But I'm not sure about his legs."

Darren just stood there. He could see Jacobsen's face writhing in pain and anger at the news. He and Michael were tight.

This wasn't right. It couldn't really be happening, could it?

God couldn't do something like this, not now, not this close, not so near the finish line. Right.

Right, God?

God?

5

First stop is Tonya, Mia, and Nia. Then Amanda right afterward. Heather knows she needs to be there for all of them.

She doesn't offer glib phrases of comfort, nor does she attempt to appear brave and strong. All she can do is hold Tonya and the girls in her arms and weep alongside them. The Bible is full of weeping men and women; there's nothing wrong with grief.

"I'm sorry" is all she can say.

They know that Michael is alive, and that is good news indeed, all things considered. But Tonya and the twins don't need to hear that; they already know it. They also know Michael has been injured and will most likely be losing both of his legs.

"They were so close—so close to coming home," a weeping Tonya says.

The timing is truly terrible. But not only that, the fear all of them have carried around has been the news that their husband or father has been killed. Being injured in this way? It's a surprising curve ball. A rather nasty one.

Heather knows all the strides Tonya, Mia, and Nia have made with Michael this past year, especially through talking with him on the phone on a regular basis. Their relationship has started to change just as Michael has. Now what will happen? What will he be like when he arrives back home? Will the bitterness return with him, or will something worse accompany him?

Heather can't do anything about that—none of them can. All she can do is sit on the couch with these friends, grieving and praying and weeping.

6

"The LORD is my light and my salvation— / whom shall I fear? / The LORD is the stronghold of my life— / of whom shall I be afraid?"

Heather sits in her car, in the early morning hours before a glimpse of sunlight can be seen. In the distance, the Bradley trailer is lit, the figures awake and moving inside. She's been sitting here for a few minutes, trying to compose herself before going in to see Amanda.

She says the words of Psalm 27, hoping they can calm her, but her body still shakes and she still feels very alone.

"When the wicked advance against me to devour me, it is my enemies and my foes who will stumble and fall. Though an army besiege me, my heart will not fear; though war break out against me, even then I will be confident."

*   *   *

Darren recalls the same verse as he stands in his quarters, restless and wanting to do more. He's been praying and reading and preparing for the words he will say tomorrow to the grieving men. They will know his grief, especially since he was particularly close with Lance. They will be paying special attention to the words he says about the death of his friend and fellow soldier, Army Specialist Bradley.

He opens his Bible and finds the psalm that spoke to his soul in the first few days of 2004, the verses that ultimately convinced him to join the army.

> One thing I ask from the LORD,
>   this only do I seek:
> that I may dwell in the house of the LORD
>   all the days of my life,
> to gaze on the beauty of the LORD

and to seek him in his temple.

For in the day of trouble

he will keep me safe in his dwelling;

he will hide me in the shelter of his sacred tent

and set me high upon a rock. (Ps. 27:4–5)

He's kept me safe, but what about others? Why couldn't He shelter others in His sacred tent?

As he paces back and forth, finding prayer difficult, finding any sort of hopeful emotion hard to grasp, he spots the gift bag from Lance. He pulls out a beef jerky, but then sees there's a card in the bag that he had missed.

Darren picks up the card and holds on to it, then he falls back into his chair, weeping.

He can't read what's inside. Not yet.

⋆   ⋆   ⋆

Heather sits on the couch holding Amanda's hand. The tears have been flowing all morning, yet they still keep coming. The poor young woman is exhausted and terrified, yet she's still strong enough to open the letter addressed to her from Lance. As she silently reads it, wiping her eyes and then occasionally laughing just as her husband would have wanted her to, Heather remains by her side. Asking God over and over again to give Amanda strength and peace. And to help her be the friend she needs right now.

⋆   ⋆   ⋆

"Do not hide your face from me, do not turn your servant away in anger; you have been my helper. Do not reject me or forsake me, God my Savior."

Once again Darren stands by dog tags hanging from upended rifles and a pair of desert boots. Speaking to the grieving gathering of soldiers, he shares some fond memories of Lance. He forgets about himself and his emotions and he does his job, helping the men understand and clasp on to some bit of hope despite what's happened. Levity is something Lance always loved and would have wanted now, so before Darren ends his speech, he sets a bag of jerky by Lance's boots. The soldiers can't help but laugh, even those with tears in their eyes.

He continues to read from Psalm 27. "I remain confident of this: I will see the goodness of the LORD in the land of the living."

He pauses for a second, the words stinging his mouth, his stomach feeling the bitterness inside.

"We are blessed to be among the living. But going home . . . we must be prepared to face new challenges."

Darren looks over to see Shonda's concerned eyes watching him, but he continues to share from his heart.

"Anxiety. Anger. Depression. Even ideas that somehow not going on might be better . . . Reject these enemies, and ask for help. Just ask. That's all we can do . . . That's all I can do. Just ask—ask, and beg God for a little help here."

After the service, Darren heads back to the medical unit, where Michael lies unconscious on a stretcher. Both legs are bandaged, and they're preparing for him to be evacuated to a hospital for amputation. Darren looks over the strong and rugged face of his friend, closes his eyes, and prays for healing and for help in stirring Michael's heart.

As Darren opens his eyes, he sees the personal belongings on the table next to Michael. He reaches over and picks up the ChapStick, then he leans down and gently rubs it over Michael's dry and cracked lips.

When the medics take Michael away, Darren fights tears and watches, feeling like he has nothing left to give or offer.

A whisper of a reminder comes in his heart, where King David's words in Psalm 27 give him the answer. A clear, simple, and straightforward answer.

"Wait for the LORD; / be strong and take heart / and wait for the LORD."

7

Darren's hands shook as he finally opened up the letter and read it. They had been in the plane for over an hour. The elation of heading home had been overshadowed by the tragedy with Lance and Michael. He was finally bringing himself to read the note the specialist had written to him.

> Dear Chaplain Turner:
>
> When I think of myself raising Alexis and Elijah, I think of you. I picture a man with strength and wisdom, but also one who carries around two very important things in this world. Humility and humor.

I hope my children will have the privilege to find a father like you.

I want to thank you. You never preached at me, but you did preach for me. I guess God's got a way of using everything, right, including mules. For me, it was beef jerky. Seems fitting enough.

Thank you for not only giving me that Bible but also explaining things from it. And thank you for sharing Psalm 39:7 with me:

"And so, Lord, where do I put my hope? / My only hope is in you."

That's the only hope I carry now too.

Lance

8

Halfway across the Atlantic Ocean, Darren decided to write one more entry in his personal journal.

He wished he could openly share these thoughts online, but he couldn't.

He was the one who answered questions, not the one posing them.

He was the one who shared his faith, not the one searching for it.

He was the chaplain who offered up prayers, not the soldier making the requests . . .

This pen marks down my heart. I'm not sure I'm still writing inside this. Not anymore. Perhaps all these words inside this journal will eventually be laid to rest somewhere, perhaps buried at sea. I began writing them for Heather and the kids to read one day, but I don't think I want them to. Ever.

Nobody needs to hear about so much pain.

I'm flying back home a wounded man. I didn't lose a limb and didn't lose my life. I have no scars anybody can see. But I carry bags and bags of hurt and sorrow.

I don't know where I'm going to be able to store them.

My prayers have been difficult lately. I've asked God time and time again the following questions: Why take a man professing his belief? And why maim one confessing his confusion? Is this an example of Your righteousness, Lord? Or is this just an example of the bitter and hard realities of this war?

I ache because I grieve and can't show it.

These wounds—I can't let Heather and the children see them. Perhaps one day Heather can, but I know I have to come back and be strong for so many.

I still have a job to do, and I'm bracing for that.

For me, arriving back home won't mean I can simply unplug and tune out. The grief I'm holding is held in some way and measured by every soldier on this plane.

They're going to need someone to go to, someone with some answers, someone with hope.

But what if that hope already came home on a plane? What if it's trapped in a coffin and buried underneath eight feet of dirt?

Where will I be able to go? Who's going to give me answers?

Will I be able to find hope once more?

PART 3

REINTEGRATION

JULY 2008

1

Amidst the family members waiting with excitement and surrounded by balloons, welcome home signs, and American flags,
a woman waited for the man she loved. She shook with nerves,
wondering how he'd act and what he'd say and what she should
say back. There were so many things Heather wanted to tell
Darren, so many things she wanted to show him, so many things
she couldn't wait to do with him. Yet she knew this was going to
take some time. Not just for her, but for all of them.

As they waited behind barricades at Hunter Army Airfield,
Heather held Meribeth's hand. In her other hand, the toddler
waved a yellow ribbon. Sam and Elie stood next to them waving
flags.

"Now remember, kids. Daddy's going to be really tired
when he gets in."

"He can't be," Elie said. "We're going to play tea party and
save the princess. And he has to watch all my dances before—"

"No way. We're gonna play Fort Bumblefoot and sword fight so I can show him my karate moves," Sam yelled.

"There will be time for all of that," Heather told them. "It just can't all happen this afternoon."

As the first sign of soldiers walking down the stairway, a burst of cheers swelled over the airfield. A few at the front of the group jogged down and ran toward their families as reunions began to unfold like flowers blossoming in a field. All around them came the glorious sounds of laughter and surprise and shrieks of joy. The photo op beloved by television news shows.

Heather's eyes quickly scanned all the returning soldiers, looking and looking until she found him. Darren walked toward them, looking taller and stronger than ever. As he spotted them he began to jog their way. Sam and Elie scaled the barricade, jumping and then running to meet him. Heather called out to them but she couldn't stop them from running into their daddy's open arms.

The cries let out by the children were a combination of inhaling this sudden joy while exhaling the sadness they'd been carrying for months.

"When did you guys get so big?" Darren said as he lifted Sam and Elie, leaving his bags on the ground.

"Babe. You're here," Heather said with a steady smile as he embraced her and Meribeth.

"We're all here," Darren said as the five of them clung together as firmly as a set of folding hands.

When they finally all let go, Darren lifted Meribeth in his arms. "Meribeth! Look at you!" he said with astonishment.

Meribeth looked uncertain and overwhelmed by everything, and quickly began to cry.

Heather stroked her arm. "It's okay, sweetie. It's Daddy."

The little girl leaned over toward her mother, so Darren handed her back with a nod of understanding.

For a brief moment, Heather saw something on his face. Something more than simple exhaustion. The expression looked different than any she'd ever seen on Darren. Perhaps it was just because she hadn't seen him for so long.

It's all going to take time. Even the simple things like that.

2

The streets they drove on and the stores they passed all felt surreal to Darren. He figured he'd maybe gotten four good hours of sleep in the last four days, so finally getting a good night's rest would help clear his head. As Heather drove and Sam and Elie talked over each other trying to tell him stories, he couldn't help but think of all the things he would need to do in the next ten days.

"Just wait till you see my karate belt!" Sam told him.

The ten days of reintegration training included many things for the returning soldiers, such as having a health checkup, seeing a dentist, dealing with any legal or pay issues, adding new babies to insurance, processing a divorce, registering cars, restoring service to cell phones. And after those ten days, they would all get an entire month off.

Thank you, Uncle Sam.

Darren knew every single soldier deserved it. He couldn't wait to spend time with Heather and the kids, go to the beach, visit family, and just enjoy being with each other.

It would be nice to just be Darren again and not Chaplain Turner.

As their Pathfinder SUV turned down their road and neared their house, Sam couldn't contain his excitement.

"There's your ribbon, Dad!"

Sure enough, a yellow ribbon was tied around their front tree.

"Yellow means welcome home," Elie said.

"Wow," Darren said. "Look at that."

As they pulled into the driveway, the kids bolted out of the vehicle as they'd done a thousand times before. Darren sat as Heather shut off the engine. He stared out at the house he'd left fifteen months ago.

"Does it look the same?" Heather half joked.

"Yeah," Darren said.

But deep down, it didn't look the same. Nothing looked the same.

He wondered if it ever would again.

3

Normally it was Darren working his magic cooking steaks and burgers, but tonight Heather was the one manning the grill. That was the one thing he had asked for when he got home: a nice, thick rib eye. Thankfully she'd had fifteen months to burn and char enough meat on the grill to finally get the hang of the gas burner.

After Heather checked on the slow-cooking steaks and the hot dogs she had just put on for the kids, she went back inside to continue preparing for dinner. It felt like a Thanksgiving or Christmas dinner, not because of the menu but because of the momentous occasion. Daddy's first dinner back home was something she had been thinking about for a long time. That and many other firsts as well. She saw Elie setting the table in the dining room while Sam was going through his collection of plastic swords, picking the ones he and Daddy would play with later.

At least one out of two of them is helping.

The baked potatoes were ready and the toppings were already on the table: butter, sour cream, bacon bits, and lots of shredded cheddar cheese. Sometimes she could make a meal simply out of these. She had gone a little overboard with the vegetables, making her garlic-roasted broccoli that she knew Darren liked, but also doing a new recipe she'd recently discovered for a brussels sprouts hash that included walnuts and crispy sage inside.

Once the steaks were finished, she put them on a plate and brought them inside. She wasn't sure where Darren had disappeared to, so she called out to him that dinner was ready. After getting Sam and Elie to bring the drinks to the table, with everything else ready to go and Darren nowhere to be found, Heather walked into the family room and saw him standing still in front of their picture window.

Staring lifelessly at the Lewis home across the street.

"Hey—did you hear me? Dinner's ready."

Darren didn't even turn. She walked up beside him, looking out the window and then back at her husband.

"Tonya and the girls left to join Michael at Walter Reed yesterday."

She reached over to touch his shoulder, wanting him to know that in some small way, she understood. But as her hand touched Darren, he flinched and jerked his body away from her.

"Whoa, gosh—sorry, babe. I called several times, but didn't mean to—"

Heather stopped as Darren shook his head without looking at her, as if to say *Don't worry about it.* Yet it felt dismissive, especially since he was still looking outside and ignoring her standing there.

Tightening her lips and breathing in, she went back to the kitchen. Dinner could wait.

4

Any moment now in the dark, he expected to hear the crack of gunfire or the roar of a mortar blast. His body ached with exhaustion, his mind fuzzy from the fatigue and his heart simply feeling heavy. Lying on his side against the plush couch in the living room, his eyes wandered around the room, watching the slight glow of the streetlight slipping through the blinds and spotting the red dot of his cell phone charger.

Everything inside swore at him, telling him he needed rest. Yet he fought it off, knowing what it would bring.

This is temporary . . . it's just tonight . . . I can control this.

Buried underneath this dam of emotions, Darren knew it was all simply due to the lack of sleep and to the stored-up pressure he'd been carrying. Tonight, it felt like the dam had sprung leaks and was starting to drown him.

This time Heather didn't surprise him as she walked into the room. He heard her steps clearly. Too clearly, in fact.

The nights had trained his ears to listen carefully, even as he slept.

"Babe . . . ?" Heather whispered in the shadows. "Did I take up too much of the bed?" Her voice felt as light as a colorful leaf gliding down off its branch high above him.

"No," he finally told her.

She waited for a moment by the wall next to the couch. "Okay . . . well . . . want to come back in?"

The smothering sensation inside of him pressed down. Darren gritted his teeth and blinked and remained silent.

"Anything I can do for you then?" Heather asked.

So patient, so soft, and so calm . . . She sounded like a dream, the sort of lovely dream he hadn't imagined in such a long time.

"Just let me stay awake," he admitted to her.

She couldn't see his tears, yet maybe she could hear them laced inside his words. It didn't matter.

She walked over toward him, then sat on the floor, leaning

against the couch. She didn't say a word. All she did was put her
hand on his arm, perhaps to simply let him know she was there
in the dark, and she wasn't going to let him go.

5

The rustling of the wind outside. Then a crackling in the background. Troops on the move and gunfire following them.
Darren stirs in his deep sleep, his mind thousands of miles away.
A voice, high-pitched and sweet, hovers over him, then another
loud, brash voice calls out.

For a moment he thinks of the dead girl in his arms and
the weeping father watching him carry her. He remembers the
medics standing over the soldier, gently covering his face with a
sheet. Darren can feel the fabric resting against his face, shifting
over his entire body.

His arm jerks up; he tears the blanket off and leaps up onto his
feet. His eyes flicker, seeing the blistering Middle East sun spilling
out across his feet. Then he realizes the ground is too comfortable,
he's standing on the carpet in their living room. Heather sits beside
him on the floor, leaning against the couch he slept on.

"Hey, you destroyed my roof," a wide-awake Sam shouts.

Elie joins Sam in pulling cushions and blankets around
them. Darren can feel the surge going through his body, the
adrenaline waking it up even as his mind is still half-asleep. All
the movement and laughter and excitement surrounding him
are too much to take in right away this morning.

"And now that you've been there, you can show us how to really play war!" Elie commands as she stands on the couch.

"Please. Stop. It's not a game."

Sam is piling cushions next to him, calling it Fort Bumblefoot, while Elie laughingly orders him to start doing jumping jacks and to stand in line.

"I said it's not a game! Now drop it!"

Both of the kids stop moving, not only shocked but scared. Darren didn't just yell, he roared at them as if they were all trying to talk amidst gunfire. Heather stands up, a startled look filling her tired face.

"Daddy?" Elie whimpers, her eyes filling.

He can barely breathe, with a head feeling foggy and a heart racing for whatever reason. Their hurt, confused expressions only further frustrate him. He doesn't know what to say. He can't figure out how to simply sit down and relax for a moment. There's a rage that woke up directly beside him.

Heather's look . . . She doesn't have to say anything else. It matches the panic inside of him. A suffocating feeling even though he can breathe. A falling sensation even though he's standing still.

"I've just got to . . . go out for a while," he says to all of them and no one in particular.

Heather guides Sam and Elie away toward their bedrooms. "Come on, kids. Go get dressed for breakfast. I'll make pancakes."

Their little steps running down the hallway only make Darren's head hurt more. That sound, the echoes, the laughter . . .

It's too much.

He slips on his tennis shoes and heads to the front door. Heather follows him, waiting for him to say something, wanting some kind of explanation.

"Hey, I'm home. Okay? Just—just give me more than a few days to figure it out."

"No one's pushing you, Darren. It's just—while we're waiting, our babies missed you a lot. And need to know their daddy still loves them."

Missed you. Need to know. Still loves.

You know nothing about missing and needing and loving and living and dying.

"I'm not going anywhere, okay? And if anyone's wondering, I love my family."

He whips the door open and rushes outside. So he can breathe and not think. So he can douse the furious flames inside of him, the ones set on fire for no reason.

AUGUST 2008

1

"It's so good to hear your voice," Heather said into her cell phone. "I'm sitting on our front steps, looking at your house right now."

Tonya gave a reflective chuckle. "I wish all of us were there right now. It's going to feel weird when the four of us are all back home."

When her phone rang this afternoon, Heather was delighted to see it was Tonya calling. They hadn't spoken in at least a week, so she wanted to hear how things with Michael and the girls were going.

"What's it like having Darren home?" Tonya asked her.

All Heather wanted to do was share everything with her friend. They had grown close over the past fifteen months, and both of them had spent many hours talking about their husbands. Tonya would have been as surprised as Heather if she heard about Darren's state of mind since he'd come back.

The last thing this woman needs is more bad news. Or anything negative.

"It's been a long three weeks," Heather said. "But another time, okay? How are you doing?"

"I think maybe I'm still in shock. Not just after coming here and seeing Michael. But . . ." Tonya's voice began to quiver, and Heather could hear the emotion in her voice.

"What's wrong?"

"It's something . . . something that happened earlier today," Tonya said, clearing her throat. "When Michael was awake."

As she waited for Tonya to continue, Heather glanced over at their house, remembering the first day they saw their neighbors. Recalling how Michael banged on the door and yelled, then took off down the road in anger. She couldn't imagine what he might be feeling right now.

"I'd been talking with my sister, so I was outside the room while the girls talked to their daddy by his bed. When I stepped into the room, I saw Michael in tears, holding both of their hands . . ."

Again Tonya paused, her voice choking up.

"He told the girls how much he loved them, and how sorry he was. He promised them he was going to do things right this time. And then he saw me and told me to come over. And he said he was going to be the kind of man the *three* of us could be proud of."

Now Heather was crying too, wiping the tears off her face as she laughed with surprise.

"Nia and Mia just loved on their daddy, telling him they

already were proud of him. It was . . . Heather, it was an answer to prayer."

"You cannot know how happy this makes me," Heather said.

2

Darren checks the dead bolt on the front door one more time, just making sure. He's been forgetting more things lately, with his head still carrying a fog he can't get rid of, so he just needs to make sure. The house is quiet with all the family asleep.

A car drives down the road in front of them, making Darren rush over to the front window and peek out from inside. Sweat covers him and he's breathing heavily. He knows there's nobody out there, surely nothing to worry about. But he still feels like they're being watched.

"Darren?" Heather asks from behind him.

He doesn't say anything, just continues to watch and listen.

"Darren. What are you doing . . . ?"

"Shhh!"

Now he's scanning the entire yard, looking down the street to make sure the car isn't coming back, focusing on the big oak tree in the front to see if anybody's hiding behind it.

"Is everything okay?"

"Quiet!" he whisper-shouts.

He's not the only one here now, the only person in possible danger. Heather's here along with Sam and Elie and Meribeth.

What if someone sneaks in from another way?

Darren rushes over the carpet to the back door to check
the lock, then back to the kitchen window to look out into the
backyard.

You just never know who's out there and what can happen.

"Is there somebody outside?" Heather whispers.

"I said stop talking!"

He can't believe Heather's up right now and questioning him
and wanting to talk. That's all she wants to do—talk. Asking
questions and wanting to know how he's feeling and if he needs
anything and if she can do anything and how things are going.
She just doesn't get it.

As he turns to head back to the front door, Heather stands
in front of him, her face tired and strained. He shoves her as he
moves back to the front door.

*She just doesn't get it. The horrors out there and the dangers in
this world.*

"Darren—you're scaring me."

"Go to bed," he says as he looks out the window again.

"Honey," she says, approaching him and touching his arm.

"Stop it! Don't—just don't touch me. Please—go to bed."

He doesn't care how loud he's being or what he looks like.

*They don't know. They can't understand this heavy load and I
don't want them to . . . they can't.*

Darren has to protect them. He has to make sure all of them
are okay. That's what he knows. That's what he's been learning
out there in the wilderness. To protect himself.

Now he has to protect them, even if they don't get it yet.
Even if they never get it.

3

In the bright warmth of morning, Darren is not next to her as she wakes up.

During the morning ritual of cereal and pancakes and television and Cheerios, Darren is not around to laugh or eat what the kids can't.

As the day begins to turn from warm to hot, Darren isn't outside jumping on the trampoline or at the park sitting on a bench watching the children.

Another dinner is served for five but only enjoyed by four.

Soldiers come home and are given a chance to take leave and relax. Chaplains, however, remain on duty, active and assisting other families.

In the cool hush of midnight, as Heather reaches out an arm to the other side of the bed, Darren is not there to be found.

Even though he's right there with them, Darren is missing in action. And the only one who truly knows this is Heather.

4

He stands by the door of his car, weary, the adrenaline beginning to leak out of him. Darren looks up at the moon and envies it, so bright and full. It's late, far too late for him not to have called home. He knows Heather is probably worried, but he knows he had to stay. He couldn't leave his friend alone tonight.

Climbing into the car, he feels his body shaking and knows the shield of strength he demonstrated back in the soldier's house was simply a facade. A disguise he wears, similar to Sam dressing up to play soldiers.

He hasn't felt strong for a very long time.

You're afraid and you're weak, the voice inside of him whispers.

The drive feels long, his frustration riding with him, picking up speed with each mile. He tries to recall Lance's face, his always-present smile, but he can't. He can't see Lance in his mind even though he keeps trying.

I still have to see Amanda. Have to see the family. But I can't.

He's been making the rounds, going to see the wives and children and families of the soldiers who have been lost. Visiting the hospitals where the wounded are still recovering, many missing parts of themselves like Michael.

We're all missing parts of the selves we brought over to Iraq. Some just aren't as obvious.

Months ago at the base, he was weary. Now Darren is exhausted, his security stripped away, his soul shredded. The night resembles how he feels. Black, draining, silent, with the bright light visible but distant.

The work he's continuing to do only shaves away a little more of his depleted reserve. Of course he wants to spend time with his kids at the park, or bounce on the trampoline, or stand in front of a grill just waiting for the steaks to be cooked. But there's so much to do and so little time. And there's only one of him.

Heather and the kids don't need to know about the nightmares the soldiers have. They don't need to hear about the
marriages destroyed or the men drinking themselves to death.
Heather has seen and heard enough tears herself, so she doesn't
need any more weight wrapped around her. She doesn't need
to know the emptiness inside some of the soldiers who've come
home. She doesn't need to carry that burden.

The porch light of his house is still on, and so is the lamp
in the living room. Darren climbs out of his car and hesitates,
knowing what's behind the door.

He's too tired to argue or to explain. Why should he have
to explain where he's been? She should understand by now. He's
explained enough about being a chaplain.

Sure enough, Heather is waiting for him on the couch.

"It's three in the morning, Darren," she scolds him in a
whisper. "Where have you been?"

*Nobody gets it. Nobody. Especially not Heather. And if anybody
should understand, it's my wife.*

"One of the guys at the base had a crisis. I still have a job to
do, Heather."

He walks past her and out of the room. He's too tired to
argue and needs sleep, even though he knows it won't come.

Part of him doesn't want it to come. He doesn't want its
dreams.

Darren can figure this out on his own. He can wade through
these waters alone. He's been doing it long enough; there's no
reason for him to stop now.

5

It could be worse, Heather thinks as she looks out the kitchen window and sees Darren sitting in the chair facing the set of trees lining the back of the yard. Nearby, Elie and Sam are playing kickball with some neighborhood friends, but Darren doesn't seem to notice them. Nor does he seem bothered by the heat in the midday sun, even though he's wearing his University of Georgia sweatshirt and sweatpants.

He could be missing his legs like Michael.

Then she thinks of Amanda, the single mother of two doing everything she can to survive each day. She shudders. Yes, things could be worse.

All she—all they—can do is get through each day.

Heather fills a glass with ice and lemonade and carries it outside. She approaches with tentative steps, walking over the grass and clearing her throat as loudly as possible so he knows she's there behind him. He doesn't look up. His hair is messy and his face unshaven, and his eyes are far, far away.

Heather leans over and gently kisses his forehead. "I brought you something to drink," she says.

He looks at the glass as if he's never seen one before, then takes it and nods before resuming his vacant stare into the backyard.

Hours later, Heather finds herself looking out the kitchen window again as the sun has already set. Still Darren sits, as if he's looking for something in the trees and refusing to move until it finally arrives.

FALL 2008

1

Heather was mad. Actually, she wasn't just mad. She was confused and concerned and angry all at the same time.

She just doesn't get it.

For fifteen months Darren had built relationships with the guys in Iraq, bonding with them and weeping with them. Grieving with them in ways nobody else could understand. So naturally it felt right to want to be around them.

I don't have to say anything around them. They know. They get it.

"You bought a *motorcycle*?" she said, the afternoon he pulled up on the black bike. "Darren, you're not a single guy anymore."

It was true, he'd been living like a single guy for fifteen months, so he was used to getting what he wanted when he wanted it. But he hadn't been able to just go to the store out in the desert.

Don't I have a right to just spend some of the money I've definitely earned?

It was a Suzuki Intruder, a motorcycle that looked a little like a Harley but didn't have the Harley price or riding experience.

His buddies joked and called it a "Hardly," but Darren didn't mind. It was fun riding it. He planned to ride with seven other guys he was deployed with.

"Haven't you spent enough time with those guys?" she asked.

How could he answer that? Yes, of course he had. They had also managed to *live*, something most people just couldn't relate to. Yes, perhaps riding the bikes was a form of escape, but that's exactly what all of them had done: escaped from Iraq. They'd come back in one piece, at least most of them. They had a reason to celebrate.

"I'm not getting loaded or high or anything like that," he argued.

"But do you think a bike is a good idea for a man with three kids? And what do you think it says to our children when you're gone on the weekends?"

Daren knew he wasn't doing anything wrong. He was having fun and spending time with some kindred souls who knew. They got it.

They understand the fears that keep us up at night.

Everything felt confusing and overwhelming. Was he dealing with stress? Absolutely. Was he being selfish? Sure. But what Heather and the kids couldn't see, and what he didn't *want* them to see, was the scary stuff he carried around deep inside of himself.

He kept trying to grab onto the man he was before leaving. But even picking up his favorite books and reading through them didn't seem to bring encouragement. In fact, oftentimes they left him empty. Even the pages of one of his favorite books by C. S. Lewis didn't offer Darren encouragement, though he thought this description of grief was accurate: *No one ever told me that grief felt so like fear. I am not afraid, but the sensation is like being afraid. The same fluttering in the stomach, the same restlessness, the yawning. I keep on swallowing.*

Every day he looked at himself and tried to hold it together, telling himself he wasn't afraid of anything. Yet those fluttering, restless feelings inside never left.

2

"So how are things going? *Really* going?"

Heather looked at Tonya and knew she couldn't keep anything from her, not anymore. She wasn't simply her neighbor or a fellow soldier's wife; over the past year and a half, Tonya had become one of her dearest friends. She took a sip of her coffee, then looked around the Starbucks to see if there was anybody who might overhear.

"Nothing like I thought they'd be going," Heather said. "It's just—everything's different these last few months. And it's not because I'm not homeschooling anymore."

"I'm sorry."

"I'm giving him time, but he just won't give me anything back. He's there, *physically*, but that's all. And even that's not always true. He spends a lot of time jogging."

"He should feel lucky he's able to do that." Tonya looked away for a moment, then realized how her comment sounded. "I'm sorry—I don't mean to sound so harsh."

"I understand. I think Darren realizes that too. He made it back to his family. But we never spoke about expectations after he came back. We spoke so much about his decision to join the army, and about which battalion to be in, and about the deployment . . . Since he's come back, we haven't talked about anything."

Tonya nodded, understanding all too well. "Michael was lost, honestly, when he came back the first time. The girls had grown and they weren't his babies anymore. I would try to talk, but he wouldn't let me in. His solution, unfortunately, was to drink away the pain. But the rest of the family started to drift downstream as well."

"But things have gotten better, right?" Heather realized the terrible irony of her comment. "At least, in some ways."

"It's all perspective, right? People talk about these seasons of life, but I don't see seasons. You fall in love but have to figure out how to pay for a wedding. You can't get pregnant and then are blessed with twins. Your husband is a hero and yet privately he's a ghost. The one thing you've helped teach me is never to give up."

Heather gave a wry chuckle. "Are you sure that was me?"

"Darren is a good man. This is typical. He'll come back around. Trust me—he will."

•

3

He walked through one aisle after another of costumes, everything from comic book heroes to Revolutionary War outfits. This wasn't any ordinary costume shop, but the sort that was open year-round and rented to people for plays and probably even movies. The racks of clothes were endless and overwhelming.

All he wanted was something he could wear for fun on Halloween. The kids were going to be all dressed up for trick-or-treating, and they had already been asking him to go with them. He didn't want to, but he knew he needed to get his act together and try. He had to start trying sometime.

Ten minutes after entering the store, Darren felt numb. All the colors of the clothes seeming to blur into one gray streak. Suddenly the whole idea seemed silly.

He turned and saw a rack of modern-day military clothes. He stopped for a moment, scanning the hanging outfits, until he came to a jacket and read its name.

Specialist Lance Bradley.

He blinked and stepped away, then looked at it again. There were no words on the jacket. Once again, he was just imagining something.

What am I doing here?

He didn't want to pick out a stupid outfit and he wasn't going to go trick-or-treating. He felt too tired and overwhelmed. The kids simply had to learn to be okay with being told no.

He climbed back into his car, turned on the engine. Then he slapped the steering wheel with the palm of his hand and let out an exasperated shout. He was angry, but he wasn't exactly sure what he was angry about. It wasn't about a costume. But something inside of him held a fury that never went away.

Sometimes Heather didn't give him space in the kitchen in

the morning, made him feel like he needed to leave while she made breakfast or fixed lunch for the kids. He'd get angry at all the things he needed to do around the house, things that should've been done when he was gone, even if Heather had had to hire someone.

The kids were loud and argued too much. His football team was doing terribly. There were too many families he was meeting with. The guy in front of him just cut him off at the red light.

It felt like every single thing throughout the day would get him angry. And as much as he tried to suppress it, Heather could see it.

She not only saw it, she often took the brunt of it.

I have to get my head and my heart in the right place.

But as he drove back home, reality smacked him in the face once again.

You can't even pick out a simple costume for Halloween. How do you think you're gonna figure out your life?

4

With Thanksgiving a few days away, Heather found herself searching to hear something—anything—from Darren, so she eventually began to reread the posts on his CaringBridge journal. She had read them all, but it felt good to hear his heart once more. Perhaps there was something inside these words that would help her understand what had happened out there. What *really* happened.

She found herself welling up at the words she had written five months ago on Father's Day. In some ways, it felt like the woman who wrote that post had dramatically changed, and the man she wrote it about no longer existed.

Darren, this past year and our journey into the army has been so amazing. When I first met you, I knew that besides the fact that you were about the best-looking thing I had EVER seen, that there was depth about you that intrigued me. You hooked me that first day, and the mystery of you still captivates me today. Watching you grow as a husband and dad these last nine years has been amazing. When I've been my ugliest you have not flinched and have even reassured me that my fits will not push you away. Wow. When you've been your ugliest you have without fail humbled yourself to say that even though you may not understand the offense, you wanted the Lord to reveal to you your heart so that you could be a better man. WOW! I talk to countless wives who have never heard those words from their husbands, and it overwhelms me that I got you! Although I know that you are just a man who sins, you have been a most excellent representation of Christ to me as a woman and to your children. Right now you are the center of their world and are a part of their conversation every day. I think that this year has gone so well for them because they are so secure in their relationship with you. I see every day children who are safe in the knowledge that they are loved and adored by their dad. I can give them some of that, but there is something about you that cannot be filled by me.

We are blessed by the gift of you.

You are my best friend and hero.

Happy Father's Day, my love.

Heather turned off the computer, wiping the tears off her face. Nothing about those words had been exaggerated or made up. They were so real when she wrote them. Yet now she questioned everything.

She no longer felt like Darren's friend, much less his best friend and love. And with each passing dark day, Heather was afraid their children no longer fully knew or believed they were loved.

Where had the man she'd written those words to gone?

God, is he ever going to show back up?

5

Christmas approached, but Darren didn't look forward to it, not the way he used to. He couldn't seem to find the enthusiasm or energy inside to be excited about the holiday or anything else. One night in early December he sat looking at the photos from a year ago, the ones shared on their site.

I have the new pictures posted. In order to tell the story better, I will narrate you through the images. Just a few words under each picture don't do them justice.

Pic 1: This was the first PB we hit on Christmas Eve. Our commander, dressed as Santa, came barreling out of the Humvee and ran into the house. The guys were floored! They thought it was hilarious. Some weren't even sure who he was. After some greetings and ho-ho-ho's he sat down and let the guys sit on his lap for pictures, which they emailed home later that night. We handed each soldier a stocking.

Pic 2: Early Christmas Day morning, about to head out to the other PBs with the commander's Personal Security Detail (PSD), the guys who drive him around and provide protection for him. This is who we usually ride with, so I know these guys well. It was about 32 degrees that morning. Sorry for the sunrise in the camera!

Pic 3: Santa getting some mirror time to make sure all his hairs are nicely aligned.

Pic 4: The first PB that Christmas morning, one of the company's lieutenants showing off his stocking.

Pic 5: A soldier and his Wilson volleyballs (remember the movie Cast Away with Tom Hanks?). Not sure why he had those, probably feels stuck like Hanks did.

Pic 6: Our encore! All the officers of the company at the PB singing "Feliz Navidad." It was a hit! I played some also on the guitar. Thanks, Calvary Chapel of Gwinnett, for the guitar!

Pic 7: A soldier taking Communion at one of the Christmas services. We stepped away from Santa and the stockings to get to the real Reason. These particular guys were waiting for "our Christmas service," as they called it.

Pic 8: Me and two Concerned Citizens. They wanted two of my Santa hats, so what could I say? ☺ A soldier in the background gets a stocking from us.

Pic 9: Great story! This little boy in the village saw us handing stockings to our guys as they had pics with Santa, and he wanted one: "Mista, Mista—I have?" Again, what could I say? He says "Shukran" (thank you). Six weeks ago, bullets were flying in his village. No more!

Pic 10: Probably my favorite picture. These guys, once they got their stockings, walked away from the group a bit to read their cards and go through their stockings.

Pic 11: And to close the day, I helped serve the Christmas dinner brought from the main base. A good ending to a great day! Thanks again.

Those last words Darren had typed out twelve months ago stung. Yes, it was a good ending to a great day. But he couldn't help looking at the one picture of the "anonymous soldier" taking Communion.

He hadn't shared Lance Bradley's name.

Yes, this had indeed been the "real reason" for them to celebrate Christmas and have fun with jolly ol' Saint Nick while
handing out stockings.

*But what's the real reason for losing Lance? Why, God? Why did
You have to take him?*

Darren didn't think he'd ever understand the real reason
for that.

January 2009

1

Sometimes Darren felt like he could keep running forever.

He went jogging in the morning, when the cold helped wake him up and the chill felt like the opposite of being in Iraq. A midday run helped clear his thoughts and revived him, while an evening jog helped repair the nerves that had been splintering apart all day long.

On this cool January evening, it felt good to run along the trails in the nearby woods leading to Freedom Park as the sun drifted away into the west. He always came back at dusk, sweaty and empty but a little more sane. Yet for some reason, Darren felt different tonight. As usual, his thoughts ran alongside him for a while, but mile by mile he was able to outrun them. The thousands of things stampeding through his heart soon only became a handful, and eventually he was thinking about nothing but the rhythm of his heart and lungs and pounding feet.

Tonight, he couldn't shake all those thoughts and emotions. He kept thinking of a *Wild at Heart* quote he'd found on a note-card: *We are hiding, every last one of us. Well aware that we too are not what we were meant to be, desperately afraid of exposure, terrified of being seen for what we are and are not, we have run off into the bushes. We hide in our office, at the gym, behind the newspaper and mostly behind our personality. Most of what you encounter when you meet a man is a facade, an elaborate fig leaf, a brilliant disguise.*

The first time Darren read this, he wrote it down as a pow-erful example and quote to use in a sermon. He understood it well, yet he also could say he wasn't hiding nor living behind a facade. But now? The words felt like they had been written specifically about him.

Every day he feared someone would discover how weak and fragile he'd become—someone other than Heather, of course. She knew well enough by now. She could see he'd run off into the bushes. Sometimes, like now, he was *literally* doing just that.

I'm a brilliant disguise. I've been hiding. For six months.

He could see all the parents weeping with him as he tried to console them. He heard the cries of the kids trying to under-stand why their daddy or mommy had died. Chaplain Turner could never show his fears, nor could he hesitate. Yet this only made him feel worse, keeping everything bottled inside, then letting it explode open time and again at home.

Memories from the past months haunted him. He recalled the argument just before the kids went trick-or-treating on Halloween. The disastrous family dinner at their house on Thanksgiving. Getting angry at Sam and Elie when they comp

lained about the things they didn't receive at Christmastime.
He didn't recognize the man walking in his skin.

I detest that man.

He just didn't know if that man would ever have the strength
to leave.

2

The wet pan was taking forever to clean. Heather kept scrub-
bing the melted cheese off its sides as the water in the sink spilled
over the side of the counter. She noticed that her jeans were wet
and simply sighed.

Her neck ached, her body was exhausted from a long day
of shuttling the kids around to swim practice and soccer, seeing
a couple of army families, and going grocery shopping. Darren
had been home when she brought in the groceries, so she made
chicken parmesan, hoping the delicious aromas would entice
him to actually sit down and have dinner with them. But as
usual, he had suited up in his jogging clothes and bolted out the
door without saying a word.

She was drying the last bowl when the door thumped open
and footsteps came into the kitchen. Darren was breathing hard
and sweaty. He quickly grabbed a glass from the cabinet and
filled it with water from the refrigerator. There was no greeting. Nothing. He hadn't said much to her since their argument
yesterday.

"You missed dinner and bedtime, again," she said.

He chugged the water and ignored her. She could tell he didn't want to hear it, but he needed to hear it. This was ridiculous. She was doing too much around this house. There were two parents living in this house, but one was doing all the work.

Darren jerked open the dishwasher to stick the glass in. He pulled out the top rack, and finding it jammed full he exhaled with impatience and searched for a place to set it. The glass caught on one of the rack pins, and he pushed and pulled it till—

"Darren!"

The glass shattered in his hand, sending pieces falling over other dishes and onto the floor. He backhanded the top rack in retaliation, and Heather could see blood splattering everywhere as another glass smashed to the floor.

"Are you kidding me?"

Darren looked angrier than she had ever seen him appear.

"Do you ever run this thing?"

"Shh! I *just* got the kids down!"

Grabbing a dish towel, Darren started to wipe the blood off the top of the counter, but instead turned it into a long smear. He wadded the towel around the gash in his hand.

"Unbelievable!" he shouted.

Heather didn't move or blink or breathe. Then she slowly began to pick up the broken glass.

"I want you to stop this *right now*," she said. "I don't want Meribeth waking up and walking in here when you're like this. You'll scare her."

Just like you're scaring me.

His eyes grew dim as he glared down at her. She'd never realized what an intimidating presence Darren could be.

"Come on, let me see that," she said, and reached for his hand to take a look at the wound.

Darren yanked his hand away from her as if she were a wild animal trying to bite it. He headed for the front door. "I'm going to base to get stitches."

She followed him, every ounce of her body seemingly on fire. "Sure, fine, walk away. I've been doing just fine on my own for the past twenty-one months."

Darren stopped and spun back around. "What's that supposed to mean? I'm here—"

"No, you're not *here!* Not with me. Not with the kids." Now it was Heather who was shouting.

"I'm going for stitches."

"I have been patient and compassionate, Darren. I've given you space. I've run interference with the kids to protect them—"

"*Protect* them? From *what?*"

"I don't know! That's the point! I don't recognize you like this. You are angry and distant and mean. All the time. And I'm totally alone here."

With each spoken word, Heather could feel herself growing more and more aggressive.

"What kills me is that you know how to show up," she continued. "You know how to be kind. Tonya won't stop talking about how you keep showing up for Michael."

"That's because he's *been* through something."

Darren looked as if he was reeling, reliving the combat

images right there in front of her. Yet it didn't matter. The anger exploded inside of her like an IED.

"*I've* been through something!" she said.

"Oh yeah? What?"

"Oh, I don't know—just raising our three children by myself—partnerless. For a year and a half I've weathered every tantrum, soothed every hurt. I have cooked every meal, washed every dish. I've carried this family and held us together despite the fact that since you've been back you've made exactly *zero* effort to share the burden."

Darren's eyes were wide open and electric as if staring at a wildfire coming at him. Heather didn't stop.

"And on top of that, Darren, I have also been holding wailing, sobbing wives, mothers, and children in my arms. While you were there, I was here. I saw and *felt* their hearts torn to shreds. And you don't think I've been through something?"

"Oh, you want to turn this into a competition right now?"

"No!" she screamed. "I want to know why! Why you somehow have it in you to show up for those men but you can't do it for your own family?"

"Those men need me," he said through clenched teeth.

"*I* need you. Your children need you! And you've abandoned us!"

The man in front of her wasn't her husband. He was a tormented and confused stranger. He shook his head and looked delirious.

"You don't get it," Darren said. "You will *never* get it. I can't look at you, and I'm not doing this right now."

He opened the door and walked out of the house.

3

Darren sat in his car, the last hour spent in the hospital getting stitches and bandaging up his hand. Most of the men coming in for a wound like this would have been questioned and suspected of doing something wrong, but not someone like Chaplain Turner. People knew him, knew he had a wonderful wife and three amazing children, so how could there possibly be anything wrong with this picture?

In the darkness, the light drizzle falling on his truck, Darren felt like his worldview had suddenly become as clear as the wet windshield in front of him.

You know how to use the wipers but you're refusing to. You don't even want to start the engine.

He was stuck and knew what he should do and where he should put all of this, but he couldn't.

No, you don't want to. You're holding on to it. To have at least one thing you can control.

Darren knew his resistance toward faith wasn't control in any way. It was sin, and it was selfish. He knew better.

Yet every time he wanted to do the right thing, to plead with God and to ask for His help, Darren stopped. He pictured a dozen different images from Iraq, each one a cord on a whip, each one lashing out as the enemy used the weapon to inflict pain.

He looked at the bandage on his hand in horror and shame.

What is happening to me?

The problem was he knew the answer. He knew what was wrong and how to fix it too.

But I don't believe it's going to work. Not now. Not anymore.

4

Even though the smell of pancakes and bacon filled their house, Meribeth was the only one in the family actually having breakfast. Or at least sitting down to take tiny swallows of orange juice from her sippy cup. Heather woke up alone in the king bed, wondering where Darren might be. Worried until she found him sleeping on the couch. By the time all the kids were up, she heard him shuffling around, heading out to the garage. Perhaps some food could at least establish a little more sense of normalcy around the house.

"Sam! Elie! Time for breakfast!"

They were somewhere, maybe in their bedrooms. Heather slid a couple more fresh pancakes onto the stack of half a dozen. Maybe she'd get lucky. Maybe Darren would walk by and decide to have some. She didn't expect him to sit down or start to decorate the pancakes for the kids like he used to. But at least maybe he could receive *something* from her. Some small gift, even if it was just a pancake.

A glint on the kitchen counter lit up by the morning sun caught her eye. She walked over and picked up a shard of glass, a remnant of the scene last night. As she threw it into the garbage can, she replayed the scene one more time, the same one that had kept her awake for most of the night. After Darren left, all she could do was pray, yet even that felt halfhearted. For one of the first times since her husband had come back a different man, Heather began to fear the worst.

Some soldiers coming back simply couldn't cope, so they would do one thing they were trained to do: kill. No, Darren hadn't been defusing bombs and being a sniper, yet he had seen more of the carnage from the battlefield than most. When the wounded came back to base bloody and dying, the medics were called in to heal their bodies. More men and women came back appearing fine on the outside, yet it was the chaplain who came in to help heal their souls.

Heather understood. She knew Darren and how he wanted to help. How he'd felt called to serve these wounded warriors, to help them carry their grief, to show them who they ultimately needed to run to.

He needs someone to help him. Someone to show him the right path. But it's not going to be me, as much as I keep hoping and praying that it will.

For six months she'd been living with a ticking time bomb. For six months she had walked around looking for potential angry landmines, fearful of emotional mortars suddenly exploding in front of her. His detachment deepened over the months, and now it was a routine of withdrawal.

Early that morning, when she saw the lights of the car move across the blinds in their bedroom and then heard the garage door opening, Heather let out a shaky breath of relief. The worst hadn't happened—it couldn't happen, right? Yet after the scene last night, she was starting to believe that anything really could happen. They were no different from any other couple battling the wounds of war. Yes, they had a faith that some others didn't have, but that faith was being tested in a mighty way.

And the enemy's been winning for a while.

She decided to not make any more pancakes until Elie and Sam came to the table. While heading to their rooms to find them, she heard Darren yelling. She stopped in the hallway, startled as she heard his booming voice, assuming he must be talking to someone on the phone. Maybe another soldier or a buddy. The voice came from their bedroom, and as she entered she saw Darren towering over the kids. They sat on the floor next to his nightstand, both of them looking up in fear at their father.

"What do you think you're doing!" Darren bellowed out.

Between the kids, as if neither of them wanted to take the blame for holding it, was Darren's worn leather journal, the one he had brought to Iraq. The journal with the opening page of WE LOVE YOU! ELIE AND SAM drawn in colorful crayon.

"Sorry," Elie said in a choked voice. "We just wanted to—"

"It doesn't matter what you wanted!" Darren snapped.

They were reading it. Oh Lord, they got it out and were reading it.

"But we gave it to you so we could—" Sam said.

"So it's mine and you read it when I *say* you can!" Darren reached down with his bandaged hand while both of the kids recoiled, as if expecting him to strike them.

He grabbed the journal and then clutched it, still glaring at them, hovering so close.

She'd seen enough.

"Darren—what are you doing to them?" She rushed over to the children and crouched down, put herself between them and their daddy.

Her expression told him everything. She didn't need to say it.

Do you see the fear you're putting in your own kids' eyes? Do you?

Elie began to cry. "Please, stop! Don't fight anymore 'cuz of us!"

Anymore.

These fights had become routine, just like Darren's distance. She glared at him, furious.

"I didn't do anything!" Darren said.

Steady and calm, Heather stood and looked at him. "Enough, Darren. Get out! Go! Right now. You're no longer welcome in this house."

Somehow he seemed to shrink down, his fury dissipating into guilt.

"No. I'm not leaving my family."

She forced him to look back down at their kids, terrified and hiding like children escaping from bombing attacks.

"You need help," she said. "And I can't give it to you. Go to the base and get some help."

Darren appeared to steady his emotions, knowing he was cornered. He knelt down on the ground while the children cowered behind Heather.

"I love you guys," he said to them. "And I'm going to find my way back."

Elie popped up and approached her father, giving him a

tentative hug on his shirt. Then Heather saw her pull out a coin from her pocket and give it to Darren.

"I think you need this more than I do, Daddy."

Without another word, Darren left.

5

He stopped at the gate of the walkway at Fort Stewart, a place he knew very well but had avoided since coming back. Then he read the sign at the entrance with the header, "Where Warriors Walk." This was a sacred place, a path where soldiers had marched before heading to battle, and a welcoming point for when they returned home.

Standing upright like the men and women they honored, Easter redbud trees stretched down the path on each side of Cottrell Field. Dozens and dozens planted for each soldier from the Third Infantry Division who died in Operation Iraqi Freedom. A concrete marker displayed the names of the deceased soldiers. Surrounding many of the trees were flowers and photos and other small keepsakes and souvenirs brought by family and friends. Those were the ones who mostly visited this memorial; soldiers were less likely to be seen striding over Warriors Walk.

In his army sweatshirt and jogging pants, Darren walked down the path and stopped in the general area where he'd been told he could find the name. He spent a few moments searching until arriving at the concrete block with the name chiseled into it.

Underneath the small American flag stuck by the tree, a blue rattle rested.

Darren knew it hadn't been accidentally dropped by some baby.

Under the gray skies, feeling the cool wind shivering around him, Darren sought for something to say, but couldn't even utter something simple. After all those words of encouragement he'd given to Lance, he couldn't say anything now. Nor could he find it in him to pray.

Perhaps Lance wasn't the only thing Darren lost that day in Iraq.

Maybe the hope he used to pass out as freely as beef jerky had departed with the young man.

Darren turned and began to walk away, then started to jog. He kept running, harder and faster, trying to get as far away from that cement brick as he could.

6

Alone in the dark, Heather sat on the edge of her bed, wiping the tears off her cheeks as she did the one thing she could.

"Lord, please come rescue this family. Please, Father, we need Your help. Something supernatural has to happen. I know that. And I know You work miracles, so please, Lord. Help Darren. Help him find his way. Please, Lord, help me find mine. We need You, God."

7

Struggling to go to sleep, Darren found himself spending yet another night on a friend's pull-out couch. He didn't have any answers, not yet. But he did have a lot of opened doors and soldiers who welcomed him in without questions.

After tossing and turning for an hour, he sat up and checked his phone, hoping for some sort of message from Heather. Instead he found a text from an old friend he hadn't heard from in a while.

There were no words, just a photo of Shonda with Colby sitting on her lap. Both of them were smiling as they held the children's book Darren had recently sent them.

He didn't smile. But the photo was a nice reminder.

Not everything had been lost and left behind under that scorching sun. Some good had come from the work he had done in Iraq.

Perhaps there were a few more things remaining that needed to be dug out of the war's hopeless desert sands.

FEBRUARY 2009

1

"I mean, by the end, I couldn't even listen to myself," Darren said to Chaplain Rodgers, who sat across from him at his desk. "Dishing up faith as reality kept cutting the legs out from under me."

Darren groaned, rubbing his clean-shaven face. He'd grown into the habit of brushing his scratchy beard, and it felt good to have finally gotten rid of it.

"Did I just say that?" he continued. "What is wrong with me? And what if Michael were here—"

"Darren, relax," Chaplain Rodgers said with his usual calm demeanor. "Michael's not here, and if he were, you wouldn't have said it."

"Wouldn't I? I never thought I'd say what I said to my family either."

Shoving out of his chair, Darren stood and paced the room, wanting to get out of there and simply breathe.

"And I *hate* that I can hear everything you're thinking this whole time!" he told Rodgers. "All the cue cards, like 'God is with you,' that Lance and Michael started buying into, and now one is dead and the other's a dad with his legs blown off! Why would he *ever* believe me?"

Chaplain Rodgers waited for Darren to calm down and sit back in his chair.

"Well, are you going to say something?" Darren asked as he fell back into his seat.

"Dang, you remind me of me. Now, let me know if you hear what I just heard. *You* stopped liking hearing *you* talk about God. *You* are afraid reality undercut *your* message and Michael's ability to believe *you* now—"

"Give me a break, you know what I meant," Darren said as Chaplain Rodgers gave him a thin smile.

"I think I do. And as can happen to any of us who try to help others trust God, the enemy got *you* trusting in *you* instead of—"

"No!" Darren interrupted. "I was trusting God! To protect those men. And He didn't!"

"No . . . You trusted God to do what *you* thought He should do."

Darren leaned over and looked at the floor, shaking his head. Chaplain Rodgers leaned over his desk to get his attention.

"You show me a believer, Darren, and I'll show you someone who's done the same exact thing, or is about to. All of us have doubted at some point, son. You went into the fire confident in the truth, but when God's divine providence didn't live up to what you asked for, you questioned it. I understand that—but I have one question for you: What kind of faith do you want to pass on to your family? Or to those who look up to you?"

2

Amanda sat on the couch holding Elijah, and Heather and Tonya sat on either side, cooing at the baby.

"That little expression is *so* Lance," Amanda said. "A mini-me version of him." She laughed and had to fight back the emotions filling her. Then she looked at Tonya. "I'll never forget what Michael did. Trying to save him . . ."

"And Michael would do it again ten times over," Tonya said. "Especially where his heart's at now. It's so . . . bittersweet."

Heather felt like she was falling again. She could feel the tears welling in her eyes.

"Heather," Tonya said gently. "It's going to be okay."

"Oh, please. Don't worry about me."

Tonya leaned over and gave her a firm look. "Why not? Pain is pain. And ours doesn't make yours any less real."

"But what is it?" Amanda asked.

Heather wasn't sure what to say, but she also knew she was carrying way too much inside.

"I'm just—the three of us . . . we are carrying so much pain. And loss. And I'm having a real hard time seeing God's goodness in all of it."

"Here's what I know, honey," Tonya said. "That IED returned my Michael to me, and to our girls. He's a different man now.

And if that's not evidence of a good God working here, bringing us something better through pain, I don't know what is."

Heather knew she needed to hear this, that God wanted her to hear these words. Tonya kept talking as she gritted through her tears.

"So at this point, *all* I can do is trust He knows what He's doing. Which better be true, because it's all that's keeping this girl together. *Just. That.*"

Heather reached over to take Tonya's hand, and then Amanda held on to both of them. For a moment they held one another, and Heather felt something that hadn't been hers in a long time.

Hope.

3

The dirt felt smooth and cool to his hands. Darren knelt down along a row of freshly transplanted flowers and thought about the first time he'd met his new boss, Bob Henshaw. He had come here to Millstone Nursery and Greenhouse at the suggestion of Chaplain Rodgers. Henshaw had been surprised when Darren asked about a possible job.

"I've had a number of vets working for us in the past," Bob told him, "but never a chaplain. So after fifteen months in the desert, you sure you want to come work in the dirt?"

Walking amidst the multicolored trees, plants, and flowers that day made Darren feel alive, more than any sort of jog in the

woods might. He had stopped and scooped up a handful of rich
soil as he smiled at Bob.

"Different kind of dirt, sir. Different kind of dirt."

Weeks later, Darren was starting over in many ways. He was
still on his own, seeing the kids on a regular basis but with nothing changed between Heather and him. The decision to resign
from the army seemed monumental, and surprising to others
around him, yet to him it made perfect sense.

A chaplain shouldn't be separated from his wife and couch-
surfing while trying to minister to other soldiers. He was the
one who was supposed to have it all together, or at least *most* of
everything together. He needed to leave.

There were those around him who came and said they'd give
him a reassignment. But they just couldn't understand. Darren
needed *out*. The military had been his mistress. All this army
stuff—his buddies and the world they all lived in—had become
an idol to him, one he bowed down to. It was time to stand up
and get away from it.

The couch-surfing had been a fine temporary fix, but he
knew he had to find an apartment to rent. Just for the time
being. Just until . . . until the seeds planted could be watered and
tended to.

An old voice from the past interrupted his reverie. "Still
livin' on your knees, I see."

Darren turned around quickly and saw Michael's beaming
face as he maneuvered toward him in the wheelchair.

"Oh man . . . I didn't hear you coming," Darren said as he
stood.

"Set it to stealth mode. Straight-up military issue."

Darren smiled and gave him a nod. It was the first time he'd seen Michael rolling around in a wheelchair, so he knew his friend felt anxious but was keeping it together.

"Man—I'm glad you're back," Darren said.

"That's the problem. I'm back, but my neighbor's gone. I wanna fix that."

Yeah, me too.

"Let's take a walk," Darren said, then realized what he'd said.

"Look," Michael said, "I'm making some strides with this whole faith thing, but I don't think I'm ready to stand up and get healed. Not yet."

Darren laughed. "Come on. I'll push you."

"Just like always—you're still in the back seat."

After strolling through the quiet serenity of the nursery for a few moments, Darren told his friend about leaving the army and starting the job at the nursery.

"Chaplain Rodgers has been helpful. Helping me see what I lost track of."

"Your armor, brother," Michael interjected. "That's what."

"Bit more complicated than that."

Michael turned his head to look at him. "Okay. So why the anger? And don't give me that look. Our wives are friends. I've heard it all, man."

"Then you don't need me to tell you—"

"Hey, I'm not the angry one."

"Michael, come on."

Grabbing the wheels and stopping the chair, Michael

turned it around to face Darren. "You angry at your wife?"
he asked.

"No."

"At me?"

"Of course not."

"Then who? Yourself?"

"You're darn right."

Michael shook his head. "Naw, not it. Come on, Chaplain.
Belt'a truth me up! 'Cuz you been in my face since the day
we met!"

Something hard hit Darren's chest and then clinked onto the
cement. He looked down and saw one of his gifts to Michael.

"A coin for a con man. 'Cause if you can't even tell *me*, that's
what you—"

"I'm afraid. All right? Of exactly—"

"I didn't ask why you're afraid," Michael said. "I asked why
you're *angry*."

"Are you even kidding me? Look at you! Look at Lance!
Look at me!" Darren reached over and jerked the handle of the
wheelchair, shaking Michael. "God is my life, so what was He
thinking? What was He thinking?"

Michael slowly nodded in approval, giving him a compassionate smile. "Now we're getting somewhere," he told Darren.
"Brother, when I picked that piece of tin out of the dirt, I never
thought it promised I'd come back in one piece. And neither did
Lance."

An unusual swell of emotion filled Michael's face. He paused
and relaxed, letting it move along before talking.

"A couple minutes after the blast, he knew he was slipping away," Michael said. "Bleeding from his head. Fading. And you know what he said to me? He said he was glad he wore his helmet. And he wasn't talking about his government-issued one either."

As his lungs filled with air, Darren bent his legs and knelt to the ground. Now he was face-to-face with the major.

"The helmet of salvation," Darren said in a whisper.

"You gave that to him, Darren. I watched him go with a peaceful smile on his face because of it. So . . . don't you go losing your faith on account of me and Lance. Uh-uh. I don't want that on my head."

Darren closed his eyes, sighing and trying to settle his wild and worn-down spirit.

Michael wheeled closer to him. "Now. What are you gonna do about that woman of yours? When's the last time you called her?"

Looking back at his friend, Darren understood.

He'd been the one for months gently prodding and nudging and encouraging Michael to do the right thing. Now it was Michael's turn to do the same for him.

MARCH AND APRIL 2009

1

Sliding down a downward spiral can feel slow and tortuous, like the time spent in a deployment overseas, yet climbing up toward safe ground can pass quickly, almost too fast to see the steady progress. But progress can come if you surrender to the right One.

A heart should never stay in place. A soul should never grow stagnant.

Darren continues to run, to stay fit and move his body and allow himself to think. To talk to God. To ask questions and to continue to ask for His mercy. He runs but he's not running away, not anymore. He's simply running to find a place to stand still.

Heather looks for life behind the lens of her camera, whether in Sam's smile or Elie's laugh or Meribeth's embrace. Whether it's framed for a family or found inside God's creation. She keeps looking and waiting, being mindful and asking for wisdom and guidance.

Every day, grace can be found in small and big ways. Starting to work on a big project for the kids, Darren finds the work refreshing and exciting, knowing he's building a bridge to something more. To something possibly better. Michael offers to help him, coming over to the barn at the nursery to paint. Soon the two of them are hanging out more often, and it feels like old times.

Every day Heather prays for Darren, for their marriage, for their children, for hope. She sees hope in Amanda, who carries a spirit of unlikely joy brought out by Alexis and Elijah. Heather sees hope in Tonya too, who proudly shares about Michael's progress in rehab.

Darren has a plan and a purpose again, yet he has to take one step at a time.

Heather takes one day at a time, wanting to rush but knowing she has to wait.

2

The classroom door was open, so he could hear the voice of the presenter talking to the third-grade class. Darren stood by the wall just before the entrance, listening for a few moments.

"I especially love photographing people. Capturing expressions. Smiles. Their memories. And moments we'll never live exactly the same way ever again. Saving them forever."

Darren smiled. It felt good to hear Heather's voice again. He knew how comfortable she felt standing in front of children, and he was reminded of her talents at teaching young students. Carrying a narrow, three-foot-long box in his hands,

and wearing his nursery apron from work, he stepped inside and
stood by the doorway. Elie's teacher, Mrs. Dykstra, motioned
him to come on in. Heather paused for a moment, surprised to
see him. Then she turned back to the students.

"You never know, when you take someone's photo, how
much it may mean to someone someday," she said, now sounding more anxious. "And that's why I love being a photographer.
Thanks for listening."

The kids clapped as Heather sat back on a chair at the side of
the room. A set of her photos was displayed on easels at the front
of the class. All four of the photos were beautiful, especially the
one of him in a uniform getting kisses on each side of his face
from Elie and Sam.

"Thank you, Mrs. Turner," Mrs. Dykstra said. "Next to
share is Elie's dad, Darren Turner."

Elie spun around in her desk. She looked not only surprised,
but a bit worried too. Darren gave her a reassuring smile as he
walked to the front of the class and sat on the stool in the middle.

"Thank you for accepting my invitation, Mr. Turner," the
teacher continued.

"My pleasure. Hey, kids."

All the kids in unison gave him an animated, "Hi,
Mr. Turner."

"So I work at the Millstone Nursery. And I'm in charge of
the trees, the plants, and the flowers." Darren glanced over to
Heather. "Flowers like chrysanthemums."

Elie shifted in her seat, still looking nervous.

"There's a lot more I was planning to tell you about that, but

I think my lovely daughter would like me to talk about something else. Until just a few months ago, I was a chaplain for the US Army."

"And he's a brave soldier and a hero who saves whole families," Elie blurted out.

Darren grinned. "Thank you, sweetheart. But I don't think I'm a hero at all . . ."

He stood up to talk to the kids properly, to make sure he had their full attention.

"But it's true that every soldier who serves in a war comes home with medals. You just can't see them all, because some are on the inside."

Sitting in her chair, Heather wiped away a tear.

"Soldiers believe so strongly that good people deserve to be safe and free, that they risk losing the most valuable of all things to go help them."

He picked up the box he'd brought and crossed the room to where Heather sat. The kids were all looking, wondering what was inside. Quite a few probably thought it was a gun of some sort.

"To me, some of the biggest heroes are the soldiers' families," he said as he neared his wife. "Who also have medals pinned to their hearts. I know my family does."

As he stood beside Heather, he opened up the box and pulled out the bouquet of chrysanthemums. He gently offered them to her, noting her flushed cheeks and complete look of surprise. All the kids in the class giggled and gave ooohs and ahhhs. Meanwhile, Elie simply beamed in her seat.

"Thanks for having me, kids," Darren said as the teacher started a round of loud applause.

Elie sprinted over to him and gave him a hug as big as the one she'd given when he first returned home.

3

It was a start. Heather knew that every good thing needed to start somewhere.

She sat next to Darren, their chairs facing Chaplain Rodgers. It was their first meeting with him, their first official counseling session. She hoped it wouldn't be their last.

"I think the kids understand that you're sorry for how you treated them," Chaplain Rodgers explained to Darren. "They believe you."

Heather saw relief on her husband's face.

"But for the two of you, I'd like to suggest you start reliving good memories," he continued. "Remind each other of what you had before you try to build new ones. So Heather? Can you pick one?"

"Sure . . . I guess . . ."

Even though she knew Chaplain Rodgers fairly well, Heather felt awkward about sharing with him. She glanced over at her husband, sitting in a chair only inches away from her, yet still so many miles removed from her life. She forced a smile as she turned to the chaplain.

"The day we met," she began, "I was taking photos on

campus when he drove by, looking at me, just as he ran his motorcycle into my shot of the chrysanthemums. And ruining both the photo and the flowers! He just kept going too, and I thought, *Who is this hotshot?* But later that day I saw him again. It turned out he was the guest speaker for Campus Ministries, and as he shared his mission work, I saw a man with a heart for God. *And* he was hot, so—"

"What do you mean, *was* hot?" Darren shot back, the first sign of any amusement from him during this counseling session.

"Hey, don't push it," she said.

Chaplain Rodgers gave her a steady nod and grin. "Okay, time—Darren? What have you got?"

Her husband's silence felt like nails pounding into her, one after another. She looked at him, waiting, willing him to say anything, watching him trying to find an answer but unable to say a single, simple thing.

"And this is where we are," she finally said. "Anything that truly matters—he shuts down."

Darren tried. "Memories have just been . . . I mean, every time I try to think back, what I don't want to remember takes over. Like there's a wall in my timeline, or . . ." He didn't finish.

Heather closed her eyes, swimming in the familiar emotions she wakes up to and falls asleep with. A lonely and drifting sensation, bobbing up and down in the middle of the ocean, with no land in sight and nobody around to hear her cries for help.

"That's very normal, Darren," the chaplain said. "And Heather, post-traumatic stress is a mind inhibitor that requires

time and intentional rebuilding of the muscles and tools we use
to control our thoughts."

"But I'm pretty much outta time," Darren said.

Heather never could have imagined such words of defeat
coming from her husband, much less hearing the tone in his
voice. But he's right. They have run out of time.

She hoped—no, she desperately *needed*—the Darren she fell
in love with and knew so well to come back home.

"Darren, I'm not putting a clock on this," she protested.
"That's not fair."

Chaplain Rodgers motioned for her to calm down and wait.
Eventually Darren opened up again.

"I mean, what do you want me to say? I was angry. At God.
At myself. Afraid of the pain. Of how I'd treat my family when
I got home. Afraid that I'd become some imposter because *my*
faith let us all down."

She let out an exasperated sigh as she faced him. "So just—*tell*
me that stuff then! Anger, doubt, fear . . . I can handle those things.
What I can't handle is the distance. You pushing me away, shutting me out. *That's* what hurts so much and scares me to death."

The toxins that leaked out of her surprised her.

This is supposed to be about Darren and his issues. Right?

"You're my best friend, but you've been treating me like a
stranger," she said. "*Why?* Why the distance, the *silence* with me
when you can just walk in here and lay it all out for him?"

"Because I'm ashamed! I don't want to admit to you that I'm
angry! And afraid! I know I'm failing you, and I want to make it
better, but I don't know how!"

His jaw clenched as he turned his head sideways toward the window, wiping his eyes before looking at her again.

"Heather, I loved those men, and He took them away, and I'm supposed to be okay with that, but I'm not I'm angry and terrified now, because I love you and the kids *so* much more. More than I can bear sometimes. So what if He takes one of you away next? What then?"

As he leaned over to squelch his uncontrollable emotions, Heather leaned toward him, wanting to simply touch some part of him. Instead of jerking away, Darren moved and wrapped her in his arms. She felt his sobs moving against her like the swells of ocean waves.

As they held one another in silence, Heather didn't even notice Chaplain Rodgers ambling out of the office, perhaps realizing the sacred space it had suddenly become.

1

Not far from the building where they'd met with the chaplain, Darren and Heather sat on a bench next to a large lawn. Fort Stewart was busy on this bright afternoon. The sun felt good to Darren, and so did holding Heather's hand.

"Well, that was fun," he said.

They both let out light chuckles. After simply holding each other in the chaplain's office as the universe suddenly stood still, they had just let the moment sit. Now in the clear light of day, Darren knew it was time. Heather had seen his anger for months, but he had finally given her an insight into his grief back there in the office.

She needs to know and understand.

He pulled the journal out of his jacket pocket along with the mini DV cassette tapes, then handed them to her.

"Some light viewing and reading material," he said. "When you're up for it."

The flicker in her eyes told Darren she knew. She realized he was trusting her again.

"Thank you," she said.

5

There were so many journal entries. Too many, in fact, to read in one sitting. After getting the kids to sleep and giving herself a little more time just to make sure they were, Heather started to read Darren's journal. Not his online posts, but the personal thoughts and feelings he had written on the pages in ink. They were his heart and soul, spoken from the man she married and not from the official army chaplain.

They were also words written for her and the kids.

All penned in the event of something happening to him.

Leafing through the pages, the Darren she had fallen in love with spoke to her. Whispering and laughing and lamenting.

It didn't take long before she began to weep as she read.

The last hour I was at the PB, some locals hit an IED and two perished immediately. A third person in the car, a lady in her thirties, barely survived. It was terrible. She was barely recognizable as a person. I helped the medics get her into the aid station and briefly spoke to her through an interpreter. She made a few moans. I could smell her burnt flesh. It's awful, I know. When the bleeding stopped, they flew her to the big hospital in Baghdad for more proper treatment.

The young medics were absolutely destroyed. They stood there, silent, staring into space. So did I. They knew they'd helped her stay alive, but they were also trying to deal with what they'd just experienced. So someone called to me to "talk with them and make sure they were okay." I worked a lump out of my throat and asked the same rhetorical questions: how are you guys doing, etc. It felt so forced. I felt like they could see straight through me, see the fear and revulsion I was carrying just like them. Soon I stopped talking and just patted them on their shoulders and looked them in the eyes. We all knew that's all that could be done in that moment.

As I got back in my waiting Humvee and started back down the road toward the main base, past the point where the bomb went off, I began to weep. It was a long, quiet ride back.

This entry was all the way back to July 23.

He's been dealing with this from the start, she realized. *All by himself, never sharing it with me.*

The journal wasn't all hopeless and sad. There were many quotes from Scripture and from the books he had read and enjoyed. Yet time after time, a tragic story was told in detail.

Soon the entries began to focus on Heather and the kids.

I miss Heather more than a simple fifteen-minute conversation can ever begin to sum up. I miss her smell and her soft skin and her smile. I miss the way she prefers talking one-on-one with people for long periods of time rather than talking to lots of people for a short time. I miss how well she can read people, and her good intuition. I miss how well she knows me.

That's the part I'm a little afraid of, to be honest. Coming home. She's going to know what this place has done to me. And she's going to ask too . . .

Darren wrote about missing the children, about feeling guilt over not being there for events and not seeing special moments. He understood his calling and that he was serving, but it still gutted him to not be with them. As the months progressed, she could hear his longing come through on the pages louder and louder.

More horrific stories and grisly details. A woman raped. Children abandoned by parents. A sniper killing one of their men. The soldier who told him he'd almost committed suicide that day. The men sharing details about their failing marriages. One after another after another.

All this sadness and pain piled on top of him.

She couldn't take it anymore. Closing his journal, Heather decided to watch one of the tapes. She connected the recorder to her computer, pressed play, and began to watch the digital recordings Darren had made in his office on the base. With each word, she felt the last ten months since he'd been back start to break down and crumble in front of her.

". . . *Please* . . . know how much I love you. And have since the day we met, when I ruined those flowers you were taking pictures of."

His somber chuckle made her do the same.

"Chrysanthemums, right? Who the heck names flowers, anyway? I miss you more than you can imagine. And I love you just the same. And I want you to know that if anything happens to me . . . that if you're watching this now and I'm not there, know how strong you are. How strong you've been."

Her sides hurt from the tears, from the ache of realizing all the damage the war had caused. To see and hear about all this hurt and pain and loss . . . It smothered her.

She shut off the tape and closed her eyes, her hands clenched together.

"Lord, I may be hurting . . ." She paused and took a long, deep breath. "But so is the man I love."

Outside she could hear the pitter-patter of rain. The thought of all the soldiers out there weeping in silence, sometimes never shedding a tear but storing them deep inside a hidden well . . .

"Forgive me, Lord, for judging what I don't understand. And leaning on Darren when I should be leaning on You. Please help us both to forgive. And help us put this marriage—and this family—back together. Heal his heart. Heal his mind. And lift this burden from him."

6

The light drizzle falling on top of the red barn suddenly grows louder, the drops pounding away at the tin roof over Darren's head. He wipes the sweat off his forehead and examines the wooden structure in front of him. Almost. Just a few more finishing pieces.

The storm outside seems to want his attention. He can hear the bellowing thunder, so he heads to the open door of the nursery barn. A wall of falling rain stands right in front of him, with flickers of water starting to splash on him.

It feels good.

Looking up at the sky, he sees a bright streak of lightning. It's a reminder of the power and might of God.

He steps out into the rain and lets the droplets cover him. He closes his eyes for a moment, feels the water soaking into his clothes.

God doesn't always have to speak through others or through His Holy Word. He can say so much simply by displaying the awesome glory of His nature. Of the heavens and the earth.

I know You haven't forgotten me, Lord. And I know You love me. That You've always loved me and never let me go.

With his face pointing upward, the rain washing his forehead and cheeks and chin, Darren grins as he opens his eyes.

Forgive me, Lord. Forgive me for forgetting You and trying to do it all myself.

There's no way he can do it all. There's no way he can do anything, in fact. That's not God's plan.

I need You, Lord. Please help me. Please help our family.

He thinks of the familiar psalm he read this morning. The words took on a new meaning, especially *"Create in me a clean heart, O God."*

Darren needed a new heart. He didn't need a Band-Aid or a crutch for it; he needed a coffin to put his old heart in.

Create a new heart in me, Lord. In both of us. And help us to start again.

MAY 2009

1

"Mom! Mom!"

The cries of both children came from outside. Heather was barely awake. What were the kids doing outside so early? She crawled out from under the sheets and rushed out of the bedroom.

"Mom, you have to see this," Elie said, opening the back door and popping her head inside. "Come on!"

Heather looked out the kitchen window and couldn't believe what she saw. She quickly got Meribeth out of her crib and carried her out to the backyard, where Sam and Elie were running around, euphoric.

Right in front of the row of trees, the ones Darren used to sit and stare at, stood a massive wooden playground structure. A house, complete with a V-shaped roof, stood on one side, a carved sign over its door reading FORT BUMBLEFOOT. Hundreds of stones were laid in front of it, making a small path to the door. Next to the house, a climbing wall with rope led up to a little walkway at the top.

Heather couldn't believe it.

How did he get this here without me hearing? How many guys did he get to help him pull this off?

While Sam and Elie climbed up the wall and ran over to the second story of the house, Heather brought Meribeth close to the sign and put up her hand to feel the grooves in the carved wood. As she walked across the front of the fort, she saw a wooden cross staked into the ground, just like the kind Darren had back in Iraq.

Darren had brought Fort Bumblefoot back to their house. Now it was time she brought Darren something as well.

"Kids! I need your help with something today."

2

The special delivery order had come to the nursery with very specific directions: deliver the flowers to the gazebo at Freedom Park shortly after dusk. Bob prepared the vase of yellow roses and chrysanthemums and asked Darren if he could handle it.

"Hey, Turner. Delivery guy's out; could you make Freedom Park gazebo after it turns dark? Special request. Think there's going to be a proposal or something there tonight."

Darren usually left the nursery at dusk anyway, and Freedom Park wasn't far from the apartment he was renting. After parking his truck nearby, he carefully held the flowers as he walked along the path leading to the gazebo. The humidity of the day had simmered down, and he could feel a slight breeze now that nighttime had arrived. As he walked along he was reminded of the many times he'd taken this very path with Heather at his side. He wondered what she and the kids were doing tonight.

As the path weaved through the trees and made a turn, the gazebo came into view. The glow from hundreds of tiny white lights made him squint, and he stopped to look at it. Along with all the hanging lights, the gazebo's posts were wrapped in yellow tulle with a bow tied around each one.

In the center stood Heather, smiling and stunning in a yellow dress and heels.

Darren slipped off his dirty cap and began walking toward the steps that led up to this angel. As he stepped up he saw a small table set for two, covered with a white tablecloth. Metal lids covered the food. Votive candles flickered in the center.

"What is this?" he asked, his voice sounding weak, just like his heart.

She only smiled, like a girl surprising the guy she had a crush on. Darren set the flowers and his cap down on a table at the side, then he looked around at the flickering strings of lights and streams of tulle.

"You did all this?" he asked.

"I had a little help." Heather looked up into his eyes. "You brought us the fort, so I thought I'd bring you the gazebo."

He wanted to take her in his arms and spin her around. To embrace her and kiss her and beg her never to say goodbye to

him again. Yet he stood a few feet away, hesitating like a high
school kid at prom.

"Are the kids gonna pop up from anywhere?" he asked.

She shook her head. "I got a babysitter. Thought it might be
a little quieter that way."

"Heather, I know—"

"Hold that thought, babe," she said as she walked over to the
table. "Let's eat before the food gets cold."

She called me babe.

That was a good sign.

"I hope you didn't go to the trouble of fixing anything—"

Heather pulled the metal lid off his plate, revealing several
slices of pizza. "From Maciano's," she said.

"My favorite."

3

Neither of them ate much. Food was the last thing on Heather's
mind, and she could tell Darren felt the same way. He was careful with his words, and patient with everything, from sitting
down to praying to even knowing when to finish. She found it
cute how boyish and insecure he acted, yet at the same time she
saw the desire in his eyes.

It felt good to see that look, to feel wanted. But more than
simple desire, Heather felt relieved to feel something else: normalcy. To feel a connection with Darren again, one that wasn't
forced or tinted with any edge. There was a charming sort of

shyness between them, one that made sense for a couple separated for a while and starting over. But the bridge they had built
in their marriage, the one that had been detonated by bombs
brought home from Iraq, was rebuilt now.

It felt good walking over that bridge.

After talking about the kids and their jobs, they moved away
from the table to sit on the nearby bench. As he studied her carefully, listening to every word she said, all Heather could feel was
love and hope from this man next to her. It felt easy and natural
to reach over and take his hand.

"You are so beautiful, do you know that? Heather, all of
this . . . thank you."

She nodded, clenching his hand in her own. "So—I
enjoyed some 'light reading and viewing materials' the other
night."

He gave her a wary smile.

"Babe . . . I thought I knew, but I had no idea what you
lived through. What you're still carrying. I'm so sorry—"

For the first time that night, she became choked up, tears
filling her eyes.

"You have nothing to be sorry for," he said.

"I get it now. You did want to talk to me. Even felt as though
you were, which means everything to me. Thank you."

He smiled and she knew. He was Darren again. The man
she loved and married and respected and wanted to honor.

"It was that moment before we got married, you know. You
were standing in the rain as I changed your tire."

She didn't understand. "What about it?"

"One of my favorite memories."

All she could do was laugh. "We'd just broken up! For the second time."

"Yeah. But you called me to help. So I knew it wasn't over." A look of sadness filled his face.

"What?" she asked.

"When I came back home, I felt like I couldn't help you anymore. And I learned that it's a hard thing to ask for help. Especially if you're the guy used to being asked."

Holding back the tears, Heather wanted to tell him so much. About the things she was learning about herself and all the lessons God was teaching her. How she'd made a conscious decision to simply humble herself and ask God what He wanted. She knew God's ways were higher than hers, and they would always be better.

God wanted her to fight and not give up. So that's what she'd been doing.

I'm choosing to stay married.

She wanted to tell Darren this, and to apologize and ask for his forgiveness, and to embrace him and bring him back home. Yet she knew there would be time for all these things.

"I want to show you something," she said, and stood up to get something.

On the other side of the gazebo stood an easel covered by a yellow sheet. Heather gave the sheet a gentle tug, revealing a poster decorated with a dozen photos. Darren walked for a closer look. Printed underneath the pictures were the words *Daddy, Husband, Friend, Son,* and *Chaplain.*

And in the middle of the poster, in big, bold capital letters:
ONE FAMILY. UNDER GOD. INDIVISIBLE.

Darren didn't hesitate. He moved toward Heather and embraced her, then gently kissed her. As she found herself in the strong arms of the man she loved, Heather realized both of them had been trying so hard to carry this impossible load. It was a load neither of them could endure.

They couldn't right this ship on their own. God was going to finish the work He was doing in them.

ONE YEAR LATER

1

Darren heard the footsteps moving steadily over the gravel through the greenhouse. He looked up from the shrubs he was watering to see a familiar face.

"Military's missing a real good man."

"Chaplain Rodgers, sir," Darren said as he shook his hand.

"Good to see you, Darren. I hear things have really turned around for you guys."

Darren nodded as he continued watering. "And I plan to keep it that way. Home is the best place to be."

The chaplain gave him a steady, secure look as always, his uniform pristine under the midday sun. "I got a call from a good friend at Fort Campbell. Their special forces team needs a chaplain."

Darren shut off the hose and turned toward Rodgers.

"With special forces, deployments are limited and brief. You'd even get the promotion to captain that Jacobsen wanted for you."

"I'm honored, sir," Darren said. "But I'm sorry. You know my story. I just—I'm not ready."

After all the time he had spent in counseling, Darren knew the older man was aware of all the "junk in his trunk."

"Your story is *exactly* what those guys need to hear."

"I just can't, sir."

Chaplain Rodgers gave him a stern nod.

"Like I said . . . Military's missing a good man."

2

The raucous activity in the minivan continued into the house when they arrived home from the grocery store. Shopping with three young children always took a toll on her sanity, so it was nice to see Darren's truck in the driveway. He opened the door as the kids whizzed by, while Heather moved more slowly, arms full of groceries.

"Here, let me get those," Darren said.

"How about you get the rest?" she said with a smile.

As the children screamed inside, he gave her a quick glance.

"They're on a sugar high from slushies," she said.

Darren stepped back into the house and called out, "I think I hear some action brewing in Fort Bumblefoot!"

Sam was already on his way. "Meet ya there in two point five seconds!"

Meribeth, now two and a half, tried to keep up with her brother. Elie, on the other hand, walked by and rolled her eyes.

"Nice try, Dad," the ten-year-old said. "But I'm still too old."

"You're never too old to play in a fort," he called as she walked to her room.

Darren finished unloading the minivan, then joined Heather by the kitchen window, watching the kids at the fort—Sam, Meribeth, *and* Elie. He was right; nobody was too old to play in a fort. Especially one as cool as this, if he did say so himself.

"Thanks for the help," Heather said as she turned to him. "You know, I think we should take the fort with us when we move."

He was about to open a box of cookies, but he stopped and looked at her. "Huh?"

"When you take the job," she said.

He put the cookies on the counter and walked closer to her. "What are you talking about?"

"Heard it through the grapevine, so I called Chaplain Rodgers myself."

"Who are you and what have you done with my wife?" he asked.

"I know, right?" She chuckled. "But we know what to expect now. How to prepare."

She put her hands around his neck, a reflective look on her pretty face. Darren followed her example, slipping his hands around her hips.

"You know as well as I do. This is what we're called to, *Captain*." She grinned. "And *Who* we're called to. Right?"

He didn't speak, just gave her a knowing nod and held her in his arms as he looked out the window. Just beyond the kids and the fort, the sun winked at him through the back line of trees.

As long as these four were by his side, he could go anywhere.

3

Sitting in front of a beautiful vanity mirror she'd recently found at a thrift store and restored, Heather removes the last roller and starts to brush her hair. She sees Darren behind her walking into the room, and grins.

"You know how I love a man in uniform."

His hands feel good against her shoulders. So does the affectionate gaze he gives her.

"I was just thinking about that day you spoke to Elie's class about medals," Heather says.

"I was thinking about medals too." Darren removes a small gift box out of his pocket and places it on the vanity top in front of her. "This one is for you. Designed it special."

She opens the box and sees a necklace inside. Holding it up, she studies the knight in shining armor on the medallion, then sees the inscription on the back.

Ephesians 6:10–18

Heather doesn't need to look up these Bible verses.

Her hand squeezes his. "Thank you. I love it."

She watches him lean over and kiss her on top of her head.

A couple hours later, she's still watching Darren as he steps onto the stage next to the podium at the medal ceremony in the assembly hall at Fort Stewart.

Chaplain Rodgers saved Chaplain Turner for last. As he begins to read the medal citation, Heather rubs the necklace she's wearing.

"Finally, be strong in the Lord and in his mighty power," reads the first verse of that passage of Scripture.

She knows they're here today not because of what they've done to turn their marriage around. They are strong because God is making them strong.

She smiles with pride as Darren looks over at her and the kids sitting in the audience.

"Therefore, this is to certify that the president of the United States has awarded the Bronze Star medal to Captain Darren A. Turner."

Darren salutes Chaplain Rodgers, then stands as a senior officer pins the medal on him. As the room erupts with applause and a standing ovation, Heather rises and looks down at the children to see their delighted pride. She wipes back tears, tears that mirror the joy inside of her.

As Darren walks over to the podium, he takes a moment to nod in appreciation of the crowd's response before speaking into the microphone.

"Thank you so much. This is deeply humbling. It is with great honor that I have served my country. But I stand before you today because Jesus is my rock. And because I have a family who loves me and believes in me, and I feel the same way about them. Which is also why I can and will continue to serve as I've been asked, to the very best of my ability."

He looks over at Heather and the kids, then to Michael, Tonya, and the twins next to her.

"My family and I—we've made a promise to each other to protect ourselves from anything that might try to divide us. We've learned the best way for us to do that is to put on the Armor of God and to seek to honor Him in all that we do. And we want to invite our brothers and sisters here and abroad to do the same."

In her mind's eye Heather sees Shonda, the sergeant Darren has told her so much about. She can see Shonda sitting with her mother in a church pew as they watch Colby sing with the kids' choir.

"So today, I encourage you, to wear by faith, the Belt of God's Truth . . ."

She remembers how she and Darren shared their testimony at a couples' retreat a month ago.

". . . the Breastplate of His Righteousness . . ."

She sees Michael in the hospital working with a physical therapist, pushing himself through pain to learn to walk again with a prosthetic, all the while being cheered on by Tonya, Mia, and Nia.

". . . the Sandals of His Peace . . ."

She thinks of their family holding hands in the living room, praying together as a family.

". . . the Shield of Faith in His power against all enemies . . ."

She knows how long the walkway is at Veterans National Cemetery for Amanda to traverse, Elijah strapped to her front, holding Alexis's little hand until they stop at Lance's engraved stone.

". . . the Helmet of Salvation, found in Him . . ."

She hears Darren reading the Bible to the family around the dinner table.

". . . and the Sword of His powerful and gracious Spirit . . ."

Once again, Heather touches her necklace. She's reminded how Scripture is alive and how it never ceases to teach and reach her heart in indescribable ways.

"Before I left for Iraq, I thought I knew what it meant to put on that armor," Darren says, looking over at them and smiling. "Here's what I learned. None of us is promised tomorrow. So I'm choosing to place my faith and trust in the One who holds all of my tomorrows. For me, and my family, it's the only way to live and the only way to die. Thank you all for listening."

4

As family and friends line up to greet and congratulate Darren, he is most excited to see Shonda's smile as she walks up holding her son's hand. He gives her a giant hug and then looks down at the boy.

"Hey, buddy! You must be Colby."

The five-year-old nods and smiles, leaning into his mother and clinging to her hand. Dressed in her camo garb, Shonda introduces herself to Heather.

"It's so nice to finally meet you," Heather says.

Just like old times, the sergeant looks at him like a knowing teacher regarding a mischievous student, then hands him the gift bag in her other hand.

"Uh-oh," he says as he studies the bag.

Shonda brushes the shoulder marks on his uniform. "The bars look good on you."

Darren nods. "Makes me look a little taller, huh?"

"Sure, just a little."

As he reaches into the gift bag, Darren half expects to find beef jerky. Instead he pulls out a framed black-and-white photograph.

In the photo, he is kneeling before the cross outside his tent at FOB Falcon. Praying.

Perhaps Shonda knows who he was praying for.

He takes a moment to compose himself as he looks at the picture.

"I had my eye on you, Captain. Which is why I'm here." She wags Colby's arm. "Why *we're* here."

"Thank you" is all he can say.

Darren turns, looking at Michael surrounded by his three lovely ladies. Tonya and the twins look hesitant, but their dad just shakes his head and gives them a grin. He sees Darren looking at him, and begins to come toward him. Without a wheelchair and without a cane.

Major Michael Lewis takes steady, deliberate strides. He looks handsome in his decorated uniform. Darren watches and waits, wearing a proud smile.

As he embraces his brother-in-arms and in Christ, Darren knows: God's not through with either of them. Not yet.

God has big plans for them.

FIVE YEARS LATER

May 17, 2014

Tomorrow I'll be speaking at Regent University, sharing our testimony while talking about King David from 1 Chronicles 13–15. Talking about how all of us want to do things on our own, and how God wants OBEDIENCE.

King David—what a man after God's heart. Yeah, he messed up big time, but he also loved the Lord. The passage in 1 Chronicles talks about how David wanted to bring the ark of the covenant back to the Israelites. Instead of doing it God's way, he chose to do it his way. King David was sincere, but sincerely wrong.

This will be the way I open the door to discuss Heather and me. Our story.

Really, though . . . I'm just going to be sharing about God's redemption. The crazy redemption of His people. The

gospel is ridiculous, right? Grace is ridiculous. I see this
every day in what God has done with Heather and me, with
the ministry He's given us.

God can take and will always continue to take messed-up
people and bring them to a place where they will find hope.
We see soldiers who already have one foot out the door
of their marriage, and after we share our testimony, they'll
come up to us wanting to know more. We'll always share
with them that it's not us.

It's Jesus Christ.

And He's called Heather and me to this. For how long,
we don't know. It might end tomorrow. But for now, we
will continue to tell our story. It's a story about hopes and
dreams. Not the ones we carried for ourselves, but the
hopes and dreams God has for us.

A Personal Message
from the Producers

Prior to my (David) first film, I wrote and directed a passion play at Calvary Church in Memphis for fifteen years. It was very unique from the standpoint that I would write a new modern-day story every year and blend that story with the passion week of Jesus' life. One Easter, I decided to write a story about a chaplain and his assistant, focusing on some family issues that both were facing during their deployment together. I love military stories, especially since I have a brother who recently retired from the Air Force after twenty-three years of service. (He's actually the soldier who pins the Bronze Star on Darren during the final scene of the movie.)

Soon after the release of *The Grace Card*, I began to work on a story structure for my chaplain film. During my research, I came across a story on a news website about a chaplain who was fighting to save his marriage after a lengthy deployment. I was immediately struck by the fact that no one is safe from the impact that a deployment can have on a marriage—even a chaplain. Despite having a relationship with Christ, and understanding the undeniable protection he offers to every one of us, every soldier can be attacked by the enemy (seen or unseen) at any time. I immediately felt drawn to this story.

I prayed and asked God to open the door for me to meet this chaplain and his family. Within a few weeks, I was able to make contact with Chaplain Turner, and my wife, Esther, and I made the trip to meet the family. We shared our hearts with Darren and Heather and prayed for His direction. After a few months of discussion, Darren and Heather entrusted us with their story and we vowed to give our all in making the film.

Esther and I did not see the Turners in person again after our first meeting for almost six years. Of course, there were countless phone conversations and emails as we struggled to get the script completed and

Six years had passed since our initial visit together, but God's timing is always perfect.

the project fully funded. The next time we saw Darren, Heather and their three children was on the set of *Indivisible*. What an emotional day! We get tears in our eyes just thinking about it.

It's been amazing to see how the film is already resonating with people even before its release. We've had a peace about that for many years, and it's one of the reasons that we've never given up on telling this story. God has done many miracles for this special film and we're so glad we can tell the story together!

—DAVID G. AND ESTHER EVANS,

CO-PRODUCERS FOR *INDIVISIBLE*

Acknowledgments

Thanks to Brian Mitchell for bringing this project to me and to David Evans for allowing me to be a part of this incredible story. It's been an honor to work on this.

Thank you, Darren and Heather Turner, for living a story worth sharing with others, both on the screen and the page. I've been privileged to have walked in your shoes through my imagination and storytelling. Darren, thank you for your willingness to answer some very big and very tiny questions I had along the way. I hope I was able to capture the true spirit of your testimony.

Once again, big-time thanks to my editor, L. B. Norton. We've traveled from the woods of Solitary, North Carolina, to the desert of Iraq. I treasure our continued partnership.

Thanks to Amanda Bostic and the entire team at Thomas Nelson.

And finally, I'm thankful for my father's father whom I called Papa. He served under General Patton's Army in World War II, driving a dozer tank in Europe. Papa passed away when I was young, so I'll never be able to hear all the stories he carried from the great war. Working on this book allowed me to understand just a tiny bit more what he went through so many years ago.

DISCUSSION QUESTIONS

1. What are the events that lead to Darren and Heather's marriage suffering after he comes back from Iraq? What are some things they could have done to avoid this?

2. Darren Turner is inspired by the book, *Wild at Heart,* when it says the following: "They may be misplaced, forgotten, or misdirected, but in the heart of every man is a desperate desire for a battle to fight, an adventure to live, and a beauty to rescue." Do you believe this is true? What are ways you or your spouse can carry out these desires?

3. When Darren leaves Heather and the children behind to head to Iraq, do they have realistic expectations for what's about to happen? Are there things they could have done to prepare themselves for the next fifteen months?

4. Have you or anybody you've known served our country during a time of war? What are ways they've been supported?

5. Throughout the story, Darren, Heather, and the children rely on prayers to God. How do you deal with prayers that seem to not be heard and remain unanswered? How can you continue to faithfully pray to God when a situation appears hopeless?

6. As Chaplain Turner begins to experience the brutal realities of the war, he shields his family from the horrors by not telling them what's happening. Were Darren's actions justified? Should he have told Heather more of what was happening to him?

7. Darren never gives up on his neighbor, Michael, even though at times it seems pointless to continue to share Christ's love and hope with him. Do you have similar people in your life? How can you continue to remain a friend and a witness to them even when they refuse to listen?

8. Heather is basically a single parent trying to take care of three young children while Darren is gone for fifteen months. What are the ways she copes and survives?

9. After seeing the loss of the young girl, and then having to deal with the death of Lance, Darren's faith is severely tested. Even with all of his biblical knowledge and his strength of conviction, Darren ends up confused and disheartened. What are ways we can continue to cling onto hope when bad things happen in our lives?

10. After coming home, Darren hides the hurt and the guilt he's carrying inside. He continues to help other soldiers going through the same thing, yet he refuses to get help

himself. Are there situations in your life where you need to stop and ask for help?

11. Heather eventually refuses to put up with Darren's moodiness and absence, telling him to leave their home and get some help. Did she do the right thing sending him away like this? Are there people in your life that need this sort of tough love? How can you get someone to realize they need help?

12. "God can take and will always continue to take messed-up people and bring them to a place where they will find hope." Chaplain Turner shares this at the end of the story. Do you believe this? Why do we need to reach this place in order to find hope?

INDIVISIBLE PHOTOS

Chaplain Darren Turner (Justin Bruening) checks in with his wife upon arriving in Iraq in INDIVISIBLE.

Chaplain Darren Turner (Justin Bruening) updates his video diary for his family during deployment in INDIVISIBLE.

L to R: Chaplain Darren Turner (Justin Bruening) and his wife, Heather (Sarah Drew), seek marital counseling upon his return after a difficult fifteen-month deployment in INDIVISIBLE.

L to R: Army wives Amanda Bradley (Madeline Carroll), Heather Turner (Sarah Drew), and Tonya Lewis (Tia Mowry) seek strength in each other upon hearing news of the troop surge in INDIVISIBLE.

Heather Turner (Sarah Drew) looks on proudly with her children (L to R) Elie (Samra Lee), Meribeth (Abigail Hummel), and Samuel (Lucas Boyle) during an awards ceremony in INDIVISIBLE.

L to R: Mia (Hannah Samuel), Tonya (Tia Mowry), and Nia (Naomi Samuel) in INDIVISIBLE.

L to R: Army wives Heather Turner (Sarah Drew) and Tonya Lewis (Tia Mowry) enjoy a moment together in INDIVISIBLE.

L to R: Chaplain Darren Turner and actor Justin Bruening on set of INDIVISIBLE.

L to R: Army wives Tonya Lewis (Tia Mowry), Heather Turner (Sarah Drew), and Amanda Bradley (Madeline Carroll) try to keep up with their kids in INDIVISIBLE.

L to R: Actors Justin Bruening, Jason George, and Tanner Stine on the set of INDIVISIBLE.

Chaplain Darren Turner (Justin Bruening) shares words of encouragement with his troops before heading out on patrol in INDIVISIBLE.

R to L: Chaplain Darren Turner (Justin Bruening) performs an Easter Baptism service in Iraq with Lance Bradley (Tanner Stine) in INDIVISIBLE.

L to R: Lance Bradley (Tanner Stine) discusses strategy before heading out on patrol with Michael Lewis (Jason George) in INDIVISIBLE.

Chaplain Darren Turner (Justin Bruening) delivers the eulogy for two fallen troops in INDIVISIBLE.

L to R: Shonda Peterson (Skye P. Marshall) and Chaplain Darren Turner (Justin Bruening) share a lighthearted moment on foot patrol in Iraq in INDIVISIBLE.

L to R: The Turner family, Heather (Sarah Drew), Meribeth (Abigail Hummel), Samuel (Lucas Boyle), Darren (Justin Bruening), and Elie (Samra Lee), pose after an awards ceremony in INDIVISIBLE.

L to R: Sarah Drew and Heather Turner pose on set of INDIVISIBLE.

About the Author

Bestselling author Travis Thrasher has written over fifty books and worked in the publishing industry for over twenty years. He has written fiction in a variety of genres, from love stories and supernatural thrillers to young adult series. His inspirational stories have included collaborations with filmmakers, musicians, athletes and pastors. He's also co-written memoirs and self-help books. His novelizations include *Do You Believe?* and *God's Not Dead 2*. Upcoming releases in 2018 include *The Black Auxiliary* about the lives of the other seventeen American black athletes who competed with Jesse Owens in the 1936 Olympic Games in Berlin. Travis lives with his wife and three daughters in Grand Rapids, Michigan.